WITHDRAWN

SAFE PASSAGE

SAFE PASSAGE

Ellyn Bache

CROWN PUBLISHERS, INC.,
NEW YORK

Published by Crown Publishers, Inc., 225 Park Avenue South, New York, New York 10003 and represented in Canada by the Canadian MANDA Group

CROWN is a trademark of Crown Publishers, Inc.

Manufactured in the United States of America

Designed by Lesley Blakeney

Library of Congress Cataloging-in-Publication Data

Safe passage.

1. United States. Marine Corps—History—20th
century—Fiction.   2. Beirut International Airport—
Fiction.   3. Lebanon—History—1975-   —Fiction.
I. Title.
PS3563.A845S34 1988   813'.54   88-373
ISBN 0-517-56807-1

10 9 8 7 6 5 4 3 2 1

First Edition

To my family . . .

Terry

Beth

Matt

James

Ben

SUNDAY

October 23, 1983

1

At four-thirty on Sunday morning Mag came up from sleep with her heart thumping and sweat pouring from her, the way she'd awakened years ago when her son Izzy was out delivering newspapers and she found him two blocks away lying on the street with a broken ankle. She sat up in bed, wide awake, sick to her stomach. She hated motherly premonitions; she thought she was through with them. Except for Simon, the seven boys were grown.

She pulled her gown in and out from her chest to cool herself, but the sweat kept coming. Once you had children, you were vulnerable forever. Alfred, her oldest, her most dependable, was plunging a knife into her heart, plotting to get her house away from her so he could live in it himself with a divorced woman and her two sons. Percival was off to war; Simon was debating his ear operation. The others were not currently in states of crisis, but you never knew. Even Gideon was so over-wrought that all he thought about was running races.

Patrick, snoring beside her, turned over and groaned. He groaned when he dreamed about going blind—a possibility, not a certainty. For the past year, without warning, his pupils would close to pinpoints and then shut entirely, leaving him with va-cant blobs of color in the centers of his eyes, but no light-absorbing black. Minutes or hours later the pupils would begin to reappear, though he did not see well until the next day. At the Wilmer Eye Clinic in Baltimore, where they'd been going since the problem started, the doctors said, finally: "This is something you just never see." But Patrick believed you either solved a problem or ignored it. When he wasn't changing his diet or experimenting with other possible cures, he pretended the blindness didn't exist. He even waited out the actual attacks with jokes and sarcasm, which the rest of the family was supposed to find amusing. But in his dreams he groaned.

Mag fanned herself, and Patrick flung a hand into her lap, making a high, wheezing sound like a child's whine. For a mo-ment she believed his thrashing was what had awakened her. It seemed unlikely. Normally his noises and bumping roused her only enough to move away so he could dream on, because maybe his dreams were a kindness that made the reality less harsh. Certainly his nightmares never left her sweating, or with this lingering sense of menace. A hot flash, probably; she'd been expecting them sooner or later. Relax, go back to sleep. Don't spaz, Mother, the twins would say. Then she thought: Why should she sleep? Was she a masochist, that she had to stay in bed with her heart palpitating and her husband groaning and sweat running down the inside of her gown?

She put on her robe and went barefoot down the dark stairs to the family room. Outside a heavy rain beat against the house. She would turn on the lights to make it seem warmer, a trick she'd learned in their poverty-stricken years. The darkness was absolute. She passed through the hallway, walked around the coffee table, touched nothing. Patrick often wandered around in darkness like this, negotiating the rooms blind. A soft, unexpected lump at ankle level. She tripped. "Oh, shit, Lucifer!" Flying, flying, catching herself on the edge of the couch. Cats! For ten years Lucifer had believed, erroneously, that the only way to get food was to put himself directly in the path of any possible provider. She flung a foot out to kick him. Missed. Heard him scurrying off. Rage filled her. An image came to her of Patrick being knocked flat by such an encounter during a blind spell—of Patrick flailing around on the floor with people looking on. *No.* The cat would have to go. In this house at least, the terrain was familiar and Patrick had a right to be safe.

But even security seemed impossible. For weeks, responsible, clean-cut Alfred had been pretending that he would be doing them a favor by watching the house for the winter while Mag and Patrick vacationed, but clearly he was only finagling to move his big-busted girlfriend Cynthia in because this house was a better place for raising her children than a little apartment. She couldn't understand it—that Alfred would try to snatch Patrick's sanctuary from him in his very time of need. Alfred, of all people, snared by an oversized bosom. Percival she might have imagined; or Izzy with his fickleness. But Alfred!

Then her rage was replaced by the sense of menace that had awakened her. No ordinary fear this, but a terrible prickling beneath the skin, called up by some awful aberration in the course of things—not imagination but something real, she knew it—and when the knowledge came it would be destructive, deadly, black. The feeling lit momentarily on Percival in the Marines, on Gideon at school in Utah, then settled on Alfred, convincing her he was probably lying dead somewhere on a rainy street. Her heart did double-time in her chest, and sweat drenched her gown. She'd never wanted children. Half her life she'd wished they would leave her alone. But Alfred was her firstborn. How could she hate him when she was having palpitations? Why—now that she had raised them—did she spend her time imagining the horrors of her sons not being there, in some permanent way?

She turned on a light, which made her feel more logical. Always be logical, Patrick said. Probably she'd gotten up in a sweat not because of premonition but because Alfred made her feel guilty. It was unthinkable—wasn't it?—to expect his parents to move out of their house for the winter when one of them might be going blind. Unthinkable to want to move the divorced mother of two in in their place, just because Cynthia needed more room for raising her boys. Alfred didn't put it that way, but there it was. Naturally Mag was resentful, no matter how benevolent Alfred made it sound. Any mother would wake sweating in the middle of the night.

But she didn't feel better for thinking it through. Her breath was ragged and uneven, edging out of control. Already she had said terrible things, and if something happened to Alfred, there would be no taking them back. "You're only twenty-four years old, the last thing you need is a ready-made family," she had screamed. "The next thing you know, you'll want kids of your own, and you'll be stuck with half a dozen of them and you won't be able to do a damned thing for yourself." Her tone had been cruel, sarcastic, unmotherly. But it was no idle threat. Mag had married young and had seven unplanned sons, and the moment they started coming, her spirit was enclosed and she hadn't been able to do a damned thing for herself. Why should she take anything back?

"Cynthia and I are sensible people," Alfred had said. "We believe in birth control. We believe in abortion." Alfred had always been practical. He had learned to dress himself at two because he didn't like to be left in pajamas while Mag tended to Izzy. Later he'd taught himself to cook French toast and eggs because his brothers were hungry in the morning and Mag was busy with the current infant of the house. At the time, Mag had been grateful for his help. Now she feared her inattention had made him too practical and superficial, leaving him with a set of rules he followed but no inner life at all. When he was nine she had started him on piano lessons to develop his soul. It was too late. He practiced dutifully, listened intently, but always (she was sure) in the interest of being able to imitate the sound, never because he was carried away by the music as she had hoped. Abortion! As if there were no more to such decisions than logic. She herself wouldn't have had abortions even if they'd been legal, no matter that she hadn't wanted children. She didn't tell him that; she wanted to let him wonder. But where was the satisfaction in that, if he was lying dead somewhere on a rain-soaked street?

The logical thing, if she was so worried, would be to pick up the phone and call him. That was what Patrick would say.

Never.

It was Alfred's idea that Patrick, blind, would be happier in the Keys. Patrick had mentioned briefly that moving south might be nice, at least for the winter. In the Keys even a sight-less man could feel the sun, Patrick said. Perhaps do some fishing.

"Nobody but you is convinced you're going blind," Mag said.

But Alfred seized the moment. "No telling what a blind man could invent for fishermen," he told his father. Patrick had been inventing things for twenty-five years and could never resist a challenge. Mag realized that Alfred had always had a diabolical mind.

"Listen," Alfred continued. "If you really want to go down there, go ahead and go. Cynthia and I will move into your house. Simon can stay with us to finish school." But Mag would no more have left Simon to Cynthia's care—sweet Simon, her baby, her love—than cut her own throat.

"Then, if you change your mind and come back, nothing is lost." Coming from Alfred, the offer sounded generous and sensible.

Mag said, "We've had money exactly twice in our life, Alfred, and not all that much, either time."

"Of course we would pay you rent," Alfred said. He meant: *not very much* rent. He was a teacher and Cynthia was a psychologist, with salaries that barely paid for their little apartment. They would never be able to afford a house of any size this close to Washington.

"The Keys are something to think about," Patrick said. The idea of wintering in the tropics intrigued him. He had once been a Hemingway fan and saw himself in a thatched-roof bar, drinking lime juice and mineral water, being Papa Patrick Singer. But what did Patrick know?

Mag squinted out the sliding glass door to the rain coming down on the deck in the dark. She had insisted on a house with lots of windows—an excellent decision, though right now she could see only bubbles of water on the glass and blackness beyond. When the boys were little, she'd been able to watch them play in the yard while she cleaned. She'd been able to supervise the babies in the family room and still catch the news on TV while she cooked in the kitchen. Later, after she went to work, she'd been able to get away with vacuuming the mottled carpets only once a week. It was a perfect house.

"I moved here from a chicken coop," she'd said to Alfred, trying to explain her attachment. "You don't remember, you were too little, but we moved here from a chicken coop."

Alfred never believed her, never understood her need for the place, but it was true. She was twenty-three at the time and they had no money. Alfred was three, Izzy was a baby, she was pregnant with Percival. They lived in a two-bedroom apartment on what had once been a farm, in a long single-story building, with a laundry room at the far end and a row of clothes lines outside in the back. Mag's life consisted of traveling from the apartment to the laundry room, from laundry room to clothes lines, then back to the apartment. She cooked meals, fed children, put them down for naps, cleaned up. She listened to classical music on the stereo in order to remain sane. She never watched TV. She got out twice a week—on Saturdays when she took the car to the grocery store, and on Tuesday nights when she went to her English literature class at the college.

After she got pregnant with Percival, she began to notice the odor of poultry in the apartment on cold mornings before the heat came up—a dank, raw smell like the meat case in the supermarket. Usually she felt all right when she was pregnant, but the chicken smell made her queasy. All day the odor rose and fell with the uneven heat from the radiators, as if chickens were running through the rooms at various times, pecking at the linoleum floors for feed—the ghosts of a thousand chickens.

"You're losing it, baby," Patrick had said. Patrick couldn't smell a thing. In those days he had nothing to do but go to work at the electrical supply company he was with at the time and then invent things, whatever pleased him. Her classroom on Tuesday evenings smelled of chalk, floor polish, cologne. "You can't tell me I don't know the difference between perfume and poultry," she said when she got home. Patrick laughed and wanted to make love. Even if Mag was not in the mood, she always acquiesced. What harm could it do? She was already pregnant. "I can't help it if my nose gets sensitive at these times," she said afterward, expecting sympathy in the mellow afterglow of orgasm. "Maybe you're under too much pressure," Patrick told her. "Maybe you should quit going to school." She said she'd keep taking classes even if she *did* go crazy; she'd get her degree pregnant or barefoot or both.

She continued to hate the smell of chickens and therefore began to envision herself leaving her family behind. She saw herself fleeing, alone, with a backpack on her shoulders, wearing a short-sleeved shirt, knee-high socks, and sneakers. Maybe she *was* going crazy. She was young, she'd never wanted babies in the first place, never even wanted Patrick. One day at the clothesline she said to her neighbor, "Somebody must have had a freezer full of chickens in our apartment before we moved in— the place smells like they're still there, it really does."

And her neighbor said, "Well, it's no wonder, with this place being a chicken coop for twenty years."

The neighbor told her the whole story. The developer who'd bought the farm had decided it would be cheaper to turn the chicken coops into apartments than tear them down. That was in the days before stringent zoning regulations. The old farm-house was rented out, too—a ramshackle white building down the street. The barn, being unconvertible, had been torn down.

Mag felt as if she'd been slapped. She whisked Alfred and Izzy back to the apartment, put them in the playpen, and turned *Gaieté Parisienne* on the stereo so loud it drowned out both her thoughts and the boys' cries. When Patrick came home Mag was still in the chair, the music playing for the sixth or seventh time, and Alfred and Izzy were both still in the playpen, asleep. "God, what a racket!" Patrick screamed over the stereo. "Do you want to get us kicked out of here?"

"I won't live in a chicken coop!" she yelled back. "I mean it, Patrick. I'm not raising babies in a chicken coop. You've got to get us a house."

After that Mag focused all of her energy on houses. She focused on houses the way years later her son Gideon would focus on running, the kind of narrow focus that stubs everything else out and makes failure impossible. By the time Percival started thrashing around in her stomach like a windmill, Patrick had sold his disposable-diaper patent to a manufacturing company. Commercial disposable diapers didn't become popular until years later, and even then it was someone else's design— not Patrick's—on which they were modeled, but the patent brought them enough to build a house. Mag insisted on big rooms, two stories, lots of windows, plenty of yard. Outside she planted anything she could buy cheaply at K Mart—azaleas, wisteria, willows and euonymous and maples. They moved here less than a month before Percival was born—a good thing, considering there were four more babies to come but no more money until last year, when Patrick sold the patent for the Velcro sweatsuit he'd invented when the middle boys were in high school. For twenty years she'd hated being confined to housewifery when she wasn't at work, but she'd always loved the house—the space, the multicolored rugs, the yard where her plants grew in wild disarray (she did not learn until later about pruning), where carpets and even grass survived years of trampling, shouting, chaos . . . where even the overgrown forsythia gave her pleasure, hanging on in the shade of the maples, with its sparse yellow freckles of bloom.

Alfred was twenty-four now, older than Mag had been when she'd been overrun by children and ached with need for this place. Watching him, his finely chiseled features hiding what might have been pain, Mag usually felt a wrenching in the back of her throat. She decided it must be Cynthia, not Alfred, who really wanted her leafy backyard and rooms with space, and that Cynthia had bewitched Alfred into asking for it . . . so she managed to choke her sympathies back. Her sons were her own flesh and she'd had no choice but to find a place to raise them. Alfred, on the other hand, could still choose his freedom until a childless woman came along.

Didn't he see? But of course she never mentioned this to him directly.

"Face it, Mother," he'd said. "Even the twins are grown now. You always said once the kids graduated from high school they were out of your hands."

"Yes, but Simon."

"He'll be better off here with us than if you tried to drag him to Florida to switch schools for half a year."

"We couldn't leave you with the responsibility."

"Even if anything happens, you're only a two-hour flight away. Listen, Mother—nothing is going to happen." But that wasn't the point. She'd needed the house then to raise her children. And now for a different reason. If Patrick went blind in Key West, in unfamiliar surroundings, how would either of them survive?

Someone was watching her. When she turned around, Patrick was standing at the far end of the family room, wrapped in his old blue terrycloth robe. He tied it tighter and then tighter again, as if he hoped to find a twenty-inch waist in the middle. His hair did not seem so gray ruffled up like this, before he combed it. His face was unlined—or maybe just puffy from sleep. "I'm closer to fifty than forty," he often said, but he looked all right. "The father of champions should stay fit," he sometimes told her. He liked to bemoan the fact that he couldn't run with Gideon anymore. Then she would say, "No father is required to keep up with champions," and they would smile at each other. They didn't talk in detail about Gideon's winning a running scholarship to Weber State in Utah, but they were both proud. "I never thought I'd get left so far behind so quickly," Patrick would say. "And I was such a good miler." "So eat more Wheaties," Mag would tell him. And Patrick would pretend to worry about his running and not to worry about his eyes.

"God, I hate when you sneak up on me," she said, though for once his sudden appearance hadn't made her jump. He had been moving stealthily ever since his eyes had started acting up, developing his blindman mode. When he thought no one was looking, he went around the house with his eyes closed, touching the furniture and the walls. He wanted to be self-sufficient no matter what. He looked like a maniac, waving his arms in front of him, sniffing like an animal at a world he couldn't see. He experimented with his manner the way he had once experimented with their toaster when it wouldn't produce enough toast for all the boys at once, trying to turn it into a model that would brown ten slices at a time. The result had been an unrecognizable wire contraption that took up half the kitchen counter, with makeshift metal grooves for extra slices of bread and insulated tape over exposed wires that stuck out in odd directions. The contraption worked, but Mag had always thought it a miracle that it didn't electrocute anybody, and eventually she threw it in the trash. Now Patrick was transforming himself from sighted inventor to eccentric blindman in the same dogged way—and she feared the final, transformed version would be as grotesque as the toaster. Lucifer rubbed against Patrick's hairy ankles, and Mag shuddered, getting a rerun in her mind of Patrick tripped by the animal and sprawled blind on the floor. Patrick gave her a curious look and leaned down to pet the cat. "What's the matter?" he asked.

"Why should anything be the matter? You were groaning in your sleep. I was trying to imagine Simon's ear. I was having visions of Percival shooting Arabs with a gun." She sighed. Patrick did not believe in premonitions, so it was no use telling him. Better to steer conversation in a more productive channel.

"Alfred's trying to con you," she said.

"Number one, I don't believe that. Number two, even if it were true, it wouldn't be the first time somebody tried to con me. I wouldn't mind living in Florida."

"I wouldn't trust him, Patrick," Mag said.

"Why not? He's always been trustworthy."

"He wants the house because his bimbo needs more room to raise her kids."

"Alfred? Honorable Alfred?"

"Even Adam ate the apple."

"Yes, and a year from now you'll deny this whole conversation when you find out he was just trying to do us a favor."

"It'll be you doing the denying, after Alfred suggests we retire to Florida so he and Cynthia can live here permanently."

Patrick smiled. "We're too young to retire. Anyway, after they get married I'm sure they'll want a place of their own." It was true that a summer wedding had been mentioned, but no date had been set, and Mag did not regard the matter as settled.

Then Patrick tied his bathrobe again, and it was such a sad gesture that her anger disappeared. He had lost weight, no question about it. He could play at being a blindman, but the truth was he was getting desperate in his effort to find out what was wrong with his eyes, now that the doctors obviously couldn't. Disappearing pupils were not as easy to invent solutions for as the wet bottoms and later the sweaty legs of his sons. And in spite of his cheerful pose, it was obvious to everyone that, for the first time perhaps, Patrick was afraid.

The eye problem had begun last fall—a year ago—just when the sale of the sweatsuit patent seemed assured. Patrick had been jubilant over the prospect of a commercial success, what with so many boys off to college or about to be. He owned a small manufacturing business where people brought their vans to be upholstered in such fabrics as shag carpeting or fake fur. It was successful enough (though not so lucrative that the money from Mag's jobs didn't help), but the recession had been a setback. The manufacturer buying the sweatsuit patent was promising a big push. There would be full-color magazine ads and even TV commercials. Male models would demonstrate the Velcro fastenings that replaced the seams in the pants and shirt, showing how easily a runner could rip the suit off, leaving him free to run just in shorts and T-top when he got warm. Similar sweatpants were worn by professional basketball players, but they had never been made quite this way, or quite so cheaply, so as to be mass-marketed for runners. The garments were being promoted under the trade name RipOffs, which Patrick said was another inspiration sure to make money, even if the name had come from Madison Avenue and not from Patrick Singer himself.

So they had not expected trouble. It was fall, and Patrick had taken a week off from the plant to conclude a series of meetings about the RipOffs. The day the problem started, he had one conference in the morning and then some domestic errands he'd agreed to do because Mag was at work. He took Lucifer to the vet for shots, had lunch, and then drove Izzy back to his apartment near the University of Maryland, an hour away, where

Izzy was a graduate student and where his car was on the blink. Mag expected Patrick home early in the evening. Instead, just after dark, the phone rang. Simon answered it.

"Dad says he's staying over in a motel," Simon yelled at her. "He says the fog is too thick to drive home."

Mag's first thought was: He's found some woman. She'd always known eventually he would. The outlying suburbs were often foggy, but Patrick liked the challenge of driving in fog or snow or downpour. At one time he had even invented some interesting—unsuccessful—fog lights for their car. She took the phone.

"What the hell do you mean, the fog's too thick?" she asked.

"It's not the fog," Patrick told her. "I have a splitting headache and I think there's something wrong with my eyes. You know how the pupil closes down when you go into the bright sunshine? Well, mine seems to be doing that now, only it's dark outside. I think it's some sort of migraine."

"Patrick, at least go back to Izzy's. What if you need a doctor? Izzy can call a doctor."

"No, Izzy has some girl there. I'll just wait it out. I've already paid for this place, I might as well stay. I'll come home in the morning when the weather clears up. I should be fine by then. I'll see the doctor at home."

They hung up. Mag was not at all sure she believed the story about his eyes. She had never heard of a migraine that caused the pupils of a person's eyes to close. She pictured Patrick with another woman. She didn't sleep. She didn't know until later that Patrick's pupils had shut down all the way after they talked. He spent two hours sitting in the motel room, completely blind. He did not call a doctor or an ambulance or anyone else. When she asked him later what he thought about, he said, "I don't remember. I was scared shitless, of course." He said that in such a matter-of-fact way. But he never really told her anything. When she pressed, he said finally, "I wished to hell I wasn't allergic to liquor and could have had a couple of stiff drinks."

Later that night his eyes had relaxed and the pupils gradually opened. His vision had stayed blurry, but he could see. He took two aspirin and went to sleep. The next morning he drove home. He didn't go to a doctor until it happened again nearly three weeks later. Now, after a year, they didn't know much more than they did then.

They moved into the kitchen, and Patrick put the kettle on. He could never get out of bed without immediately preparing himself a cup of tea. He stood by the stove until the water boiled. He took a mug from the rack and a tea bag from the cannister. He poured the water on top of the tea bag and dangled it up and down in the cup six times. He always did precisely that. Then he let the bag steep. When the water was almost black, he threw the tea bag into the sink. Later Mag would remove the tea bag to the trash. They had been doing this for twenty-five years. She had always hated cleaning up after him. She had resented his freedom to leave trash in the sink and her need to remove it. But she didn't hate it now. She thought: He'll be able to make tea for himself even if he can't see. He could do it in his sleep. She thought often of the tasks she would have to perform for him if he went blind and those she wouldn't. He would hate needing her help—he was so independent—and she would resent giving it. For years the boys had demanded so much from her that a clinging husband would have been unbearable. Now, with the boys mostly grown, she looked forward to abandoning her domestic-servant role, and she did not relish the thought of taking care of a blindman. She was ashamed of herself for being glad he would at least be able to make his own tea, but she couldn't help it. Her sense of menace clung to her. Patrick would say she must not imagine things. She must be practical. They must discuss the issue of Alfred as if he were all right.

"I'm too young to be a step-grandmother," she said.

Patrick squinted at her. "You're not that young. You have a few wrinkles."

"Blond hair, though. No gray." Patrick said he had married her because of her blond hair. She believed this. He said he stayed married to her because she had a nice ass. Her ass was not as nice as it had once been, and this was frightening in its way but not something she dwelled on. At the same time, she had married him partly because of his turquoise eyes—and if he went blind, that would be frightening, too, or perhaps only ironic.

"Alfred is really acting like a prick," she said.

Patrick got up from the table and brought over an Olan Mills portrait the seven boys had given them for their twenty-fifth wedding anniversary a few months ago. He pointed to Darren and Merle. "My sons the twins," he said. A finger on Gideon's face: "My son the athlete." Percival: "My son the Marine. Izzy and Simon, my sons the students. And this is Alfred the oldest. My son the prick."

Mag gave him a disdainful look.

"There are worse things he could do than support another man's kids," Patrick said.

"I hate when you try to make me laugh." She got up and turned away from him, walked into the family room, turned on the television. A test pattern. A real-estate pitch. The twenty-minute workout.

Three perfect-looking women in leotards and leg warmers were doing jumping jacks against a background of pure white: white floor, white walls, as if they were exercising in midair, perhaps on clouds; maybe they were angels. The camera focused on their faces. They were smiling; sweat trickled down their cheeks. A shot of their glistening shoulders, a close-up of their legs, their rear ends.

"That's more like it," Patrick said. The music was simple, a pounding rhythm punctuated with screeches, parrots screaming in the jungle. Beasts. Mag was a music lover. The pounding was so jarring that she was amused. She felt calm. It was true that she had gotten up in a sweat when Izzy's ankle was broken, but no permanent harm had come of it. Her premonition over his broken ankle then had meant nothing—and her waking in a sweat now would come to nothing, too.

The perfect-looking exercise women disappeared. "We interrupt this program," a voice said, "for a special news bulletin." A man in a newsroom appeared on the screen.

"Forty-three Marines and fifteen French soldiers are dead this morning after a dawn explosion at the Beirut airport where the American contingent of the multinational peacekeeping force . . ."

"That's where Percival is," Mag said. She spoke but did not register the information in a logical way. Her premonition had not been about Alfred after all, but about Percival. The morning Izzy had broken his ankle, she had rushed into the twins' room first. Her premonitions were never very specific. Percival was off to war. She had woken because of Percival. Of course.

"The blasts apparently occurred when a terrorist suicide force drove into the two buildings with trucks loaded with explosives."

"Oh, my God," Mag said.

Patrick was holding Lucifer in one hand and pressing the top of his nose with the thumb and forefinger of his other. "There are over a thousand men there," he said woodenly. "Only forty-three were killed. That isn't so many. It probably wasn't Percival." But he kept pressing on his nose, which was what he did when his eyes were starting to bother him.

"Preliminary reports indicate that the blast leveled the four-story administration building where an undisclosed number of Marines were sleeping. Other Marines, housed in a nearby barracks . . ."

"It isn't even supposed to be a combat zone," Mag said. She had not wanted Percival to join the Marines, but had thought to herself: At least it isn't wartime.

"Did he live in that building? Did he say?"

Patrick shrugged. They had his address, of course, but it was just an FPO box number, and his letters home were never very specific about his location. Percival would turn twenty next month; he was not yet twenty and they didn't know where he lived.

"When he was little," she said woodenly, "I used to throw him out of the car when he started acting up. I used to leave him miles from home sometimes. I used to make him walk."

"He never minded," Patrick said.

"If he was sleeping in there—he could have died in his sleep."

"Oh, Christ," Patrick said. He was still squeezing his nose.

She could not bear for Percival to die in his sleep. As a child he'd never had a clear concept of tomorrow. "You mean when it gets night and gets morning?" he would ask. Later when he cut school so much, she believed it was because he still didn't understand an abstraction like tomorrow: the consequences that would come tomorrow. Maybe even now he could only relate to concrete darkness and light.

She thought of him sleeping, and willed him to wake up. She refused to see an explosion, a bomb, limbs detached and catapulted through the air. This is what she believed: that if anything bad happened to her children, no matter that they were thousands of miles away—if anything bad happened, it would be her fault. She had not wanted them in the beginning, and the sins of the fathers (in this case the mother) might well be visited on her sons. She had listened to music when she should have been tending babies—and Simon had been born without an ear. Her sons swam in a sea of menace—pastel cartoon figures in a video game, surrounded by black mouths that grew larger and more menacing the more they escaped. Having not wanted them, she could not protect them, only wish them safe passage through their lives. There were no guarantees. When she learned Simon's ear could be rectified by a surgeon's knife, she should have known another son would become the sacrifice . . . but she would not have predicted Percival. Percival had always been active and skinny, had never been charming; he had been bright

— 19 —

and bored and given to tantrums. He had not been able to run as fast as Gideon. His life had not been easy. She had loved him the most.

Outside the darkness was absolute and a heavy rain poured onto the wooden deck. In the family room Simon appeared before her. She thought for a moment she was hallucinating, because Simon liked to sleep until the moment he had to wake up to deliver his papers. Sometimes he liked to sleep longer. But it was Simon all right. He had even put on his bathrobe over his underwear. He was stretching and yawning and snapping his fingers. He always snapped his fingers when he was content, though he never knew he was doing it. He arched his back. He had grown so much that he looked even skinnier than usual, almost anorexic: tall, lazy, lovable Simon, nondescript and still prepubescent. His dark hair hung straight down over the ear that wasn't there.

"What's going on?" he said. And even in that moment, when she missed Percival as if he had been cut from her, in that moment she could think only of how it would be to tell Simon what had happened, because then he would stop snapping his fingers—maybe for good. He had been snapping since he learned at six or seven and was still doing it at fourteen. Knowing that, she could hardly bear to tell him, because Simon was the most beloved . . . and if Gideon had appeared, or Izzy or Alfred or the twins, she would have known at once that *they* were the most beloved, until her mind bogged down with it all. *Each* was the most beloved.

"They've bombed the headquarters in Beirut," she said. "Where Percival is."

Simon stopped snapping. He looked at Patrick. "Is he dead?"

"They didn't kill that many," Patrick said. "We don't know. They don't know anything."

Patrick had stopped holding his nose now and put his hands to his temples. The cat jumped to the floor. Patrick turned his face toward Mag, and she saw that his pupils were growing smaller, as if he'd looked at the sun. The turquoise irises grew larger and the pupils kept contracting. The headache had come, and now the blindness.

"Dad's eyes," she said to Simon.

Simon stood there for a moment and then opened the door to the little phone room—the room she'd had put in specially, off the family room, because with seven boys in the house, how else could anyone hear?

"What are you doing?" she asked.

"I'm calling Alfred."

Whenever there was a crisis, everyone called Alfred.

She had been foolish to think something terrible had happened to Alfred. Alfred handled crises, he did not get embroiled in them. Alfred would come over and make everyone feel calm. It was good Alfred was all right. She did not think she could stand for Percival to be dead.

Patrick was trying to look at her and then at Simon, but Simon was in the phone room, out of sight. Patrick's head bobbed awkwardly, in odd directions, like Stevie Wonder's. The pupils were shutting to pinpoints, little by little, like muscles pulling more than their accustomed weight.

"I never wanted children," she told him. "This is the punishment."

Patrick opened his eyes then, but the pupils were gone. The turquoise irises for which Mag had loved him had become two round blanks with no pupil in the middle, the perfect dead blue of cataracts. She had not wanted children and had not wanted Patrick, and this was the price.

2

"Mag—this isn't the punishment. This isn't the any-thing," Patrick told her. "An explosion went off in a war zone. It happens. You have to take it one step at a time."

She could not look at him. He put his hands to his temples to fend off the headache and stared in her direction with pale saucers of unseeing eye. Her throat, her heart, her whole chest was clenched into a fist—and Patrick, blind, seemed to be carrying on as usual.

"It wasn't supposed to be a war zone," she said. "Just a peacekeeping force."

"Semantics." Patrick started to get up, turning toward the kitchen. Mag realized he was going after his medicine, which he wouldn't be able to identify in this state, and which he would resent not being able to see. His dozen visits to the greatest eye specialists in the world had yielded no miracle drugs, only Valium for nerves, Darvon for the headache, and a muscle relaxant that was supposed to control the opening and closing of the iris but did not.

"Here, sit down," Mag said. "I'll get your stuff." The twenty-minute workout had resumed—parrots screeching, a steady drumbeat, the three models doing jumping jacks during which their bosoms remained absolutely motionless and flat. Mag turned the volume down.

"At least get a newscast," Patrick said. "It's torture knowing those ladies are there and not being able to see them." He might have been lusting for them without another thought in his mind.

Mag changed the channel. A sermon. "No preachers," Patrick mumbled. He was proud of avoiding preachers—of having quit the Catholic Church after high school and later refusing to send the boys to any sort of Sunday school. But Mag believed his approach to life had been shaped by the religious upbringing his mother, Angela, had given him—a woman who was widowed when Patrick was nine and spent the rest of her life going to Mass every morning in the freezing Maine weather and refusing to eat meat on Friday even after it was allowed.

"It's too early for the news on Sunday morning," Mag said. She found a weather forecast and walked into the kitchen.

Patrick made a show of listening as if he were absorbed, not at all concerned with what was happening in Beirut. She knew his stoic mode well. On their infrequent trips to Maine, his mother had served meager meals at such widely spaced intervals that the boys were irritable and light-headed by the time they sat down—but Patrick had starved silently along with Angela and expected his children to do the same, as if graceful endurance were more important than their hunger. And his calm facade now was apparently as important to him as Percival. Or rather, what was important was not to show emotion, no matter what. It was something like fasting before Communion, even if lack of food made you faint in church every week, as he'd told her one of the girls in his high school used to do.

She poured the pills into her palm and wet a washcloth for him to put over his eyes. "Here," she said, not kindly, shoving the medicine into his left hand and a glass of water into his right. He swallowed and then lay back, folding the washcloth over his eyes. He liked the cloth not for its dampness but because the material would prevent him from seeing anyway, and he could pretend he was normal. The weathercaster gave way to a newsman in a brown suit. Patrick didn't change position. Behind the reporter, invisible to Patrick, was a large photo of a sand-colored building surrounded by fences and barbed wire.

"The blast apparently collapsed the four-story Marine administration building, which had—in addition to sleeping quarters—a mess hall, library, gym, and other facilities for administering the sixteen-hundred-man force. More than sixty men are known to be dead at this hour, and efforts are under way to rescue others still trapped beneath the debris," the newsman reported.

"More than sixty dead," Mag said. "They said forty-three a while ago. It could be a hundred. It could be all sixteen hundred."

"That's unlikely," Patrick mumbled from beneath the washcloth. "There's no sense in imagining it worse than it is."

Simon emerged from the phone room and stood completely motionless in the middle of the family room carpet, listening, his hands hanging at the end of too-long arms, face white as an egg. "Alfred's coming over," he said. Mag could not imagine that until five minutes ago this had been a child who was continually snapping his fingers. "What else do you want me to do?" he asked.

"Just deliver your papers," Patrick said. "There's nothing we can do right now but wait for some news. We have to assume everything is going to be all right." Patrick's voice was steady.

Mag should have been grateful for his trying to reassure Simon, but she was too disturbed. She saw chunks of cement pillar, cinder blocks, shards of wire trapping sleeping men. Heard screams, and groans not unlike Patrick's when he dreamed of blindness.

"Percival could be under that building," Simon said, echoing her thoughts. He stood unnaturally still, as if he were rooted to the floor.

"Simon, don't imagine what might not even be there," Patrick told him.

"It's hard not to."

"I know."

"I can't do it," Simon said.

"Just make your mind blank."

"I don't mean that. I mean I can't deliver the papers."

"You don't have any choice."

"Patrick," Mag began.

He held up the hand that wasn't holding the washcloth. "It's . . . what? Five-thirty in the morning? Where are you planning to get a substitute?"

Simon didn't move or speak.

"It's your responsibility," Patrick told him.

"You act like you don't even care," Simon said woodenly.

"It's not that I don't care. It's just that I don't see going into a panic unless we have to."

Mag hated Patrick's calm. She saw Percival, who was always graceful, always fast, trapped beneath a building, unable to move, much less run. If he were crushed, Patrick would not think of it, though he had cared for Percival and trained him to run and loved him more than the others. But now Percival might be dead or dying and Patrick would not think of it. And if Patrick went blind, he would ignore that, too, claw his way along a beach somewhere, as if he had no needs, no grief, no pain. He expected the same of his sons: that they remain in control, do what was needed, never lose focus. To please him, Alfred had learned to practice piano in spite of a tin ear and Gideon had run track until he threw up—whatever was required—and even Simon pretended not to care about his ear because he was afraid of surgery. But it seemed too much to ask him to deliver his papers. Simon's face was white, drawn, as if at any moment he would issue a great roar that would engulf them all. Mag heard the cry in the recesses of her mind, not Simon's voice but Percival's—her son—beneath the rubble of a building in Lebanon, not calling for help with the calm face of a stoic, but screaming out of control. And because she knew Simon was close to that, too, and because in spite of everything she knew Patrick would make him deliver his papers, she said to him, "Come on, Simon, I'll help you."

Five minutes later they sat on the cement floor of the garage, stuffing the papers into transparent plastic bags. It was too wet outside just to rubber-band them. The overhead light was on, bright and unshaded. The only sound was the rain. She had delivered papers hundreds of times and never hated it like this. First she'd helped Alfred and then the others—ten years of it—whenever it rained or was too cold. She'd helped on Sundays and Wednesdays, when the food ads made the papers thick and the boys either had to make two trips on their bikes or get her to take them in the car. They argued that otherwise the complaints would start coming in, because deliveries were supposed to be completed by seven. In those days Mag only listened if she felt like it; they all understood that. There were eighty-nine dailies, ninety-four Sundays—fewer in Alfred's and Izzy's time, before their subdivision was complete. Mostly she didn't mind. She liked the neighborhood early in the morning, the webby green feel of it in summer, with rabbits running across the grass; and in winter getting hot from the exercise, especially if she knew she'd be sitting at a desk all day at work. But now it was the last week of daylight savings time, dead dark, and it felt colder than it really was because of the rain. The *Freestate Sentinel* banner head passed under her fingers forty-odd times as she slipped it into bags. There was no mention in the paper of Beirut, or of Percival, because the explosion had come too late to make the deadline. But tomorrow Lebanon would be front-page stuff, and Patrick would make sure Simon delivered it to the neighbors by seven A.M.—photos of buildings blown up, leveled, obliterated, and perhaps the graduation picture of that local boy, Percival Singer, who was or wasn't dead. And for the first time since the morning Izzy had broken his ankle, Mag felt that the job was obscene.

Simon began to load the back of the station wagon. He worked slowly, mechanically, his face still very white.

"Applewood first, all right?" he said. But she already knew: Applewood first, then Lynwood, Canterwood, Trevor Circle; they had their routine. They would park halfway down the block on each street, and she would deliver one section, he the other, each of them moving away from the car to do the houses on one side, back toward the car on the other.

The darkness and the cold rain were all-consuming. She carried fourteen papers on Applewood, her big canvas bag pulling at her shoulder, Sundays always so heavy. Her hood did not protect her. Soon her face was wet, and water seeped down under her collar, down her neck, ending in a cold puddle on her chest. She didn't care. In the dark she could not see where she was going. She knew these lawns, these landmarks, but in the blackness she tripped on an uneven driveway, on vines growing at a property line, on a branch lying on the grass. She didn't fall. She caught herself, righted herself, as if the larger force of her terror were holding her up. Simon, too, moved swiftly, unthinkingly, and when they got back into the car to drive to the next block, she saw that he had let the hood of his slicker fall free. His hair was soaked, hugging his head, showing the clear outline of the right outer ear that was there and the flat place on the left where it wasn't. Simon always wore hats, or sweatshirts with hoods, and never in the past two years had he let his hair get wet in public.

"At least the rain keeps people inside," Mag said, needing to draw some response from him. All the boys had hated it when people came outside wanting to complain or pay or exchange greetings. They said it slowed them down.

"You'll be surprised," he said woodenly. And Mag knew he was thinking he couldn't bear anyone to come out today, oblivious of the news, and ask him how he was.

She could hardly stand it. It seemed to her that Simon suffered enough. When he was born, the first thing she'd noticed about him was the small round hole in his head where his left ear was supposed to be, but no outer ear whatsoever. It had seemed to her then that he was bearing the punishment for her failures. Now it occurred to her that this additional burden of Percival's fate might be just too much for him.

"He's deaf," she'd said to the doctor when she first saw him, suddenly realizing both the enormity of her guilt and of his suffering. It was her fault. Four years before, when the twins were born, giving her six sons at the age of twenty-five, the obstetrician had said, "You ought to consider having your tubes tied. You can't do this forever." She had been giddy then, feeling superior for having produced two sons at once, and refused. Also, she believed if she had her tubes tied, the children might be kidnapped or run over by a tractor trailer as an irony to remind her she hadn't wanted them—leaving her alone with a useless reproductive system. Later, when Darren cried with colic and Merle cried in sympathy, when she was snowbound for a week with all six of them (only Alfred was in school all day), it occurred to her that lower animals also produced their young by the litter. But she was too busy then, for irony or surgery, either one.

She had almost begun to believe she was through with pregnancies when Simon came along, squalling and red and earless.

Knowing he was deaf, understanding he was heir to her punishment, she loved him the most. She had her tubes tied before she left the hospital, reasoning that nothing worse could happen. She hadn't wanted children, had listened to music, not heeded them, and it seemed fitting that Simon was born unable to listen at all—though hideously unfair to Simon. It was a pure gift when they learned Simon's hearing was normal, and another when he began to snap his fingers when he was happy and snapped them all the time.

Before his hair grew in, she dressed him in hats to hide the defect, but Simon pulled them off. People stared; Simon smiled back. He lived in a closed universe of brothers who did not regard his earlessness as abnormal, so neither did he. "Where's your eye?" the boys would ask when he was little, and Simon would point to it. "Where's your mouth?" When they got to his ear, he would point to the normal one unless they indicated the left side and asked, "What's that?" Then Simon would smile with delight, put his hand on the hole, and answer gleefully: "No ear!" To guffaws all around.

Other times when they were small, three or four boys would pile on Patrick as he lay on the family room couch on Sundays, watching basketball games. "Oh, I see," Patrick would say. "What we've got here is an ugly sandwich. I'm the bottom bread, Darren's the mayonnaise, Simon's the top bread—and Percival is the *ugly*." This formula could be expanded to accommodate lettuce, pickles, and onions and any number of players, with the child closest to the middle singled out for insult as the ugly. Usually it was Percival, but often Darren or Merle, since everyone enjoyed the idea of one twin being ugly and not the other, when they looked exactly alike. Simon invariably ended up high in the pack so his older brothers wouldn't crush him— and maybe he believed, truly, that he was always the top bread and never the ugly.

Once his hair grew in, it covered the naked hole and made him look normal. Mag almost believed punishment had passed them by until Simon was five and had to have his tonsils out. A week after the surgery his fever shot up to 103, he broke out from head to toe with welts, and his lungs filled with fluid from an allergy to an antibiotic. Allergies came from Patrick's side— but when Patrick had grown allergic to beer, he had only sneezed uncontrollably, while Simon, sweet Simon, would die.

But Simon lived, Simon lived! Mag took her first full-time job as soon as he got better—canvassing neighborhoods for a product survey—because she knew she couldn't stand it if one of the children died while she was home doing nothing but tending them, when all she'd ever wanted was a life of her own. Yet in the morning, packing lunches, she would hear a boy coming down the stairs and know it was Simon because he was snapping his fingers. And that, as much as her work, made her happy.

She would have been content, then, having a defective son who didn't recognize his flaw. She would not have asked him to change. But then adolescence overtook him, and though his voice didn't deepen and he didn't stop snapping his fingers, an inner turmoil had been shaking him for a year. He went around the house making the strange dancing motions favored by his black friends at school. He spent hours looking at himself in the mirror. He stopped playing basketball—his favorite sport—and refused to run in races, though like his brothers, he ran well. He played baseball instead, though he was never any good at it, and soccer because they let him be goalie. Mag believed he switched to those sports because at second base and goalie his head was reasonably still. She believed he'd given up basketball and running because when he was moving fast or jumping, the air blew his hair back from his face and exposed his missing ear for everyone to see.

When Mag saw a newspaper article about a surgeon who re-made parts of people that were missing, hope bloomed in her chest. She consulted the doctor herself before mentioning it to Simon. The doctor said Simon was at the perfect age for ear reconstruction, because ears reached almost their full size by eight or nine. Though the surgery had to be done in several stages—two or three operations in all—the process would be complete in a year, with no corrections needed later to compensate for further growth.

When she brought up the possibility of surgery to Simon, he turned to her with a face the color of wax. He said, in a voice she had heard before only from a cute little black kid on TV: "What you talkin' about, Mama? You want me to *die?*"

And today, in the dark rain, she felt the unfairness of his having to contemplate not only his own death from surgery but Percival's from war. She was not sure he could bear it.

He appeared out of the darkness, shouting something at her.

"What?" she yelled back.

"I said I'll take the path over to Trevor Circle."

She saw that he had finished his papers on Canterwood and even refilled his bag. He moved across the lawn swiftly, angrily. She understood. He was racing against himself, playing a survival game. The more he exhausted himself, the less he would think.

"Meet me over there in the car," he shouted, not slowing down. Then he was gone, down the wooded path between two houses, onto the street behind. Though the two streets butted each other, you had to go all the way around the block to get to Trevor Circle in the car, and he did not want to wait for her. On foot, it was faster to take the shortcut through the trees.

She was finishing her last few houses when a dog began to bark. She could not place it at first; it was somewhere in the distance. The barking grew louder, more violent. Then both the pitch and the direction of the noise became unmistakable. Monster! The dog lived on Trevor Circle, terrorizing the residents. In ten years she'd known many animals, but only one like this. A growl, deep and vicious, then the frenzied sounds of attack.

She ran to the car. She could imagine it: Simon emerging from the woods, loaded down, at the bend of the road. Monster sitting in silent ambush on its porch until he approached. Now the dog was racing toward him, snarling out its fury, baring its teeth—a wide, yellow, knee-high burst of anger. She imagined Simon fending it off with threats, with great wavings of a rolled-up paper, but she didn't know if it would work. Monster had bitten Simon on the calf during the summer. He still had the scar.

Her heart beat so fast that she felt ill. She could take the footpath, but the car was a better weapon. She got in and drove down Canterwood wildly, around the block toward Trevor Circle. She lost the sound for a moment and then picked it up again—a fierce, untamed mix of barking and growling. She had begun to tremble.

She turned onto the street. She would honk, weave back and forth, let Simon jump in. But in the small silence before she took action, the sound modulated. It became an ordinary bark, no longer the anguished fury of attack. The sweep of her headlights caught Simon far on the other side of the circle. The dog was not at his heels. It was trotting back toward its home. Simon was jogging across a lawn to drop a paper, having escaped from the attack. Monster's house was on her section of the route, not his; it was only that he had to walk past the animal to get there. Now the dog saw the car and hastened toward her. It resumed the frenzied barking. She stopped at the bottom of its driveway just as the dog reached her car. The door of the house had opened and a man was standing on the porch, sheltered from the rain.

"Daisy!" he called. He didn't venture off the porch. Daisy indeed! *Monster.* Her heart still pounded. That such people should be warm and dry in their houses, and Simon should have to fend off their dog in the rain. That such a dog should be allowed to exist . . . The man in the doorway wasn't someone they knew; he'd lived there less than a year. Mag turned toward him, hoping he could see. She stuck her arm out the window, slipped the paper out of its plastic sleeve. There was a little puddle in the middle of the driveway. She dropped the paper into the water. The dog barked faster, louder, and ran for her arm. She pulled it back.

"Here's your paper!" she called to the man on the porch. "Come and get it!"

"You better not leave it there! You're supposed to bring it to the porch!" The man didn't move from the doorway.

"Not with that dog out here. Ever hear of the leash law?"

"You put it on the porch anyway!" he yelled at her. "I'll call and complain."

"Be my guest."

"You get it up here!" he threatened.

"Next time I'll drop it in the intersection," she said.

The dog had retreated, was heading for the porch. She put the car in gear and drove around the curve, toward Simon. He had finished delivering his papers and was standing in the street, listening.

"He get you?" she asked. Suddenly her voice was shaky, thin.

"No. Usually I wave a paper at him and he goes away. Toreador-style, you know? But he surprised me. Barry Kline says the neighbors are getting up a petition to make them keep him inside, and I guest mostly they are."

"Bastard," Mag said.

"Language, Mom."

"That idiot—standing on his porch so he won't get wet, while the dog chases you halfway down the street. He even said he'd complain. I hope he does."

"He never complains."

"I took the paper out of its bag and dropped it on his driveway."

"All *right*." Simon snapped his fingers.

"There was a little puddle in the driveway."

"I know it well." Simon smiled and his fingers snapped. Then he remembered what day it was; they both did. As if a switch had been thrown, the sound of the snapping stopped. The car was cold and silent except for the rain. Mag's hands were shaking. She wrapped her fingers around the steering wheel and willed herself to drive.

There was one more block to do. She forced herself to load papers into her bag calmly. They would finish, and this would be over. That was what Patrick would say.

It was still quite dark and the rain had not let up. In an odd way, the darkness and rain were like a veil around her, protecting her. The trembling began to lessen.

As if to mock her for thinking she was safe, a porch light went on as she approached the next house. An elderly woman in a robe cracked open the front door. The old never sleep, Mag thought. She recognized the woman, but vaguely. "Simon?" the woman said.

"No, it's his mother."

The woman squinted. "I believe I used to see you back when those twins used to bring the paper."

"All my boys have had this route," she said.

"They've got you out on some awful morning."

"Yes," Mag said. She wouldn't explain.

The woman laughed. "Well, they've probably just got you well trained—all those boys for so many years."

"Probably," she said. Water was running down her neck. The truth of the statement struck her. She was a middle-aged woman delivering newspapers in a predawn rain because she was well trained. She was here because of a principle her husband believed in and she didn't. She should not be delivering papers while Percival might be lying dead five thousand miles away. She should not be bringing Simon out into the rain because Patrick expected it. She was so accustomed to his demands that she had lost her own good sense. And it was not just today. Had she followed her own instincts years ago, she would have stopped having babies before they overwhelmed her. Percival would not have been sandwiched into the middle of such a large family. She would have had more time for him, and he might not have needed to join the Marines. In the darkness it did not occur to her that if Percival were the baby, she would not have had Simon at all. She only knew that now the punishment would fall on Percival because she had let Patrick train her to a life she didn't want. The porch light went off in front of her and the woman disappeared into the house. She was shivering more than she had been in the car.

Her name was Margaret. She was seventeen years old and everyone called her Peggy. "What's your real name?" Patrick Singer asked, staring down her bathing suit at the only tan she'd ever had. Her breasts were not large, but the skin on her chest was golden and the bathing suit gave her cleavage.

"Margaret," she said.

"Mag." Even that first day, he never called her Peggy. Always Mag.

"Short for maggot?" her father asked later. "Magpie?"

They were at the beach for a two-week vacation. Her father came on weekends, between his business trips, and her sister, Sally, stayed the whole time, with her baby. Sally's husband, Wayne, drove down as much as he could. When Patrick threw a Frisbee into their blanket, Wayne remembered he and Patrick had taken a class together at the University of Maryland and introduced him around.

Mag liked Patrick's dark hair and light eyes. She liked his height and his leanness and particularly the way he stared at her. She was attracted but not overwhelmed. She was just seventeen, about to enter her senior year of high school and then go on to college. She had other things on her mind besides boys. She was only playing.

Patrick admired her hair, which had bleached almost white from so much sun. He admired her tan. Like many blondes, she normally didn't tan and was happier in winter. She liked crisp dry air; she liked to be cold. Heat and humidity made her feel untidy, and sitting in the sun made her dizzy. That summer she baked herself for hours because she was so restless. Her mother drove her crazy, sweeping the beach cottage clean of every scrap of sand. Sally wasn't much better. Peggy fled. The first day she burned a little from staying out so long. Later her skin turned beige and then golden. A sweaty, light-headed feeling stayed with her from so much sun, but she didn't mind.

"This is my first tan ever," she told Patrick. She did not want him to expect more from her appearance than she could deliver. "Probably my last. We almost never come to the beach. Too much sun makes me feel sick."

"Biologically, you must be a northerner," he said. "I like northern hair." He touched her hair, which was caked with salt from swimming, the texture of straw. She was embarrassed because normally her hair was silken. "I also like your tan, even if it's just a temporary aberration." He stroked her arm, right there in front of everyone. Her stomach began to cramp.

He took her to a miniature-golf course, introducing her to his friends as Mag. She didn't like his friends much, or being called Mag. She did like the way he kept touching her. She had been touched before, but less confidently, and never in public. Still, she was only seventeen, she didn't take it too seriously. After they went home from the beach, Patrick called almost every night, though he was at the university in College Park, an hour away, and had to pay long-distance rates.

She dated him all her senior year because he was less dreary than the boys at school. His calling her Mag annoyed her, but it seemed less important than his eyes, which were the exact turquoise color of the neighborhood swimming pool. Soon her mother and her sister were calling her Mag when Patrick was around. Sally's baby, Rachel, stammered out among her first words a hesitant "Ant Mag." Her father stuck with Peggy—Margaret when he was angry—but even he was not immune to Patrick's ability to fix cars and rig up insulation blankets for an aging hot-water heater—all those practical qualities his family of women lacked.

Patrick got his degree in business administration two weeks before Peggy finished high school. He came to her graduation, where her friends stared at him and referred to him as her Older Man. All summer she necked with him in the back of his car, warding off the boredom of her summer job. In the fall she went to Hood College, commuting forty minutes because there was no money for her to live in the dorm. She took courses in biology, music appreciation, history, and English. At night Patrick fondled her until she was sick to her stomach, in such odd positions in the front seat of his car that she would often wake the next morning with sore shoulders or a stiff neck.

"Don't, Patrick," she would say, not removing his hands. He would continue to a point and then reluctantly stop. It was fashionable then for girls like Peggy to save their virginity until marriage.

Living at home was duller than ever, with her mother ironing shirts and discussing toilet training with Sally over the phone. Peggy had no wish to emulate either of them. She would get her degree and then take a traveling job like her father's. She would never be like her mother, who vacuumed the carpets twice a week and ushered her family to occasional services at the Presbyterian church. College and Patrick were a temporary escape. Patrick unbuttoned her blouse in the semisecrecy of his car, put his hand into her pants. When her parents went out at night, they spent hours lying naked under the covers in the guest room, rubbing against each other, drunk with the sense of being alone in private, until her parents seemed likely to return. Otherwise they were relegated to the car, because Patrick lived an hour away with three roommates. They declared their love, though Peggy wasn't sure if it was love she felt or only passion. In his spare time, Patrick redesigned the seat of his car so that it went down all the way, turning the entire vehicle into a double bed. Peggy, too, had come to depend on his practicality.

In her own spare time, she studied less and thought more about having sex with Patrick, though she resisted the ultimate act. Some nights she refused to let him put the car seat down, to show him she was serious about preserving her virtue. During one of these nights Patrick slid her underpants off completely—something he had done before only in the spare bedroom. She held onto them. "Come on, we're sitting up, nothing's going to happen," he said. He turned her so she was spread-eagled on his lap facing him, her knees on the seat on either side of him, her breasts cradled in his hand. He rubbed her nipples with his fingers and her lower parts with his penis. After a time she realized he was moving not only *against* her but in, just a little. She was too curious to resist. They had waited so long. She was only slightly astonished when her hymen broke, suddenly, with a few drops of blood and a pop like a bursting balloon, but no pain.

"I thought it was supposed to hurt," she said afterward.

"I think, Mag," Patrick told her, "that these past couple of months we loosened it up."

Patrick had gotten a job in Washington. It was 1958. Peggy told him she was going to stop having sex with him, she was going to concentrate on college. He said that was ridiculous, he loved her, he respected her, what difference did it make. She argued with him but discovered that once you started having sex you couldn't stop. To offset the arguments, Patrick offered marriage. The day of her wedding, her father, the last holdout, started calling her Mag.

Alfred was born a year later. Her water broke before she went into a labor, with the same balloonlike pop that had marked the end of her virginity. Mag believed that this was some kind of sign—the pop of the hymen precursing the pop of her waters, indicating that Alfred's birth had been preordained. This reassured her, because she had not planned a baby so soon. She had intended to continue school and work part-time, since Patrick's salary was enough for them to live on but didn't allow for any saving. But as her pregnancy advanced, she gave up her part-time job and dropped all her courses but one, a survey of English history from ancient times to the present. Even then she sensed that Patrick was training her to live according to his plan and not her own, but she resisted in her own way. The baby arrived just as she was studying Alfred the Great in school, and it was Alfred she chose as his name. The original Alfred had saved his country from conquest, laid the basis for the unification of England, written a great code of laws. Mag did not know if she chose the name for herself, since she was only nineteen and hadn't done anything yet, or her hopes for the baby, who was unplanned but cute enough, and apparently preordained.

Izzy came along two years later, when she was studying ethnic modern literature. Patrick wanted to name him after his late father, William, but Mag thought a baby named Isaac Bashevis Singer would be nice, in honor of the writer. Patrick disagreed. Isaac Bashevis Singer was famous for his ethnic Jewish stories, and Patrick was not only not Jewish but had given up religion years ago. Why foist it on his offspring? Why name a son Isaac Bashevis and open the whole Judeo-Christian can of worms? Mag didn't give in. Patrick's father had been a Methodist, she argued; his mother was a Catholic; a Jewish patriarch generations ago had given Patrick's branch of the Singer family its name. How could he get away from religion? Besides, there was another Isaac Singer in recent history, not a writer but the inventor of the sewing machine—and since Patrick was already something of an inventor himself, what would be wrong with passing that name on to the child? They compromised by calling the baby Isaac William instead of Isaac Bashevis, and dubbed him Izzy right away.

For the next few years Mag was busy tending babies and not pursuing a career, but when she looked at her sons, she saw Isaac Bashevis and imagined an intellectual; she saw Alfred the Great and envisioned a leader of men. She hung her dreams for a great career on her children, figuring she would get her chance later. Even so, she was restless. She hated hauling diapers back and forth to the laundry room, washing diapers, hanging diapers out to dry. She hated diapers even after her complaints led

Patrick to invent the makeshift disposable diaper she rarely used but that turned out to be good enough for the manufacturing company.

She might have wised up then, but she didn't. Patrick stroked her thigh under the table even as the babies were mashing strained peas between their fingers. Watching the green mess did not keep her stomach from cramping with desire, or her thoughts from imagining Patrick's mouth on her breasts. His eyes were turquoise; his chest was broad. He woke her from a dead sleep in the middle of the night, with his hands between her legs and her crotch already wet. He was training her. She not only let it happen; she kept going back for more. Percival was born on November 22, 1963, the day Jack Kennedy was shot. Patrick wanted to call him John, but Mag insisted on something grander, more knightly: Percival. She had just read Malory's *Morte D'Arthur* and named her son for Camelot. Did she think it would make any difference? Did she think it would gain her her career? The jobs she began to take when Simon was four were always just that—jobs, not careers—and now, twenty-five years since the beginning, nothing had changed.

In her office at the county public-relations department, her colleagues called her Mag, not Margaret or Peggy. Her parents called her Mag, and so did her sister Sally and her two grown nieces. She was so well trained that she had gotten used to it. But the truth was that Patrick had changed her completely—from Peggy, who was young and free and ambitious, to Mag, with all those sons. To Mag, who at his request would go out and deliver papers in rain and darkness with Simon, wondering if Percival were still alive.

3

lfred woke the instant the phone rang, before Cynthia had a chance to stir. He had been expecting a middle-of-the-night call for months—some emergency about his father's eyes. He was prepared to get up in the darkness and rush Patrick to the emergency room, even to Hopkins in Baltimore if necessary. He did not expect an incident in Beirut. When Simon gave him that and his father's eyes at the same time, a sharp pain cut through his belly—adrenaline probably—and settled into a knot that would not go away.

Cynthia turned over as he hung up. "What is it?" Her voice was hoarse with sleep and her large breasts moved beneath her gown. He did not expect to be affected by the sight of her just then, but she was wearing flannel against the cold, and the thick material made her seem softer, more vulnerable than she did in cotton or lace. For a moment he was filled with such a sense of her lushness that Simon's call made him feel like a man in exile—suddenly barred from his bed and what seemed, in retrospect, perfect happiness. He foresaw days of waiting, sorrow, tragedy, when happiness would be inappropriate and he would feel guilty even for his desire.

Her hand was on his wrist, and her breasts moved against his arm. "My mother overreacting again, I think," he said in a voice pitched to let her go back to sleep. "Probably nothing." Watching Cynthia roll back over, he felt exactly as he had as a boy in his grandmother's house in Maine, aware of the Lifesavers he'd stashed in his pockets to hedge against the skimpy meals, but too ashamed to eat them because his brothers were not similarly fortified and his father expected him to make do with Angela's cooking. Now he knew he wouldn't be able to touch Cynthia for as long as it took to handle this crisis, and was embarrassed for wanting her. The knot in his stomach grew tight. In the living room, dressed, he closed all the bedroom doors to shield Cynthia and her boys from sound. Then he turned on the TV to learn what was happening in Lebanon.

When he got to his parents' house an hour later, his father was lying on the couch with a washcloth over his eyes, and his mother and Simon were sitting there soaked from delivering the papers, which gave some indication of their states of mind. The TV was on full blast, though for the moment no newscaster was on the screen, but rather an evangelist. Patrick never watched religious shows of any kind.

"Give the most you can, sisters and brothers," the evangelist was saying, "the most you possibly can to spread the word of *Gawd*."

They were all absorbed in it. Alfred had come in the front door, not silently. None of them said a word to acknowledge he was there.

"And tell us your want," the evangelist said. "We'll put your pledge to work and we'll do our best to pray over your want."

"Your *want?*" Patrick echoed.

Alfred strode across the room. "I can't believe you're watching this." He changed the channel.

"Oh . . . Alfred," Mag said, suddenly aware of him. "The program comes on when they take off the news."

Patrick, still on the couch, said, "If God really cares how people act in the world, I have to believe He's pissed off at that guy."

"Patrick, don't," Mag said. She never liked him to speak disrespectfully of God, just in case.

Alfred had anticipated their disarray. The first thing he intended to say was that, statistically at least, it was unlikely Percival had been killed or even hurt. Alfred wasn't sure it would help, but it was logical and they would all feel the need for logic.

"That dog went after Simon again," his mother said in an expressionless voice. "It bit him once already."

"Twice," Simon said.

"Twice!" his mother yelled.

Simon opened the Velcro leg seam of his RipOffs sweatpants, to reveal a dark bruise on his calf. "It didn't break the skin."

"He can handle the dogs, Mag," Patrick said. His voice was muffled under the washcloth.

"I called Camp Lejeune," Alfred told them in the calm tone he had prepared. Percival had been stationed at Camp Lejeune in North Carolina before he went overseas. "They say only one building was involved in the blast. There are a number of buildings."

Mag and Simon stared at him. It seemed as if Patrick was staring, too, though the washcloth was fast against his eyes. The knot in Alfred's stomach contracted like a fist.

"Yeah, only one building," Simon said. "Only the headquarters."

"They don't know much about the casualties," Alfred said.

"Does that surprise you?" Patrick asked.

"It's only been a couple of hours."

"A couple of hours."

"More like eight hours," Simon told them. "It was just after midnight here when it happened. That's more than a couple of hours."

"You should take your shower," Alfred said, noticing that Simon was hugging himself into his dripping sweatshirt, looking pale and ill.

His mother studied Simon, though she was equally wet. "You're going to catch a cold."

"That would be just some tragedy right now, wouldn't it?" Simon said. "Me catching a fucking cold."

Mag ran her hand through her hair. "Simon, don't. No F-words. Not now." Simon stared at the floor.

A newscaster had come on. He was retelling what they already knew. Alfred turned the sound a little lower. He did not see the value in hearing such things over and over again.

"I called Izzy," he announced. "He's picking up the twins and bringing them home." Darren and Merle were freshmen at the University of Maryland; they lived in a dorm and did not have a car. As a graduate student there, Izzy had his own apartment in College Park and a car that had been in the family for years. "I thought we'd wait a little to call Gideon. It's two hours earlier in Utah. We might as well wait till he gets up."

His mother was not listening to him. She focused on the TV set. "Ironically," the announcer was saying, "casualties may be higher because on Sunday morning many of the men were asleep. Sunday is the one day most of them did not have to report for duty."

"I can't listen to this anymore," Mag said. She rose and went into the living room. Her shoes were so wet that they made a sucking sound as she walked across the carpet. They could hear her flip through her record case. A moment later she turned the stereo on, loud enough to drown out the news on the family room TV . . . and also, Alfred suspected, the thoughts that must be racing through her mind.

His father shifted on the couch.

"You want me to say something to her?" Alfred asked.

"No. Give her a few minutes."

"Christ," Simon said.

"This would be a good opportunity to shower," Alfred told him.

"Not yet," Simon said.

The walls of the family room vibrated with the crashing music from the stereo. Simon watched the TV, though the sound was inaudible over the music. Patrick lay still on the couch and seemed to be asleep. Alfred didn't think he really was. It was unlike his father to abdicate in times of stress. After five minutes of the music playing at full volume, Alfred trailed his mother into the living room. She was curled into the corner of the sofa, knees up, chin resting on them, arms wrapped around her legs—a fetal position, catatonic, staring into the music. The position struck him as even more unbalanced than her wet clothes. He turned the stereo down so he could talk to her.

"Mother, don't," he said. "Everyone will be coming home soon."

"Every time the doorbell rings," she said, "we'll think it's bad news."

"It won't be. It'll be Izzy and them. And then the neighbors. As soon as they hear, you know they'll start coming over."

"A social event."

"They'll bring things to eat. It will be out of kindness."

His mother rose from the sofa and turned up the music again. It was Mussorgsky's *Pictures at an Exhibition*. He knew the piece well. It had been one of his favorites when he was a child—full of horns and cymbals, not too violiny. But his mother only played it when she was upset. Her music always reflected her moods: opera when she felt sentimental—*Madama Butterfly* or *Aida*, always Puccini or Verdi; sweet ballet music when she felt nostalgic—*Swan Lake* in warm weather, *The Nutcracker* in cold; Chopin polonaises when she was restless. When he was in grade school she'd always played *Gaieté Parisienne* on the nights his father stayed out late—wild, untamed-sounding stuff—and now that he was living with Cynthia, he felt he understood. But *Pictures at an Exhibition* she saved for when she was upset about the children.

The last section of the piece was playing—"The Great Gate at Kiev." He was six or seven when she'd told him about it. Each part of *Pictures* represented a picture at an actual exhibition, she'd said. One painting was of the city of Kiev, of the gate. The music was about the painting. "Try to imagine it. It makes it more fun."

So he'd tried. "Kiev is in Russia," she'd announced, setting the Q–R volume of the encyclopedia before him, opened to the section on Russia. He was too young to make out most of the words, but he'd looked at the photograph of the domed Russian church in Red Square. Afterward, listening to the music, he'd imagined tall wrought-iron gates leading into a city named Kiev. Beyond the gates he'd pictured a domed church like the one in the encyclopedia, but surrounded by a grassy yard and stone paths instead of sidewalks.

In the music, bells rang. There was a sound of stars falling, or maybe confetti—*star* confetti—and then a gong. The music sounded like springtime, so he'd pictured church bells ringing on Easter morning, summoning people from the countryside to the church inside the great gate. The sun was shining, and the grass was new green after the winter. The music grew larger inside his head. People in peasant costumes poured through the gates as the star confetti fell. He knew from the music that they had come to celebrate the Resurrection, a genuine Resurrection. Alfred didn't go to church, but his father had told him the story of Jesus. The star confetti fell on the people, and there was the possibility of perfect joy. This struck him now as strange, not only because he knew so little of religion then or because his mother was listening to the music now in anticipation of Percival's death, but because at six or seven he'd been too young, he thought, to get caught up in that kind of power. Later, when he'd taken piano lessons, it was the feeling inspired by "The Great Gate at Kiev" that he'd tried to recapture as he sat practicing.

A note of triumph, then a silence that let the mumble of the television through from the other room. Alfred turned the record off, annoyed for having listened, for getting involved in it again, especially right now. "You ought to get out of those wet clothes, Mother," he said. "Before anyone gets here."

"You have it all planned, don't you? This death watch."

"Chances are he's not dead."

"I woke up this morning with a premonition," she said.

"That doesn't necessarily mean anything."

"What about the time Izzy broke his ankle? What about Simon's tonsils?"

"They both got better."

She sighed. "Is Cynthia coming over?" she asked.

"She wasn't up yet when I left."

"I think most women would wake up if the phone rang in the middle of the night."

"I told her it was nothing. I didn't want to disturb her until we knew something."

"I see," his mother said.

But she did not see. She had told him his living with Cynthia was setting a bad example for his brothers, even though Izzy had several different female roommates a year while he, Alfred, was practicing fidelity. She objected to his raising Cynthia's sons even though she'd always demanded that he be responsible; she objected to his plans for marriage. Alfred felt no compunction to explain. It was none of his mother's business that he had said "I love you" to other women before but "I need you" only to Cynthia. His feeling for her was as powerful as it had been for certain pieces of music when he was younger. His mother had nurtured the one, why not the other? As a teenager he had tried to play Chopin's polonaises on the piano and she had not tried to talk him out of that. When the music refused to come from his fingers the way he heard it in his heart, he had gone instead to his mother's records, needing to hear them so badly that he could think of nothing else. She had not objected to that, either. She had watched as the music built and filled him—its teasing, its cresting, its great crescendos that he recognized with some embarrassment as musical orgasms. Later his mother had been sympathetic to his need for women, which drew (he believed) from the same underlying passions. But now with Cynthia— when there was both the yearning and pleasure the music had once inspired, and also solidity and permanence, his mother was immovable in her disdain.

He had been surprised and hurt at first, striking back by refusing to defend the relationship. But his timing had been bad. He saw that his mother was disturbed by his father's eye condition and Simon's refusal to have ear surgery, and he did not wish to add to her distress. She was not unpleasant to Cynthia outright—quite the opposite really; she saved her lectures for when she could get Alfred alone. So he searched for some gesture of appeasement. When his father began talking about spending the winter in the Keys, now that the money from the RipOffs had come in, Alfred saw his chance. He offered to move into his parents' house with Cynthia and her boys, so his parents could sample Florida for a few months without worrying. He thought perhaps it would smooth things over, though it would not be an easy thing to do.

At first, Cynthia was reluctant. She wanted her own house someday, not Alfred's old one, and liked being in the apartment because the babysitter lived just downstairs. She was afraid of what might happen to the place if she sublet it and didn't relent until Alfred explained how much this meant to him. He had in mind that he might do some repairs while his parents were gone—repaint the bedrooms, prune the overgrown bushes in the yard. He thought that in the long run everyone would be pleased. Finally, with some misgivings, Cynthia had agreed.

"She has a friend who's willing to take her apartment through the winter," he had told his mother, though that wasn't entirely true. "You and Dad can just go, just enjoy yourselves, and we'll look after everything here."

His mother, hearing that, had looked stricken. She looked equally stricken now, hearing that Cynthia was still asleep. And though he had always seen it as his duty to intervene in times of crisis, he felt at a loss.

"I won't ask her to come over unless you want her to," he said.

"It's all right," she told him. But he could tell by her tone that it was not.

Mag decided she would not fight Alfred about Cynthia today. There was no point. The situation was already horrible beyond words, and Cynthia could not make it worse. Anyway, Alfred always got what he wanted because he was so good at passive resistance. What he lacked in passion he made up for in endurance. She had to pick her battles. Let him have Cynthia. Under no circumstances was he going to get her house.

How could she think about that now?

But she did. She remembered how Alfred had always waited her out, even as a child when he wanted the tiny fourth bedroom that was too small for more than one boy. He would use the same tactic now. Back then, Percival had screamed that he should have the bedroom for privacy, and Izzy had sulked that he needed a place for his experiments. But Alfred, more clever, had only said calmly, "I just don't want to live in a pigsty like the rest of them," and eventually he had won out. Every time she thought of giving the room to one of the others, Alfred's words would remind her of Percival's and Izzy's detritus—scraps of balsa wood for a model, overdue library books on snake breeding, clothes uprooted from the drawers—and finally she gave the room to Alfred because he would keep it neat. Alfred had prevailed.

And if he wanted Cynthia here today, he would prevail in that, too. Even the way he had presented Cynthia to them was an exercise in persistence—so tentatively at first, bringing her to the house alone, letting them notice her slick dark hair and pale skin and outsized breasts; and then bringing her with her sons—not asking for anyone's opinion, just bringing them to a backyard barbecue, to a race Gideon was running, casual occasions where they would not get in the way, letting everyone adjust, until Cynthia and the boys seemed inevitable, and even the idea of their living together did not send the younger ones into dirty-minded whoops of delight.

So let him have Cynthia. Because on the matter of the house Mag would be unswayable. Her passion for the place would save her—the one thing Alfred could not fight against because it was a quality he lacked. Cynthia was the sort of sweaty pleasure Mag's grown sons needed, but real feeling carried over twenty years was something else. When it came to Mag's house, he would be hindered by his coolness just as, years ago, he had been unable to master the piano—able to pick up the technical knowledge but never to experience the great, transcendent joy Mag had hoped he'd get from the music.

Alfred was staring at the floor. He seemed to be anticipating his next move. "We probably ought to call Beth O'Neal," he said finally. The idea wiped any other thought right out of her. It was the sort of logical, bloodless thing Alfred would think of.

"I'll call her if you want," he offered.

"No, I will." Now that he had mentioned it, there seemed to be no other choice.

They've got you well trained, the woman on the paper route had said this morning. It was quite true. She rose, turned the music off, and headed for the phone room.

Her fingers were unsteady as she dialed. Beth O'Neal and her son, Tim, were responsible for Percival's being in Beirut. The two boys were stationed in the same unit, though the truth was, Mag had not thought once about Tim. She resented Beth even at this moment. This call was no act of friendship, or even of charity—but of contrition, the sort of thing her late mother-in-law would have enjoyed. If she made the phone call, perhaps Percival would live.

To Mag, Beth O'Neal had always seemed the essence of those big-boned, hulking women she could never bring herself to be— the primal mothers who appeared at school and baseball games not to socialize with other parents but to hover over their young like animals scenting out the threat of danger. The children of those mothers were always treated well by the adults in charge of them—even Tim, who was as small and feisty as Percival but smiled upon because of Beth's everpresence as recess aide, lunchroom proctor, field-day volunteer.

In those days Mag was home with other babies and had no time to stand guard over Percival, even in a subtle way. She sent little threads of thought out to follow him, blanket him like protective fingers, but she never managed to provide her actual presence. Instead, she let Alfred know he would have to keep his eye on Percival, because Izzy, the closest in age, was too distracted by his own deep thoughts. Alfred's vigilance didn't help. In middle school, Tim and Percival both cut classes, but while Beth conferred with the school psychologist (a form of parental penance), Mag was finishing college course by course and yearning to go to work. A difficult child could drain you, she had decided; she needed something for herself. She took part-time jobs. Then full-time. Tim had only Beth to encourage him, she reasoned, and the Singer boys had each other. She prayed for her sons' well-being—she did that honestly—but she was no match for Beth's attentions.

In high school, after a race at Brunswick, Percival stopped speaking to Gideon, the brother with whom he'd been closest. That was when Percival and Tim O'Neal became inseparable. Beth encouraged it. She fed the two of them dinner, lent them her car. Mag thought her boys would have reconciled if the O'Neals hadn't gotten in the way. But Tim was always there with his friendship, and Beth with her support.

And then, of course, Tim propagated the myth of the Marines, making it sound like a grown-up version of scout camp. His cousin, Brandon, was a drill sergeant, adding to the glamour. Percival was at the community college, looking for a way out. Mag believed that without the O'Neals, the restlessness would have passed. On the day Tim and Percival signed up for the Marines, both so pleased with themselves, Beth had said, "Maybe it will settle both of them down." *Fat chance.*

Mag never forgave Beth her complacency. She ignored the fact that the Marines did seem to suit Percival. He grew confident, strong. Home on leave before he left for Beirut, he even made a guarded peace with Gideon. Patrick said there were worse things he could have done than join up, but Mag never believed it. The phone rang in Beth O'Neal's apartment, and the other woman answered at once.

"I was going to call you after a while," Beth said. "I was hoping maybe you were still asleep and didn't have to know about it yet."

"We can't find out anything," Mag said.

"Me neither. I called Brandon. He's trying to find out what he can, but so far it's not much more than what they're saying on television. I know it must be even worse for you—with no Marine Corps ties." She sounded kind, as if she were concerned with Mag's well-being.

"Do you know where Tim and Percival lived? If they were in that building?"

"Brandon's trying to find out."

"Alfred called Camp Lejeune," Mag told her.

"Yes. We did, too."

Of course, Beth had done everything. She was so efficient.

"I guess all we can do is let each other know if we hear anything," Mag said.

There was a long pause.

"When they identify the bodies, they send someone to notify the families," Beth said finally. "That's what the Marine Corps does. They don't tell you by phone."

"Yes."

There was nothing else to discuss. After all these years, being a good mother or a bad one might make no difference. Beth might have more justification for hoping her son was alive, but still. . . . When she hung up, Mag felt it was good to have called, but she had no sense of having been helpful or kind. Outside, a rain-soaked day had dawned, illuminating a soggy yard and fallen leaves. All the lights in the house were on, but the world was gray.

"There's really just no way to find out anything," she said, walking back into the family room and addressing Patrick and her sons. "It's like a wall between us and whatever has happened. Even Beth doesn't know any more than we do."

"Shit," said Simon.

"Take your shower," Alfred said.

Simon looked down at his clothes as if he'd noticed for the first time that they were wet. His hands hung oddly at his sides. Mag had not realized how unaccustomed it was for his fingers to be still, how constantly he had snapped them. He headed up the stairs.

Alfred turned to her. "Mother, there's nothing we can do," he said.

"That's quite a situation, isn't it? When there's nothing you can do?" But it occurred to her that, with regard to Percival, there had never been anything she could do. He had yelled and fought more than the others; he was never calm like Alfred was. He was different, and he had eluded them. Not for a moment had they ever had him under control.

From the time he could walk, Percival could get out any door—and often did—to race his tricycle down the street. She was busy listening to music then, imagining the career she would have when she finished college. She tended the children, but distantly. Percival was three years old, vanished into a damp afternoon. She was busy with year-old twins and with Gideon, who was two. So when she noticed, she called all the louder: "Percival, for God's sake, answer. *Percival!*" But he was no-where—an angry middle child, often ignored, given to riding off on his tricycle when she was tending the others.

She went out to the street, dragging Gideon along, leaving the twins behind in the playpen for Alfred to watch. A nasty drizzle was falling; the gray road was empty. They walked around the block. At the bottom of their hill Percival's tricycle sat, overturned at the edge of the Durrells' lawn, its front wheel lodged in a rut it had made on the soggy grass. The Durrells wouldn't be gracious about the rut—property-conscious people, childless, staid. There was no sign of Percival.

Then they heard him but did not see him. A cry, faint and far away, as if he'd been caught in the drainage culvert that ran underneath the driveway. Mag bent to examine the culvert, but of course he wasn't in it, and still the cry came: her son, tortured, trapped.

She expected to faint but understood she wouldn't until she found him. She became surprisingly strong. Holding Gideon's hand, she followed the sound toward the Durrells' house. Realizing that he was inside—inside!—she did not knock on the door but opened the screen, which was not locked, and pulled Gideon in with her. The crying was louder now, and the sound of a woman's harsh voice led them through the hall and into the kitchen. By the sink stood her neighbor, Susan Durrell, dressed in fashionable slacks and a sweater, holding Percival by the arm, preparing to bring a long-handled metal spoon down on the back of his jeans.

"What the hell are you doing?" Mag screamed. She started to lunge for Susan but Gideon held her back, clinging to her leg like a ball and chain. Her heart knocked unevenly and a black rage grew in her chest. Susan Durrell, startled, let go of Percival. He ran to Mag and grabbed her other leg. She couldn't move at all.

"If you can't discipline him," Susan said through her teeth, "someone has to."

Mag's rage grew until the room was black with it, but the boys held onto her slacks and whimpered. "You stupid bitch," she said. "I could have you arrested for assault."

"On what evidence? The word of a three-year-old street urchin? *Your* word?" Susan smiled, more like an animal baring its teeth. "Obviously you don't care what things look like, but we have a nice home here and we're trying to grow *grass.*"

"Grass," Mag said. "You were going to beat my child because he put a dent in your *grass?*"

"We don't have any children here, and we don't want any." Susan's face was a maniacal white.

"You really are out of your mind," Mag said.

"Do you understand what I'm saying? We *do not want* your six or eight little maniacs putting ruts in our yard and tearing up our bushes and picking our flowers. If you can't keep track of them, someone has to. I think now this one at least"—she pointed to Percival—"will stay the hell away."

"I think," Mag told her, moving the children toward the door, "that if you want so much privacy and no kids on your lawn, you better start building your moat and drawbridge."

"Just keep them off our property," Susan said.

"If you ever lay a hand on one of them again—if you ever so much as talk to them—you can kiss your sweet suburban life good-bye. I mean that literally."

Susan Durrell blanched, though Mag would not have thought that possible on top of her previous pallor. Percival stopped crying.

"If she ever says anything else to you, I'm going to beat her up," she told him as they wheeled his tricycle back up the hill in the rain. "Don't tell Daddy."

Percival clapped. She believed he was undamaged. She'd swatted him many times herself, on a bare butt, with a hand and not a spoon. But still.

She never mentioned the incident to Patrick. The next day

she bought a complete herbicide at the garden center. Early the following morning, before the sun or the twins were up, she walked down to the childless Durrells' yard, and sprayed and sprayed. A week later, the lawn began to die—first in patches and then all over, where she had sprayed. Susan Durrell, knowing full well who'd done it but with no hard proof, left the children alone—even Alfred and Izzy, who sensed what had happened and began to make a path across the Durrells' lawn every day on their way home from school. The next spring the Durrells sold their house. Mag understood that she was in control absolutely—of protecting her children, caring for them, defending them, nurturing them. Until then she had been a child herself, not wanting children, wanting only an education and her career. But at that moment she ceased to regard herself as the center of her own life and began to think of herself as a mother (not without resentment), and, spraying herbicide just before dawn, was astonished at the violence of her love.

But it didn't make her into a Beth O'Neal.

"Never in my life, not one time," Percival would yell at her, "have I ever gotten anything I want." It was true. Alfred had insisted on having his own room, Izzy wanted lizards and snakes. But Percival stumped her. No matter what she did for him, he never went off happily like the others, never seemed content, never left her alone. If she'd been like Beth, Mag might have invested whatever extra energy it took to figure him out. But she didn't. And if he were trapped beneath a ton of concrete now, it would be as if nothing had changed.

A bitterness filled her. She had tried. When Percival was seven, she'd even sent him to take piano lessons from Alfred's teacher, thinking that would calm him, but it didn't. Waiting for Alfred after his own lesson was over, Percival would be sitting livid on Mrs. Wellman's couch when Mag came in to get them: hateful, challenging, furious.

"I'm thirsty," he would say in a stage whisper audible over Alfred's scales.

"There's nothing to drink here. You can wait in the car if you're going to act up."

"At least *ask* her. She has a kitchen."

"No."

"I'm really *thirsty.*"

Alfred, smug, would look around from the piano bench, exercising the brilliant passive resistance he knew would eventually remove Percival from the situation.

"Shhh," Mag would say.

"Don't talk to Mrs. Wellman, either," Percival would hiss. "At *all.*"

"What if she asks how I am?" Mag would ask. "Am I allowed to reply?"

"Just don't get into one of your conversations."

Then Mrs. Wellman would glance into the living room, making Mag feel as if she'd walked into a formal dinner in jeans. Weeks later, when Percival complained about practicing, Mag let him quit, while Alfred continued his lessons for years— Alfred with his measured playing, his indifference to music, his rational soul. She'd expected from Percival's music something akin to the spell of a snake charmer—Percival slithering up from the piano bench mesmerized, obedient—but they had no such luck.

"I never get anything I want," he'd yelled at her later, "and I never get anything to eat."

She tried, but there was nothing she could do. Percival's blood sugar plummeted after he ate sugar or if he missed a meal. He held her responsible, never feeding himself a single morsel she didn't set before him on a plate. He shot imaginary enemies in the yard with a stick, climbed trees, fought with his brothers in the car—and then crept into the house, hands shaking, too weak to move. She found him lying under the kitchen table, groaning. "I don't *feel* good," he accused her.

"You don't feel good because you need to eat."

"It's your job to feed me."

"It's not my job. You're old enough to feed yourself." Seeing the situation, Alfred started making him a peanut-butter sandwich even as Mag railed. "What are you going to do when you move out someday?" she yelled at Percival. "You can put a slice of cheese on a cracker. You're not an invalid. Alfred shouldn't have to feed you."

"I'm probably dying." He rolled back and forth on the floor, crying, groaning, making a display. "Why are you letting Alfred do it, anyway? You make stuff for *them*," he said, pointing to the twins. "And *him*." Pointing to Gideon, who in those days loved him so much he would have starved rather than take food from Percival's mouth.

"Oh, for God's sake, Percival." She plopped the sandwich in front of him with a glass of milk. He ate, and ten minutes later his blood sugar was normal, the crisis had passed. Yet sometimes he was in a corner of the house doing push-ups or imagining himself an astronaut, and she would forget. He was one of seven; she had other things to do. He was difficult—would not eat food he thought anyone else had touched, would not buy the school lunches but hated hers ("You give me such barfy sandwiches. I couldn't touch it—God, tuna fish on *rye?*"), blanched at the sight of a purple inspector's stamp on the fat of a pot roast. "Make me macaroni," he demanded. She, busy, did not. He starved morosely, never gained weight. Always lived too close to the surface. And at times—at times—she didn't care.

He was ten the first time she threw him out of the car. He always fought with his younger brothers in the car unless Alfred or Izzy was there to stop it—especially with Gideon and the twins. He didn't pick on Simon because Simon worshiped him so openly.

That day he was beating on Gideon. They were only a year apart and almost the same size. Percival was gritting his teeth, and Gideon was pulling at Percival's jacket. They were grunting and hitting and making noise. Each one was trying to bellow louder, to gain ascendancy. Even their heads—Percival's dark, Gideon's blond—appeared and disappeared in the rear-view mirror like animal hides, disheveled and wild. The twins cheered Gideon on. Simon woke from his nap in the back of the station wagon and began to cry. Mag couldn't stand it. As soon as they got home they would be friends again. It was only being confined in the car that reminded Percival of his station in life—a middle child, packed in—that roused his fury against the younger ones.

Percival was choking Gideon. Gideon was gasping, clutching at the air. "Stop it!" Mag yelled. "Do you want to kill him?" The truth was, Percival did. He was grunting, panting, crying—as if his life depended on his brother's death. Until at last, a dreamer waking, he would see himself as if from a distance and pull away, shamed, horrified at what he had done. Mag thought she would scream. She pulled to the side of the road. The boys looked at her expectantly. The fighting stopped.

"Out," she said to Percival.

"You've got to be kidding."

"*Out.*" She grabbed his arm. He resisted. He was feisty, but skinny for his age, and she was stronger. The other boys looked on with wide eyes; even Simon stopped crying. Breathing hard, angry, she pushed Percival out, onto the blacktop. She closed his door, locked it before he could get back in, and drove off.

He got home half an hour later, enraged and humiliated, red-faced from running.

"That should teach you not to start fights when I'm driving," she said.

It didn't.

She shoved him out of the car a second time. A third. She made him get out farther and farther from home. At first he tangled with her when she tried to exile him, but finally he stopped—tired, she supposed, of her overpowering him in front of his brothers. She made him get out even when it was raining. "It isn't fair when the weather's like this," Gideon said. That was true but she did it anyway. When Percival started

fighting in the car (regularly, inevitably), a hate rose up in her—
a hate, yes—until she could not stand the sight of him: the noise,
the anger inside him, the very sight. And she would hear herself saying, "Out"—driven by her anger and her hate. Then one
day after stopping at several long lights, they turned a corner
into their block and saw Percival already standing in the driveway. He had run that fast.

That was how Percival became a runner.

"This is his way of getting his emotions under control," Patrick said.

They joined a track club. They signed him up for the county
elementary school meet. Percival won. In the evenings Patrick
took Percival to the track and timed him. "Pick it up, Percival,
you're a little off the pace," he would yell to him. They learned
the difference between a 220, halfway around the track, and a
440, a quarter-mile. Patrick had been a miler in high school. He
taught Percival about splits and running intervals. The track
club coach gave him special workouts. Percival basked in the attention. He stopped fighting with his brothers in the car.

When Percival was eleven the track club went to a qualifying
race for the regional Junior Olympics. It was Percival's first time
in statewide competition. He came in fifth.

"God, I ran so *awful*," he screamed, coming home. Tears
trickled down his cheeks and his face was splotched with anger.
Gideon, coming into the yard, said to his brother, "How did
you do?" Percival shoved him into the dirt. It was the old Percival.

"You qualified to run in the regional," Patrick said.

"Yeah, but I came in *fifth*."

"You can't expect to win your first time in big competition."

"Gee, thanks for having confidence in me." He pulled leaves
off the bushes with vicious swipes of his hand.

"Get yourself together, Percival," Patrick said. "You have a
month to train for the regionals if you want to go."

Percival sniffed. He looked a mess. He wanted to go.

He started running four miles in the morning and four miles

at night. It was summer, humid. Percival hated humidity, but he ran. "No pain, no gain," the track coach told him.

"He's only eleven," Mag said.

"Let him learn to get himself under control," Patrick said.

Patrick ran with him sometimes, barely keeping up. They ran in the rain. "No rain, no gain," Percival said, dripping onto the floor. He was smiling. Stoic. He was too tired to fight with his brothers.

Most of the best runners did not show up for the regional race. They were training for the East Coast Invitational the following week. The day was sunny, not humid, cool for July. All the boys in Percival's race went out together—teeth clenched, too fast, a little uneasy. Mag could not breathe. One boy took the lead on the first turn, and another in the backstretch. Then both leaders fell back and Percival and another boy were in front. Percival's legs rose and fell in a great arc, like the legs of a deer. He stayed on the other boy's shoulder, as Patrick had said he should, letting the other boy do the work of leading. On the last lap he passed just as Patrick had told him to—going around him fast, so that the other boy could not repass. He ran as if he'd been racing always. He beat the other boy by at least ten meters—panting, white-faced, victorious.

Mag shouted until she was hoarse. Shouted him around the last turn, down the straightaway, through the finish line. She knew if Percival could keep running like that, he would live easy in his spirit, like a deer. For a moment, she was as dedicated a mother as Beth O'Neal. She did not know then that Percival would hold himself together and be under control and be the stoic only when he was winning. She did not know that Gideon would run faster. She stood in the stands, shouting, thinking: Let the running consume him. Let him not fight in the car. There is nothing I can do with him. Let him leave me alone. But that was not really what she wanted.

Alfred had turned her records off. Patrick shifted position on the family room couch, blind. "Dad, you used to say the worst

—— 61 ——

thing that ever happened to Percival was winning so early," Alfred said.

Mag looked from father to son, startled. "I was just thinking about those early races," she said. She did not like Alfred reading her mind or appearing to agree with Patrick. Patrick believed those first victories accounted for Percival's troubles later—that winning had come too easy, so the rest of life came hard. Patrick said that cutting school, quitting the track team, joining the Marines—all were a form of running away. Alfred must agree with him or why would he mention it? Father and son believed Percival deserved whatever fate he got.

Mag said bitterly, "Better to win early than not at all, if that's all you're going to have."

"What?" Patrick mumbled. The washcloth was hiding his eyes.

"Nothing."

Alfred walked over to her, touched her on the shoulder. "It *is* better than nothing, Mother. No one's saying it's not." And then, in a strange, fatherly tone: "Mother, you better get dressed." As if he were the parent. As if she were the child.

Everything was coming around. If Alfred wanted to send her upstairs to dress, why should she be surprised? Hadn't she said, "You are the oldest, you have to look out for the others"? Percival's death would be as chaotic as his life, ending in a blaze of fireworks. And responsible Alfred would spend his life caring for another man's sons. It was the punishment. She turned and went up the stairs, not even noticing the sound of Simon's shower in the bathroom or considering that—as usual—he would stand under it until all the hot water ran out.

4

If the spray came down hard enough, it would always block out what was in Simon's mind. Little knots of water would hit him all over, and he would be skin under a hot rain, nothing else. He rubbed soap into his hair, mushing it in with his fingernails. When he was a kid, his mother had told him that was a good way to get his nails clean. He'd rub his temples with the balls of his fingers, and he'd actually be able to feel his mind inside, under the scalp and the scrubbing fingers, going empty.

Today it wasn't working. He rubbed, but he kept seeing the picture of the headquarters building on the TV set. He kept seeing the building falling down, like a little kid's blocks. That image had been with him even when he was out delivering the papers, even with his hood down and the rain slopping all over his face. The only time the picture had gone away was when Monster chased him—and it seemed wrong, selfish, to forget another person's welfare when you were caught up in saving your own skin. He'd even laughed when his mother told him she'd dropped the owners' paper in the puddle. But as soon as he'd finished laughing, he remembered the headquarters building. It was like a curtain coming down. A cry had been gathering in his throat ever since they heard the news, and at that moment it had come back bigger than ever.

He was trying his damnedest not to let it out. Downstairs his father had a headache and couldn't see, but it was as if his father were looking at him all the same. Patrick said Percival might be all right, it was even all right to deliver papers. In a way, actually delivering them wasn't so bad—knowing he could do whatever he had to. But there was nothing he could do for Percival. He hadn't even been *thinking* about Percival when the dog came at him. So the cry had kept piling up in the back of his throat like cherry pits, heaping up until he could hardly swallow.

The water ran tepid and then cool. He climbed out of the shower and knew he needed some way to keep himself together; otherwise he'd lose it, go off in all directions, and his father would have a fit. So he said to himself: It's yesterday. His father said you could believe anything you wanted if you worked at it hard enough. "You can believe you're a winner or you can believe you're a loser—and that's very powerful, don't think it's not," he used to say to Percival, back when Percival was running in races. So maybe he could believe it was yesterday, and maybe that would keep the cry from flying out of his throat.

He put on his underwear and stood in front of the mirror. Yesterday he was a tall kid whose muscles hadn't filled out. He was too skinny and his voice hadn't changed. He was a kid who could never keep from arguing with Hope Shriber, the Jesus freak in his class. He loved telling Hope the things Patrick liked to say: "You can believe God is watching your every move if you want to, but since you can't ever know for sure, it makes more sense to act as if the power isn't with God but with yourself." Hope always started to get red in the face when he said that, but Simon went on. "It's crazy to put responsibility for your life onto some Higher Being," he'd tell her, in exactly the tone his father used. Red color would spike across Hope's face then, in little jagged streaks, but Simon would just look down at her in a superior way. He was six inches taller than she was, easy.

Finally Hope would say, "I don't see how you can talk like that, Simon," in a real small voice. Then she'd quote the Scriptures and her voice would get stronger. Sometimes she'd yell at him, and once he almost made her cry. He knew that was wrong, but it took an effort not to argue with her. That was all he had to worry about yesterday. He would make it be then.

But he couldn't. Yesterday Percival had been alive. Yesterday the headquarters building had been standing. No matter how much he believed, he couldn't make time go back to that. The things he had done yesterday seemed separate from him, like games he had played back when he was a kid.

He looked at himself in the mirror. Usually when he looked in the mirror he would pretend he was black like his friends Pooter and Boozer and even talk to himself as if he were black. "You call me a scruff, punk?" he would say to his reflection, in a voice as close to Pooter's voice as he could get. "I ain't no scruff." But that seemed impossible now. In the mirror he saw that his hair was wet, slicked back from his face to reveal the smooth flat place where his ear was supposed to be. Usually it was not the ear but his hair that he noticed, and the way he had to wear it so long that it wasn't in any kind of a style. If it were yesterday, he would be worrying that he couldn't have a hairstyle like Pooter's—black fuzz shaved short all over his head— or Boozer's braided dreadlocks. He knew that as straight and thick as his hair was, he'd be able to wear dreadlocks himself if he didn't have to keep his ear covered up like an overgrown Buster Brown. But today that didn't seem important at all.

Today he didn't care about his hair. He cared about the walls of the sand-colored building tumbling down in Beirut. If Percival was under the building, he knew how it would be. He knew because of having his tonsils out when he was five. It seemed to him that being crushed under the building would be exactly the same. The feeling of cherry pits in his throat slid down as if he'd swallowed it and settled in a heap in his chest. He remembered pain and fear and nightmares.

He'd felt pretty good before the surgery. His mother said he'd had one sore throat after another, but he didn't remember that. He only remembered the hospital. They took blood from his arm and made him pee in a jar. Then they made him wear a nightgown like girls wore, the kind that tied in the back. They wheeled his bed to the operating room. His parents couldn't come. The light was bright and the operating room was cold. They strapped him onto a table. He was crying but his parents couldn't come. "We're going to put you to sleep now," they said. They strapped his arm to a board. They put him to sleep by sticking a needle into his arm. He woke up feeling like he was coming from under water. He'd been swimming underwater and he'd had trouble coming all the way up. His throat hurt and he was sick to his stomach. He threw up all over the warrior action figure his parents gave him.

After he went home, his legs felt rubbery when he walked. He didn't feel like his regular self; he felt like he was dreaming. When he looked down at his stomach, there were big red blotches all over it. He might have been dreaming except that they itched. His mother told him not to scratch. More blotches came out on his arms and legs. "He's blooming," Darren said. Simon didn't think flowers bloomed like that. Flowers were bright, clear, good. He felt really lousy.

Something had gone wrong with his feet. His mother tried to put his shoes on to take him to the doctor, but his feet had swollen so much the shoes didn't fit. He thought they would keep growing, get big and misshapen like the pictures he'd seen in the Medical Museum of people with elephantiasis. One of those people was sitting on his own leg. You had to look at the picture for a minute to realize it was his own leg and not a bench. His feet would get so big he'd be able to sit on them. He wouldn't be able to walk. He walked across the room while he still could. He was sick and the bottoms of his feet felt cushiony. He was cold inside.

His mother put Merle's outgrown shoes on him so they could go to the doctor. The doctor gave him a shot. The welts got smaller and didn't itch so much. Back home he slept a lot, but not a nice kind of sleep. He slept because he couldn't get enough air inside him to stay awake. Sometimes he woke up choking. He would start coughing while he was asleep. If he woke up, his mother would give him medicine to make him breathe right. A lot of times he didn't wake up right away, or his mother didn't hear him coughing because she was busy with the other kids. He kept sleeping, dreaming how he was coughing, with the gunk in his lungs rolling over and over. Really he *was* coughing, and he was dreaming it, too. Sooner or later somebody would shake him awake and give him the bitter-tasting medicine. Sometimes it was Alfred but usually it was Percival. He would be all right for a while and then he would sleep again, and cough.

It took a long time to get better. The whole time he was sick he felt like he was on the other side of himself, a dark side. That was how you felt when you had an operation. His mother said no, that was how you felt when you had an allergic reaction to some medicine they gave you *after* the operation, but Simon never believed that.

He thought of Percival under the building. If he was crushed, he might feel the same dark way Simon had when he was sick. The dark feeling was how you felt before you died. Nobody could go into the dark with you, and you were alone. You hurt and then you died, alone.

For a long time after he got well, Simon kept having the

choking dreams. He shared a room with Darren and Merle, and if he woke up making a sound, they would tell him to shut up. If *they* had a bad dream, they'd both have it at the same time, and they'd wake up together. It was creepy. So on the nights he woke up, he took his pillow and his cover into the room Percival shared with Izzy and Gideon and tapped on Percival's shoulder.

Percival never woke all the way up, only put his hand on Simon's head, which made him feel better. "Simon?" he'd say.

"Yeah." Simon would put his covers down on the floor next to Percival's bed and go to sleep. Or if he was really scared, he'd talk some more and Percival would get up and listen. "The scary thing," he'd said once, "is that when I wake up, it's like I'm still sick, like it's happening again."

"One thing you have to remember," Percival told him, "is if you were really choking to death, you wouldn't be dreaming about it. You wouldn't be doing anything."

"Yeah, I guess," Simon said. He always felt better after Percival talked to him that way. Later he realized that what Percival had said wasn't really very comforting. He didn't like the idea that if he were dying he wouldn't be dreaming. But he supposed it wasn't what Percival said that made him feel better, it was just Percival's talking and touching his hair while he lay on the floor beside his bed. Sometimes Percival's hand would still be on his hair when he woke up.

It wasn't as if Percival had gone into the darkness with him; it was more like, little by little, Percival's being there had made the darkness go away.

He didn't think he could keep the cry in if Percival was under a building hurting or maybe dying, feeling the dark side of himself. In Simon's mind the cry was bursting out, echoing around the rooms. He imagined his father saying, "Simon, toughen up, boy. All we can do is wait." But he thought there must be something else he could do.

He was still standing in front of the mirror, fooling with his hair. A little idea started to form in his mind. When Merle got sick, Darren always felt bad, too. Then as soon as Darren felt bad, Merle would feel a little better. That was because they were twins. One twin could take the other one's pain. But maybe you didn't have to be twins. His father said you could make a lot of things happen if you believed hard enough. Simon didn't know if you could take another person's pain after the pain was already there. Or if you weren't twins. But maybe you could. The idea got bigger in his mind. He looked at the smooth place where his ear was supposed to be. He thought of the ear operations his mother wanted him to have, and the cry began to draw its wings in a little inside his chest.

Up until now, he had only argued with his mother, saying he didn't want his ear fixed because it didn't bother him and it was senseless to make himself sick for no reason.

"It's not like I have a hideous, scrunched up, deformed ear," he told her. "I just have *no* ear. What's so bad about that?"

She would roll her eyes and turn her back to him. If one of his brothers was around, she would say, "Me—I'm just his mother. What could *I* know? Maybe he'll listen to you." Alfred was the only one who ever tried to convince him. "I think you should consider what you want in the long run, Simon," he would tell him. "You have to consider that if you ever want your hair cut, people will make fun of you."

Well, of course his hair *did* annoy him, and also when Alfred said to think about a thing, it was usually a good idea to do it. He thought about getting a short haircut and being teased. He remembered being teased, usually by the twins, when he was smaller. If they wanted the bedroom to themselves, Darren would jump on top of him and twist his arm back, yelling, "Get out of here, you earless freak!" Darren was four years older and a lot bigger, so Simon would have to leave. He didn't love being called an earless freak, but he didn't get too upset about it, either. Darren called Merle a hook-nosed shithead when he got mad at him, and the twins looked exactly alike. Also, the twins were pretty ugly; Simon thought he was better looking than they were, even without his ear.

And the truth was, even if he'd cared about being teased, he wouldn't have wanted the surgery. He just didn't want an operation that would make him go into the dark side of himself again. He didn't tell his mother that, but she seemed to know.

"It's crazy to get hung up on the idea that surgery will kill you, because it didn't the first time and they're certainly not going to give you the same antibiotic again," she said. "Not to mention that this is an external thing—you're not going to wake up with a sore throat."

"It's not that," he lied. "It's more that I have this vision of how I look. First I get so tan that I'm about the same color as Pooter. Then I let my hair grow out and wear it in dreadlocks. Then either I glue an earring where the ear is supposed to be, or else I have the skin pierced so I can wear a pierced earring. I think a pierced earring would be better."

It wasn't that he *thought* something bad would happen if he had an operation, it was more like he knew it. But if he made a joke out of it, everything would be all right.

His mother never laughed. "Simon, I can't deal with you, I absolutely can't deal with you," she would say. She would turn to his father. "Patrick, speak to him seriously instead of letting it be a joke. Talk some sense into him."

His father never helped her. One time Patrick even turned the TV on louder than usual to drown her out and switched channels until he came to "Soul Train." Normally he watched only news and sports shows. But that day he stared at "Soul Train" like he was really interested in it. A group called the Fat Boys was on, doing one of their rap songs. "Is that actually music?" Patrick asked.

"Yeah. Sure. Don't you like it?" Simon liked it a lot. He had just bought a Fat Boys album with some of his newspaper money.

"Aaauugh," his father yelled.

"You're avoiding the issue," his mother said.

His father turned the TV up. "I don't think I can talk about ears," he said. "I feel this awesome backspin coming on." He crumpled onto the floor, rolling over in an imitation of Simon's *truly* awesome backspin, which he had learned from Pooter. His mother snapped the TV off and yelled: "And what if some girl doesn't want to go out with you because of your ear? Some girl you really like? I don't think I could stand that—watching you get hurt when it's completely unnecessary."

"I don't even like girls," he'd said. Hope Shriber had great honey-colored hair, but she was always blessing you or saying, "In Jesus' name." Anyway, he thought they had been through this already.

When Percival came home last summer, before he went to Lebanon, his mother must have figured he was her last hope. She brought up the subject of Simon's ear every time Percival walked into the same room with them.

"Percival, *you* tell him," she kept saying. "He's old enough to do it—why should he wait until later, when he can't afford it or he has to go to work every day?

"Percival, tell him it would look better," his mother went on. "It would look better, wouldn't it? Percival, please."

"Of course it would look better," Percival said. "A kid with no ear—I remember kids starting to barf when he walked up to the bus stop, they were so grossed out."

"Percival!" his mother yelled. She was looking from Percival to Simon and Simon to Percival with her mouth open.

"There's no question he should have it done. But why should he stop with his ear? Look at his nose—not the greatest nose. His chin makes him look like he has a strong opinion about everything, but really he only has opinions about dancing and being black." He was holding Simon's shoulder at arms' length, walking back and forth to observe his face. "I say the ears first and then the nose and then take out the jut in the chin."

"Percival, be serious."

Percival lifted Simon's arm. "And maybe a silicone insert in the biceps to give the appearance of muscle." Percival had just come up from the basement, where he'd been lifting weights. Usually it was Gideon who lifted weights, but since Percival had been in the Marines, he had started lifting again, too. Percival's face was red from exertion, and he was laughing. He looked at their mother. "I think you should let Simon make up his own mind," he said.

"At the very least, he should go for a consultation," his mother added.

Percival winked at him. The whole family joked and yelled about his ear, and sometimes they were serious, but what they didn't know was that behind it, all the time, was the darkness.

Simon looked at himself in the mirror again and then turned away. The idea that had started in his mind got stronger. The thought of the darkness frightened him, but if he kept his goal in mind, maybe it would go away. If you concentrated hard enough, his father had always said to Percival, you could block out everything else, even the guys who were trying to psych you out. The cry in his chest drew in its wings further. He was cold and needed to get dressed. He rummaged through a box of stuff the twins had left when they went away to college. He found a faded red T-shirt with white letters saying FREESTATE STRIDERS. It looked like it came from the thrift store, but really it used to be Percival's. He put it on. It made him feel calmer, the way he'd felt when Percival put his hand on his hair. He thought of Percival in Lebanon, under the sand-colored concrete building. He knew what would happen if he had the ear operation. It would be worth it if he could take Percival's pain away or, at the very least, share it. He knew what he was going to do.

Passing Simon's room on her way back downstairs after dressing, Mag was struck by the motionless silence that seemed to have settled over him. Usually he danced around or snapped his fingers, but now he was kneeling on the floor in his underwear, going through a box of discarded clothes in a silent, deliberate way. He did not even notice her walking by. A dark bruise throbbed on his calf from the second dog bite. She was suddenly hurt that he hadn't told her about it. He would have said his usual thing: "Mother, don't go into a hyperspasm about this. It's no big deal." But at least she would have known. And now it seemed that it *was* a big deal. After the first bite she'd called Monster's owners repeatedly, but nobody was ever home. It turned out that the family had left for vacation. Though there was no danger of a dog in this neighborhood not having its rabies shots, she'd been furious. She meant to take action. Yet nothing had come of it. By the time the family got back, the bite had been forgotten. Watching Simon now, she vowed that this time she would not forget. She would call the SPCA. She would sue. But it seemed a small, shabby thing to think about right now.

When Simon came downstairs a few minutes later, she saw what he had been looking for in the box upstairs—a tattered running shirt Percival had worn hundreds of times and then passed down to the twins. Oddly, Simon had put it on along with a pair of good trousers instead of his usual jeans. The ludicrous outfit touched her. Normally, he would never wear such a combination. Only yesterday he had strutted around this very room, moving his hands in short, jerky angles to imitate the dances his black friends did, snapping his fingers, and pointing out in his imitation black-boy accent what he was wearing.

"See my *Lee* jeans?" he'd said to her, modeling. "See my *alligator* shirt? I'm a J-Street regular, lady. Don't you tell me you think I get my clothes at the *mission!*" He had made a menacing face at that. J Street was in the black section where most of his friends lived, and the Rescue Mission was there, too. It had a thrift store with old clothes and furniture the residents of the area were supposed to be able to afford. But Simon insisted the black kids would no more buy their clothes there than come to school naked.

"See, Boozer'll come in with a sharp new belt or shirt and Pooter'll say, 'Hey, man, where'd you get that—the mission?' So then Boozer says, 'No, man, I got it at the mall, but I seen *you* buying them pants at the mission the other day.'" Simon had shimmied his shoulders and slid backward on his toes as he told her these things, doing a dance step called the moonwalk that his friend Pooter had taught him at school. Pooter had taught him the moonwalk in the cafeteria, in front of everyone, even that idiot Jesus freak Hope Shriber—who, if Mag wanted to know the truth, liked to dance as well as anybody. He'd snapped his fingers and made his fist into a microphone, pretending he was Michael Jackson: "Uh . . . Billie Jean, is not my lov-er," he'd sung. He'd danced and snapped his fingers and described the rotting smell of the Rescue Mission. As far as Mag knew, Simon had been to the mission only once, when they dropped off the remains of her last yard sale. But he spoke as if he lived on J Street and went there every day—talking in a loose, irreverent way that he had learned not from his black friends, but from Percival.

And now he was wearing dress pants and a faded running shirt, and his hands were absolutely still.

At that moment an odd thing began to happen. The day began to take place outside of Mag. She had not felt this way for fourteen years, since her pregnancy with Simon, but she remembered the sensation well. Whenever she was pregnant, a fine veil would lower in front of everything beyond her, leaving her hazy except for her own workings. She would have preferred to concentrate on school, or later the jobs she had begun to take, getting down to the real business of her life—but she was helpless to stay the process. Each time, she drew back to her own center, monitoring the quickening in her belly, becoming absorbed. But then it had been births she was waiting for, and now it was a death. She was helpless before either of them. So without meaning to, she stood separate from herself, watching as if she were not really taking part.

The front door opened. She knew before she turned that it was Izzy and the twins, arriving after their ride up from College Park. She greeted them from her distance, having no power to propel herself nearer, yet noticing them with surprising clarity. As they crowded into the hallway out of the rain, she was struck by Izzy's dark beauty and the twins' homeliness, as if she were seeing them for the first time. She thought with perfect coldness that it was unfair her most brilliant son was also her most handsome. The twins' hair hung limp and almost white over high foreheads, while Izzy's dipped down onto a perfect dark brow—crisp, shiny hair, full of body and almost black. Izzy had a bright, intelligent gaze, too, while the twins had the vacant look of pale-eyed, lashless blonds—identical brooding Hamlets, though neither of them brooded much, and there were no Danish ancestors on either side. Then she recalled that the twins received attention because there were two of them, and she saw Izzy with his face contorted as it had often been when he took notes on suffering animals in the interest of science. From her distance she understood that Izzy's beauty did not help him, no more than Percival's ever had, coming so late—and she felt sad for all of them: the homely twins and Percival and Izzy all at once. And yet she felt removed from it, beyond it.

Izzy kissed her, having grown to that level of maturity where kissing did not embarrass him; and the twins nodded and shuffled away. She saw that Merle looked different—worse—but before she could figure out why, Izzy said, "Heard anything yet?" and she forgot Merle, thinking instead, very objectively, that this question—"Heard anything yet?"—was to be the refrain from now on, until they actually did hear something. People would want to react appropriately to the news, though of course it was a matter of indifference to her how they reacted.

Neither Izzy nor the twins had brought laundry home with them. This had never happened before. She saw—in a cool, detached, probing way—that even in her grief, she was relieved they had brought no clothes for her to wash. She registered that as a strike against herself. And registered another: that in spite of the crisis, she still felt crowded by the boys' physical size as she always had since they had grown so large, and still hated feeling dwarfed, in her own house, by her own sons. She saw that Percival's death would make no difference in this regard— that she would not wish, even then, to have four or five grown boys so close to her. She was not capable of making even so small a sacrifice. And she was bruised by her selfishness.

When everyone had been greeted, they resumed their vigil in the family room. Patrick lay down on the couch again, listening to the TV with the washcloth over his eyes. Simon, immaculately clean in his odd clothes, sat at the far end of the couch on Patrick's feet. It was something he had done when he was a small child trying to maintain contact with an adult. His hands lay in his lap as if they had been paralyzed. The sight of them saddened her. Once, a few years ago, he had made a difficult basket in a game at the Y, and the coach had yelled in a voice that the whole gym could hear, "Nice play, Simon Singer." Trying to be nonchalant but unaware that he was giving himself away, Simon had walked down the court snapping his fingers. But now she feared the snapping was gone forever.

This seemed quite clear to her in her distant state. And not just that—but that all the boys would now lose something precious and irreplaceable. The joy in Simon's fingers might have been Percival's life. Or Izzy's occasional peace of mind when he was not worried about killing laboratory dogs, or Gideon glowing from exercise after a race. As if, inside her, all of that was the same.

"Guess who, Dad," Merle said, sitting down on the couch so that Patrick had to move over to make room. She saw then that Merle had grown a mustache. A fine, bristly fuzz of hair above his upper lip. That was why he looked so terrible. The mustache seemed to be thicker on the right side than on the left— unbalanced—but the worst part was that it was spotty in places all the way across, pale and uneven, so that he gave the appearance of an unkempt animal. Odd that she hadn't noticed.

Patrick let his washcloth drop and felt Merle's face. "*M* for mustache," he said, smiling. "I didn't think you'd do it."

It was a sick joke. During a recent blind spell Patrick had noticed that the twins' voices were exactly alike. She had imagined the terror: of having your son speak, your own son, and not knowing who he was. But Patrick had said, lightly, "To tell the truth, one of my main concerns is how I'm going to tell the two of you apart if these eyes don't let up one of these days." As if there were no terror at all in the possibility of going permanently blind, but only practical matters to be dealt with. That afternoon he had made a show of reaching for the twins' feet, because often in warm weather Darren would put his shoes on and Merle would not. But both of them were barefoot that day, so nothing had been resolved.

"I guess one of us could grow a beard," Darren had said, in the high, thin tone their voices took on when they were upset.

"Nothing so spectacular, please."

"A mustache?"

"Let Merle grow the mustache. Then in case I go senile as well as blind, I'll have an easier time of it—*M* for Merle, *m* for mustache."

"God, Dad, don't be so morbid." But they had all laughed, and no one had expected, then, that Merle would actually grow the mustache. Now he sat on the couch, with fuzzy hair sticking out above his lip to please his father, and Patrick's face registered not his headache, not blindness, not Percival crushed . . . but delight. Mag saw herself in the Keys all winter, living under a hot sun, laughing at the sick humor he would require from her to deny the darkness: making sport of his bumpings into the wall, the crash of dropped dishes, the awkward journey through a rented cottage, unfamiliar terrain. If he would say simply, "Help me," then she would resent helping—another strike against her—but she would do it. And helping would be simpler than pretending that nothing had changed, just as they were pretending now that nothing had happened in Lebanon. Yet even those observations, much as they hurt her, seemed slightly distant from her, as if she were not quite there.

Merle got up from the couch, jostling Lucifer off Patrick's lap. The cat immediately climbed back up and draped itself around Patrick's neck instead. The sight unnerved Mag: of Patrick, looking cataract-eyed, acting as if he weren't, and the cat hanging over him like a shawl. For a moment the once-removed feeling vanished and she was filled with anger. "God, how can you stand that?" she yelled at Patrick. Ten years ago Simon had slung Lucifer around his neck when he was still a kitten, and the beast had never understood, later, that he was too old and too large for such a position.

"I'm putting him out, Patrick," she said. "I wish you wouldn't let him hang on you." She picked the cat up.

"Out in the rain?" Simon asked.

"A little rain won't hurt him."

She hated animals. Or rather, having seven boys, she hated the extra caretaking. They had had only one other pet, years before, and Mag regretted that one, too—a puppy who contracted distemper but instead of dying had recovered to a sort of listless invalidism, having convulsions every afternoon on the basement floor until she finally took it to the SPCA. Alfred had named the dog Moanin' after the sounds it made, and Izzy had taken notes on its condition for a science fair project. "That's a disgusting thing to do," Mag had told him, but Izzy was so hurt by the dog's suffering and yet so intent on studying it for the sake of science that she hadn't pursued the matter. She had only outlawed pets entirely, and except for Izzy's snakes, which he insisted were scientific specimens, she might have succeeded.

Then Lucifer wandered into the yard the year Simon was four. Earless and brotherless six hours a day (the others were all in school), Simon had pleaded to take the cat in. Mag had relented. But she named it Lucifer to vent her feelings and grew more resentful as Simon lost interest in it and the cat transferred its affection to Percival. Years passed. Finally Percival left, Gideon was too busy running to pay it any attention, and the twins were absorbed in each other, so it began to cling to Patrick. She lifted the beast from Patrick's shoulders, carried it by the belly to the sliding glass door, and threw it out. "If he doesn't like getting wet, he can go into the garage," she said.

"Sadist," Izzy told her.

"You're the animal lover, not me. Take him back to College Park if you feel so sorry for him. Put him in one of your labs." That was cruel, because Izzy really *was* engaged in animal research and had a horror of being dubbed a vivisectionist. But Mag did not regret saying it. A slogan came on the TV screen, announcing a newsbreak. They all turned toward the television.

"Because of the vast number of inquiries from families of the Beirut peacekeeping contingent," the announcer said, "the Marine Corps has announced that it will take the unprecedented step of preparing a list of survivors. However, spokesmen say that because rescue efforts are still under way and some units are scattered, a definitive list may take several days to prepare. For further information, relatives of those stationed in Beirut may call the following hotline number, which has been set up at Headquarters Marine Corps." A phone number was flashed on the screen.

"Alfred, call," Mag said. But Alfred had already disappeared into the phone room. No one moved to turn down the TV, but they all strained to hear what he was saying beyond the door that separated the family room from the phone. There was only an unintelligible mumbling. When Alfred finally emerged, he had a deliberately blank expression on his face.

"It's just like he said—a list might take a couple of days to prepare. Each Marine has to be seen by a first sergeant or an officer. Then they'll make the list. Then they'll give the list to the hotline number and you can call in to find out who's on it."

Izzy, scientific, said: "And what if they're hurt? What if they're dead?"

"Then it takes even longer. They don't announce it over the phone. First they make positive identification. Then they send someone to tell you—an officer or a chaplain."

There was a silence that touched Mag even in her distance. This was exactly what Beth O'Neal had told her. Everyone looked at the floor. A long moment passed. Then Patrick, as if to break the spell, said in a light, flip voice: "No chaplains, please." But he shivered as he spoke, and Simon rose from his position on Patrick's feet and covered his father with the afghan that was folded on the arm of the couch.

5

Patrick had not meant to shiver. It was not at all what he'd intended. He only wanted to bring the situation back under control, what with Mag throwing the cat out of the house like a madwoman and Izzy bringing up the subject of injuries and deaths when clearly that was premature. They must not assume Percival was injured until they heard. But tending to that and his eyes at the same time . . . He had been having trouble all morning.

He thought his vision would have returned by now. It had been—what?—five hours? Six? The Valium had worn off and he hadn't taken more. Heart rate up again. He was full of the sensation of light having receded all around him, going dimmer and still dimmer, and of his pupils pulling shut, like overtense muscles clamping down, creating a charley horse in his eye. Then full darkness—five hours of it—and the sense of being trapped inside himself. His heart pounding like a kid's, slapping against his chest. Imprisoned, blind, caged inside himself. His head throbbed like a punching bag beneath a fist.

Enough. Simon put the afghan over him, thinking he was cold. He was not cold. He was concerned about his lack of concentration. Even when they weren't talking about Beirut, he kept waiting for the newscast to come on, and then he couldn't think about anything else. Important to keep things in perspective. Blindness under control, then Beirut. But the two kept getting jumbled up.

Head throbbing. He put the afghan aside, rose from the couch, felt his way around the coffee table.

"You need something, Dad?" one of the twins asked. He couldn't tell which one but would not resort to feeling for the mustache.

"More cold water on this washcloth," he said.

"I'll get it."

"Thanks."

He turned, took two steps back toward the couch, tried to be careful of the coffee table. He had a bruise on his shin from bumping into it the other day. Easy does it . . . sliding his foot around the table leg, sitting down again.

"Here, Dad." He was always amazed that the twins had exactly the same inflections in their voices. . . .

Washcloth in his hand, closing his fingers around it. Lying down, he put the cloth back over his eyes and felt the cool dampness, something he could pretend was closing him in deliberately—something he himself had chosen—and not that he was trapped inside himself by forces outside his control.

The Keys . . . focus on the Keys. Usually that helped. Replace every visual sensation with a sensory one . . . go where it was hot enough to feel the sun, let it replace the light; feel sand, water, the tug of fish on his line—keep so busy with the other senses. . . . But each time, on the edge of blindness, he understood how much world his eyes let in. Only Alfred seemed to sense how he felt. He could stand everything except the feeling of being trapped in his own head. In the Keys, where the heat would be strong enough to hold his attention, to overpower his need to see, he could be practical. Swim. Fish. Maintain a little dignity.

Imagining sunlight on his skin now. Warmer. Not shivering so much. He breathed slowly through his nose to calm himself. It only reminded him that the passage of air into his nostrils during these episodes made his eyes hurt as if his sinuses were infected. Actually, a sinus infection was one of the theories the doctors at Hopkins had embraced and later discarded after they'd given him antibiotics. They'd rejected it the way they'd rejected the brain tumor theory, the virus theory, the exotic disease theory (had he traveled in the past year, say, to Africa?), the nerve disorder theory. But surely some bacteria were resistant to the drugs they had tried. Very likely that.

In the Keys he could work on his problem. Get out of the house, away from Maryland. Away from pollen, mold, dust, even the carpet swatches and vinyl at work; you could be allergic to those things as well as to beer. Mag said no; at Hopkins the tests showed he was allergic to most everything but not enough to close down his eyes. Some seasonal thing, then? The eye problem had started last fall and now it was fall again and it was worse. If he could just gain the proper distance . . . He had changed his diet, started taking vitamin pills. Sometimes you waited. You took aspirin till you had a cure. You broke problems down into logical components and didn't try to tackle too much at once. He had taught Izzy this method, and look how well Izzy had done. You suggested alternatives to the doctors. You assumed your son was all right until you heard otherwise.

Your son?

Enough.

Concentrate. You could break things down, you could change your physical location. But first—oh, shit—you had to convince your wife that going was a good idea.

Mag was rarely impressed by logic, but in this case it seemed so obvious. . . . If he went blind permanently, who did she think would support them? Who would keep his business going, to pay the bills for five boys still in college or high school? Did she think they would live on the little pittance of money she made working for the county, taking a different job every year? She said: "Why waste the RipOffs money on a sunburn?"—but the truth was, winter was the only time he could get away from the plant for any length of time. It was the off-season, and the foreman could take charge. In spring they would be swamped with vans to upholster.

"Why Key West? So you can learn to live like a blindman in some strange place while Alfred is enjoying your house?"

"That isn't the point," he'd told her. He would not consider the possibility of living like a blindman. If you did not have a retreat plan, you did not retreat. But nothing was resolved.

"For all we know, Percival could be lying under that building and it'll be three or four days before we hear about it," Simon said.

That jolted him back to the present. "Simon, what did I tell you this morning about imagining things?" he asked.

"Isn't that exactly what they're saying on TV and at that hotline number?"

"It could also very easily be true that he's perfectly all right and would not admire our imagining him otherwise."

"I think he'd like knowing someone was thinking about him," Simon said.

"Thinking about him, yes. Not falling apart over him whether it's necessary or not."

Hear me, Simon. You do not crumble because of blindness, or even because of a death. You concentrate on whatever's left.

He had learned that after his father died, and he had shivered a few moments ago because when Alfred said the Marines would send a chaplain to announce a death, he'd gotten a perfect rerun in his mind of Father James, the priest, coming to tell him about his father the year he was nine.

He'd been in school that day. This struck him as odd suddenly, because hadn't Simon delivered papers this morning, under the same conditions? But no . . . this morning he'd wanted Simon to get on top of the situation; forty years ago there was no possibility of that. He'd gone to school because no one told him to stay home. His father, William, had been in and out of the hospital so many times that Patrick had gotten used to it—a short stay for transfusions and tests, a quiet homecoming. William had looked gaunt but remained cheerful toward Patrick, so nothing had forewarned him of a death. He did not know his father had one of those violent, acute forms of leukemia for which, in those days, there was no cure. But when Father James appeared in the door of his fourth-grade classroom, whispering to Mrs. Treadmore and looking in Patrick's direction, he understood completely. When a priest came, it always meant bad news.

Watching Father James's lips moving close to Mrs. Treadmore's ear, Patrick had felt as if time had slowed down. In a strange, detached way, he knew absolutely that his father was dead. Two nights before, William had hugged him before leaving for the hospital, saying, "Take care, boy," in his usual way. He'd ruffled Patrick's hair and given him a kiss. Patrick had smelled illness and aftershave and felt the rough beginnings of his father's whiskers against his face. That would never happen again. In the slow, creeping passage of time in that classroom, Patrick remembered that when people died, their whiskers grew. A gray, gritty light came through the window. His father was dead at that very moment. It had happened while Patrick was reading and doing math. He was *not inside his body anymore*. But still his whiskers were growing. The memory of his father's living, stubbled face became sharp and painful. A sob formed in his chest and finally lifted and burst from his throat.

With the same slowness with which he had imagined his father, Patrick watched his classmates turn to stare at him. The children seemed to move and fix their eyes on him in unison. In the skewed passage of time, there was opportunity to look at each of them through the blur of tears. Some wore curious expressions, others seemed uncomfortable. A few of the boys shaped their mouths into tight smiles.

Father James walked toward him. Patrick's father had not liked the priest, who always said, "I hope we see you in church next week with the rest of your family, William." But his father never went to church. Once he'd replied, "I was raised Methodist and I didn't like that much, either, Father James," and he had winked at the priest, who then jumped away a little, barely perceptibly, as if William had slapped him or spit.

Patrick did not mean to let the priest touch him. The children were watching. If his aunt Kay had come, he would have been all right, but he knew she was probably home with his mother. Patrick rose from his seat. He could not stop the tears. Father James was beside him, talking. Soon he would say William could not go to heaven. Only the faithful went to heaven. That was so crazy. He did not mean to let Father James get too close. Someone giggled. Patrick felt Father James's sleeve against his shoulder. Father James's arm went around him. He had no power to stop it. The tears came harder. He walked out of the classroom with sobs breaking from him, and his head buried in the black, black, black of Father James's suit.

Everyone in the class had witnessed this. His humiliation was absolute. When he'd finally summoned the strength to pull away from the priest, Patrick vowed never again to feel so helpless. It seemed to him that now, blind and with Percival unaccounted for . . . perhaps this was the ultimate test.

"Well, *fuck* that—not hearing for a couple of days," Simon said. "Just fuck that."

"Simon, don't," Mag began.

"I'll tell you what I'm going to do," he said. "If he's okay, I'll have my ear fixed. If he's not okay, I won't."

"I thought you'd decided definitely not to do it," Alfred said.

"I changed my mind," Simon told them. "Is it such a crime to change your mind?"

"It sounds to me like a bargain with God," Patrick said. "Always a dangerous kind of bargain."

"Percival said it'd look better fixed, but I should make up my own mind—that's all. What difference does it make?"

"None, except that I have to believe God would concern himself with larger issues than your ear and Percival's well-being," Patrick said. He knew his voice sounded calm, but his heart thumped in his chest. He would not allow this.

"If Percival comes home, he'd probably like to see me with an ear, right? But if he's dead, there's no point having it fixed for him to look at because he's not going to be around to see it."

"Oh, I see," said Patrick. "The Angel Solution."

"Come off it, Dad."

"Well, it is, isn't it?" The term Angel Solution had been derived from Patrick's mother's name—Angela—and the way she always lit candles in church and struck other religious bargains to ensure the safe passage of Patrick's family from Maryland to Maine, as they drove the perilous roads north every third summer. Patrick had always pointed out that it was his good driving that got them there safely and not Angela or her angels—and hence the Angel Solution, which he always felt was a disrespectful term to use with regard to his mother, but useful to prove his point. He wanted the boys to understand that you yourself, not God, were responsible for getting you there.

"This has nothing to do with Grandmother Singer," Simon said.

"I still don't like to see you making rash decisions based on something that may or may not have happened four thousand miles away," Patrick said.

"I can't argue with you about it," Simon said.

"No, I can see that. That's because there's no logic to it."

Simon sighed in a dramatic, irritated way. Then he sat back down on the couch on top of Patrick's feet. Patrick was flattered that he'd turned to him for solace in the middle of a reprimand, but he felt it was no more constructive than the Angel Solution, especially since he was sure this wasn't the end of it.

"Simon, if you think numbing my lower extremities by sitting on them has taken my mind off my headache, you're mistaken," he said. "Now get up and make yourself useful. Get a decent channel on the TV. Then make sure the room is picked up so when people start coming, they won't think we've lost it."

He did not think he sounded convincing, but he could hear everyone picking up papers and rearranging things that had been displaced. He was disturbed that Simon would be ready to trade off his ear for Percival's life. It was too much like what his mother had always done, the joke about the Angel Solution aside. After Patrick's father died and for the rest of her life, Angela had become so helplessly religious that she couldn't take care of herself, and this is what Patrick had tried to avoid in his own life and to teach his sons to avoid.

The first year of her widowhood, Angela had relied heavily on Father James. Patrick would not have minded if he hadn't seen at once that while the priest's attentions were comforting, he had no more grasp of mortgages and fuel bills than his mother did. The only practical help he finally provided was to get Angela a job in Dorothy Whitmore's dress shop.

"See, God is providing," Angela had said. "All we have to do is trust." But it was hard to trust when God was providing only minimum wage.

"Ask her for a raise," Patrick begged his mother as the years went by. "You certainly deserve it."

But Angela wouldn't. She went to Mass on her way to work, she fasted and visited the sick. God provided, Angela said; she would not ask for more money. In the end her rituals seemed inspired less by religion than by fear, just like Simon's offering up his ear.

Angela had become even more helpless as time went on. When the plumbing leaked, she prayed for endurance while Patrick borrowed plumbing books from the library and took the pipes apart. Patrick learned to fix the furnace and took a paper route to earn spending money. When he was fourteen, he realized that Dorothy Whitmore was too ill to run her store alone and depended on Angela to manage it. Nervous but determined, he went into the shop on his mother's day off, hinting that she had been offered work elsewhere and might take it unless Dorothy raised her salary and provided a retirement plan. Dorothy Whitmore gave in. It was then that he decided you had only your own good sense to rely on and must not turn the responsibility over to God or anything else.

"You've done all right so far, but you can't expect everything," Angela had said when Patrick announced he intended to go to college. She feared he was proud, setting his sights so high, and cautioned him to be humble, lest God do worse than deny him a university education. "You'll always be able to make a living, you're so good with your hands," Angela maintained. "Think about taking the vo-tech course at school." But Patrick signed up for college prep, got a part-time job at the lumberyard on weekends, and continued to deliver newspapers every morning. He also made the track team. He was a good miler and hoped for a running scholarship. Angela wasn't surprised when he didn't get one. "Think of Job. You don't understand everything, but usually it works out for the best," she said. When Patrick won the Paper Carrier's Scholarship, she changed her mind, saying God had sent it after all. But Patrick credited his own hard work. He left for college in Maryland, a long way away. He never went back to Maine except for visits, though he arranged through friends to have the repairs kept up on his mother's house until the day she died. He never argued with her about religion, but he stopped going to church when he left home and later never foisted it on his sons.

His self-reliance served him well. Watching Mag insist her life was hopeless if it consisted of soaking diapers in the toilet twenty-four hours a day, he'd invented disposable diapers to show that even a houseful of babies was manageable. Seeing that he would never make enough money working for someone else, he'd done a market study and finally opened his upholstery plant. He'd invented a ten-slice toaster to stop the fighting at breakfast and made RipOffs to keep his sons running in the cold. Even when his blind spells came and the doctors at Hopkins couldn't help him . . . even then he wasn't surprised because he already knew nobody else would ever bail you out. He was going to find his own solution. If God was up there, His mind was on larger matters. Why should He let Percival live just because Simon offered up his ear?

Yet he understood. If Percival were lying beneath a building, unable for once to rely on his own wits, how could a bunch of nineteen-year-old Marines—boys who had just been through a blast themselves—be trusted to pull him out? Of all Patrick's sons, Percival had needed most to be unfettered . . . and now he might be trapped even more permanently and more horribly than Patrick was trapped inside his own head, blind. He knew Simon offered surgery because he found the idea as unbearable as Percival's entrapment, but all the same it was like trying to buy grace the way Angela had, with her candles and Spartan ways and strict attendance at Mass. A perfect hollow formed in his stomach. He was exhausted—from the aftereffects of Valium, from the headache, from the stress. A trembly weakness filled him. Blind, and thinking of Percival dead, he felt very nearly defeated.

Then he remembered something Percival had said after losing a race in high school. He had said, "Sometimes you just don't have anything left."

And Patrick had replied, "That's why you slow down, that's why you psych yourself out, because you think in the end you aren't going to have anything left. But what you'll find out is you always have something left."

Of course it was true. Perhaps, five thousand miles away, Percival would remember that. Willing the weakness away, Patrick took the washcloth off his eyes and sat up.

"What time is it?" he asked.

"Almost eleven," Alfred said.

"Don't you think it's time we finally called Gideon?"

"It's only nine out there," Alfred said.

"Still, we should call." Usually he kept his eyes closed during the blind spells, but he made himself open them now. The world in front of him was not black but grayish, flecked with orange, as if he'd closed his eyes tight and clenched them shut. But his eyes were open.

"I'll dial," one of the twins said. Whichever one it was sounded like a child excited about speaking with his big brother on the phone. The twins still worshipped Gideon. In high school they'd gone out for running because of him—not because they were good at it or even particularly enjoyed it, but just to be with their brother. But Patrick was disturbed by their exuberant tone now. Calling Gideon was going to be no joyride. "You can dial," he said. "But I want to talk."

So Merle—or Darren—dialed. The headache was a weight, and the orange dots floated in the gray distance of Patrick's vision. In Utah, the phone rang three times. When a voice answered, it wasn't Gideon's but a roommate's. Patrick remembered. It was Sunday morning. Gideon would have let himself sleep a little later and then gone out for his weekly twelve-mile run.

He had thought at least to get this conversation over with. He left a message for Gideon to call back. He would have to pace himself, allow himself just so much stress, to get through this day. "Wait a minute," the roommate said as he was about to hang up. "I see him coming."

There was a long pause while Gideon came into the apartment. For a moment Patrick wished he hadn't caught him after all, only to give him bad news at the end of a grueling workout. He regretted that his role with Gideon was always to make difficult demands. When Gideon had started running, Patrick had not only seen how talented he was, he'd also discovered how well he responded to criticism, while Percival did not. So he was easy on Percival and hard on Gideon, and the harder he was, the better Gideon ran. It was not always wise. There were the inevitable difficulties of having two sons who ran competitively, the difficulties of Percival's having started first. After the race at Brunswick that changed Gideon's career, Patrick had acted badly toward him. He still regretted it. He remembered Gideon running track as a high school freshman, throwing up after every race, enduring. Such capacity for pain. Later Patrick suggested to the high school coach that Gideon wasn't really a miler, and when the coach put him in the two-mile, Gideon stopped throwing up. But more often, Patrick inflicted the pain rather than eased it. As now. Gideon's voice came suddenly on the line, tense and expectant, and Patrick almost shuddered.

"Hello? Dad?" Gideon was out of breath. Patrick pretended that his headache was a black ball outside of him, hanging in the gray air of his blindness, several feet away. He told Gideon what he could.

"I'll come home," Gideon said.

Patrick breathed deeply. "Christ, coming home is the last thing you should do," he said. "Aren't your conference championships coming up?"

"This puts the conference championships in one hell of a perspective, Dad."

"Until we know something, the best thing is to stay right where you are. Train. Besides, Percival is probably all right. We all have a good feeling about it."

Horsecrap. But what good would it do to have Gideon home, thinking how he'd beaten his older brother in every race that mattered—including, perhaps, the ability to stay alive?

The orange dots danced in front of Patrick's eyes. He smelled Mag's bath powder as she took the phone from him. He went out of the phone room, feeling his way along the wall.

"Gideon, do me a favor," he heard her say. "Stay where you are. Your father is having a difficult time trying to entertain all his sons."

She believed he was trying to entertain them.

"No, not his eyes, just stress," she lied. "But humor him anyway."

When she hung up, Patrick said, "We didn't even ask him how his team did in that big cross-country meet yesterday."

"He doesn't care about that now," Mag said.

"We should have asked." Gideon would always care about such things. Not thinking meant that he was not as much in control as he had tried to be.

Patrick felt as limp as the washcloth he had used to cover his eyes. He could not go on like this, setting the example. And then, just at that moment, it seemed to him that the gray he was seeing was not the gray of blindness but of light outside his eyes.

"I feel it easing up a little," he said.

"What?"

"The eyes—easing up."

"Can you see?" Izzy asked.

"I'm starting to." The headache was still very powerful, but daylight was clearly visible as he looked through the windows. The orange dots had disappeared. Inside the room the light was a cozy yellow, almost golden. He could see one of the twins.

"Focus on my mustache," Merle said.

"I can just make it out." Yes, yes, his vision was definitely returning. "It looks like a disease," he said to Merle. "Or maybe a fungus."

"That's just how I would have described it," said Darren.

The relief was enormous. He looked down at his clothes. "I can see well enough to go upstairs and get out of this bathrobe," he said. "I didn't realize I was still in my bathrobe. Maybe I'm going senile."

"How's the headache?"

"Hurts."

"Probably low blood sugar," Izzy said. "You need to eat something."

"Maybe." It was generous of Izzy to try to offer a solution. But if it was just the headache, he could cope. It was a trifle compared to the feeling of entrapment when he was blind. His eyesight was blurry—it would stay blurry for hours—but it was functional. It would get him through the day. He felt that his vision had not returned just then by accident. He felt that he had willed it.

Mag could not believe how pathetic Patrick was acting. Pathetic. There was no other word. Pretending to concentrate on Merle's mustache as if that were the important thing, and not his eyes opening up. Acting as if he was shocked to find himself still in his bathrobe. Pretending he'd been in charge all along, when in fact everyone had been doing for him all morning— getting his medicine, wetting his washcloth, dialing the phone. Patrick the Stoic, replaced by Patrick the Clown. And all the time pretending Percival was in no particular danger, that this was some sort of cheerful family gathering. Telling Gideon not to come home—and she going along with him, *trained* to go along with him—when Gideon had every right to be here if he wanted to. If it were not for that sense of separation that surrounded her, she would have screamed or shaken Patrick. But now he was upstairs dressing—he had been up there much longer than he needed to be—and his absence unsettled her, too. Every moment things were becoming more bizarre.

At first, in the early hours of TV bulletins and interrupted shows, the phone and door had both been ominously silent. Then suddenly they both started ringing nonstop. It was as if everyone had absorbed all they could of the TV fare and wanted the drama raw.

The first newspaper that called was the *Freestate Sentinel*.

"Yes, Percival Singer is over there," Mag heard one of the twins say from inside the phone room. The voice was wobbly, the thin whine the twins always lapsed into when they were upset. "No, no—you better talk to my mother," the voice said. Then Darren poked his head out and handed her the phone.

"We understand you have a son in Lebanon," the reporter said. "Have you any word. . . ?"

What nerve! She knew why Darren sounded so upset. To call at a time like this . . . She knew what Patrick would do: He would keep his voice firm, deep, as if to say, "Listen, fellow, I'm in charge here." He would talk the reporter into finding out what he could and calling them back, saying that if you were clever you could even turn their curiosity to your advantage. But Mag could only stand there with a sour rage burning in her throat.

"I'm sorry, we don't know anything," she managed finally.

"Of course, Mrs. Singer. In the meantime . . ." The dramatic pause. "We'd like to come out and speak to you. We know it must be difficult. . . ."

A fine thread of pain wended its way through her skull. "No. We couldn't do that right now." She wanted to say something tactful: This is difficult not just for us—for all the families. She wanted her voice to sound inscrutable, especially since Darren had sounded so terrible. But nothing came. She put the phone back on the hook.

Darren was staring at her. "You'd think at a time like this, at least they'd leave us alone," he said.

"Are you kidding?"

She intended to put her music back on. But the doorbell rang. The Warrens came, the Jacobis, the Haverfords, neighbors from blocks around, saying, "Oh, Mag, how terrible. What have you heard?" Bringing casseroles, banana bread, cloth-covered jars of jam made last summer for Christmas but ferreted out now in October: offerings in exchange for information. Alfred took the food and ushered them back out, but Patrick did not appear. Mag had to talk when his old Aunt Kay called from Maine, had to explain to his entire staff from the plant. . . . Her own parents and sister phoned too—she didn't mind that—and she told them there was no need to come just yet (where did they think she would put them?), but she felt abandoned when she had to deal with people she didn't even know.

Where was Patrick?

Two more small newspapers called wanting interviews and finally the *Washington Post*. The local TV station offered to send a reporter any time the family deemed convenient; a talk-show host from Radio 63 called, claiming to be an old high school friend of Izzy's.

"Not me. Never heard of him," Izzy said afterward.

"This is ridiculous," Mag said. "I'm not talking to them anymore."

So the twins dealt with the media people, though it seemed odd, what with their upset-sounding voices, which usually embarrassed them but now did not seem to. The only sense Mag could make of it was that somehow they had taken over because they had been attached more to Gideon than Percival all these years and therefore would be less emotional. But she felt selfish for thinking that, and of course their voices gave them away. After more than an hour Patrick finally appeared, shaved and showered and dressed as if he'd never been blind. She wondered why she had missed him.

"We should eat," Alfred said, though by now it was well past lunchtime. They had not eaten all day, had only had endless cups of tea and snacked on a coffee cake a neighbor had brought, so that crumbs now lay all across the family room carpet. Alfred put one of the casseroles in the oven to warm. Izzy got out paper cups and plates, and Patrick opened a jar of homemade pickles someone had put on the counter. Everyone seemed awfully calm, unaffected by the phone calls and visits and lack of information on TV—calm in the face of crisis. Mag would have preferred them to scream and cry and pound on the table.

When they all sat down, Simon began digging dirt from under his fingernails with a steak knife.

"Don't do that, it's disgusting," Mag said. She did not actually care that it was disgusting or have any real reaction to it. She was looking at his missing ear—or rather the hair that covered his missing ear. She would not forgive Patrick for trying to talk Simon out of plastic surgery just because he thought Simon was making one of those infamous deals with God. She herself had no such objections to such deals, if they did you some good. Sometimes they were all that was left, though in her mother-in-law's case they had been carried to an extreme.

Alfred dished out the casserole—a glop of different cheeses, holding together noodles and chopped meat. Simon ignored his plate and dug harder under his index finger until a little line of blood appeared beneath the nail. She wondered if he would always mutilate his fingers now, instead of snapping them.

"Put the knife away, Simon," she said. "I mean it."

"Better take it to have it disinfected," Merle said.

"Yeah, boil it for a couple of hours," Darren said.

Simon got up and dropped the knife in the sink. He did not wash his hand. Blood seeped out from beneath the nail and reddened the tip of his finger. The sight of it made Mag turn away, though she was not usually squeamish. Something terrible occurred to her. If Simon had the ear fixed, it would be bloody like this. If Simon had the ear fixed, he could die.

"I think Dad's right," she said suddenly. "I wouldn't make any grand commitments about having the ear done right now."

"I thought you wanted me to," Simon said.

"Yes, but not like this. You don't make a decision like this during a crisis."

"Your mother's making sense for once," Patrick said. He had no right to make it sound as if she was normally unreasonable. She saw with perfect clarity that the situation was beyond reason. Simon's difficulties after the tonsil operation had been a warning for him never to have surgery again. That was why he was so afraid. He thought he was trading his own life for Percival's. It might be true. Or Simon might die and Percival, both. The punishment could be two sons. Three. All seven.

"You're the one who's been pushing the operation," Simon said.

"I know, and I'm not saying don't do it," Mag said, although of course she was. "I just don't want you to decide right now."

"Well, I'm having it done," Simon said.

Alfred was watching her, as if he expected her to eat. She was so far from eating noodles and meat and cheese.

"Mother, I don't understand you," Alfred said, trying to lighten the mood. "I'm not condoning Simon's methods, but you have to consider that when Percival comes home now, you've got Simon on the spot. He'd never back down on something he says he'll do for Percival. You should exercise your advantage while you've got it."

Simon wiped the blood from his finger with a napkin. It was Simon's blood and also the blood of Marines, sinking into the dusty soil of the Beirut airport. "Percival might not be coming home," she said.

"Mag, don't start that," Patrick said. He put some of the noodle glop into his mouth, to show how irrational she was being, to stress the need for calm. They were all eating.

It was possible at this moment, while Patrick was chewing noodles, that Percival had been under the rubble for more than twelve hours. The weight of it would have been bearable at first and then not. Breath squeezed out little by little, and no strength to draw more.

"Please, Simon, I don't want you to decide right now," Mag said. Her voice was strained, almost hysterical. Patrick looked at her with disgust.

"I told you, I've already decided," Simon said.

She saw him dead on the operating table—a slow numbness—and Percival crushed. She saw everything. Her heart being cauterized one-seventh at a time, annihilated, leaving the flesh dead and useless and the pain spreading out and out. And Patrick continued to eat.

At four P.M. Mountain Time (six Eastern Daylight Time), Gideon was sitting in the Denver airport waiting for a plane to Chicago, where he would get a flight to Baltimore or Virginia or D.C. and find his way home over land from there.

He was having considerable difficulty moving his limbs, but even so, he made himself walk to the pay phone a hundred feet across the concourse to call the hotline number they'd been posting on the television. He'd watched the news in the airport snack bar long enough.

"Major Williams," a voice said. Gideon's immediate thought was that if a major was answering, the situation was at least as bad as they said on TV, maybe worse. It was a lot more serious than his father had made it out to be.

"My name is Gideon Singer and I have a brother, Percival Singer, stationed in Beirut," he said. "I wonder if you have any word on him yet." As he spoke, he felt he ought to know Percival's unit number or other details—and that the lack of them made him sound foolish and suspect. But the major did not seem to care.

The major gave him a long explanation of the procedure they were following to identify the surviving Marines—how each one would have to be seen personally by a first sergeant or company commander before his name could go on the list, and how fragmented the units were at this time, and how this made the procedure painfully slow.

"What if he's wounded?"

"He would be moved out. Again—it could take time."

"And if he's dead?"

"Son," the major said, "you might not hear anything one way or another for a couple of days."

The heaviness in Gideon's limbs became something he could see, not with his eyes but with his muscles. It was an odd sensation. He made his way back to his chair.

The day had started out like any other Sunday, which seemed quite ironic now. The most ironic thing was he'd thought about Percival while he was running this morning, which was something he never allowed himself to do. Sitting in the plastic airport chair, his legs felt heavy and he was afraid. Until now he'd always been able to count on his body reacting a certain way, even when he couldn't count on his father or his brothers or anything else. Now his legs might have been full of lead. He thought this morning's run over again because he was afraid it would be the last one he would actually be capable of making.

Sunday was the only day he ran alone—twelve miles, on the road. "Long slow distance," his coach always said. "Very good for endurance." He always reviewed his Saturday cross-country races as he ran on Sunday because they were fresh in his mind and gave him something to do. If he waited for the week to begin, his thoughts would be too jumbled, what with his three-hour physics labs and running workouts twice a day—pace work with the team, barriers, hills, speed training. But on Sundays he ran alone, and he could think clearly.

He'd started out in his usual way. After sleeping a little later—a gift he allowed himself—he rolled out of bed into the chilly air. He put on shorts and a top and a pair of RipOffs over that and went downstairs out of his apartment onto the road.

Maybe it was the landscape that started him remembering. After a year at Weber State, he usually didn't notice it, but this morning the stark Utah autumn seemed strikingly different from Maryland's, where humid green Septembers gave way to wine and gold Octobers before the trees went bare. Here, the colors had faded quickly to yellow and then were gone. Cold from coming out of the warm apartment, Gideon wondered if the leaves were still on the trees in Maryland and thought they were. He remembered running home with Percival when they were much younger, on an October day just like this, after their mother threw them out of the car. The main thing that had kept him going, he remembered, was looking at the leaves.

It was one of the first times he had run with Percival. He'd gone because he felt his mother was unfair to put only Percival out of the car when he himself was equally responsible for the fight they were having. Percival was noisy and had attracted her attention, but Gideon had started it by silently pinching Percival on the arm.

He ran as close behind his brother as he could, once their mother drove off. He had a hard time keeping up, but he was afraid to let Percival get too far in front, leaving him behind in a neighborhood he didn't know. To keep from thinking how out of breath he was and how his chest ached, he counted the trees along the road. They were mostly sugar maples, orange and gold in the autumn sunlight. With the light coming from behind them, the leaves looked as if they glowed. Finally, they reached their yard. Gideon started coughing because his lungs were so tired. He didn't want Percival to hear him cough. But Percival said, "I used to cough all the time after I ran. It's because you're not in shape. When you get into shape it'll stop." Percival did not hold him in contempt for coughing. Gideon was glad. After he got used to running the mile or two miles from where his mother threw them out, the coughing *did* stop. Then he discovered a lightness in his body and was able to rely on his legs to carry him as fast as he wanted to go. It seemed to him that Percival was responsible for the joy he had discovered.

Later, there were other Maryland autumns, which he would remember because of cross-country season. In middle school, he and Percival shared their paper route, meeting at the 7-Eleven for doughnuts when they were finished. But on one particular Sunday there was a cross-country meet in Harford County, two hours away—one of Gideon's first big races. They wanted to get substitutes for the papers, but their father wouldn't let them. "You're responsible for those papers first and running second," he said, even though they would have to leave home by seven to get to the meet.

So they got up at four-thirty that morning, earlier than they ever had before. Their father drove them to pick up their papers at the *Freestate Sentinel* loading dock, because it was too early even for the delivery trucks to be out. The air was dark but not very cold, and the streets were deserted. Gideon had never been out at that hour. Piling the papers into the station wagon in the electric-light glare of the loading dock, he and Percival had looked at each other and broken into grins, thinking how urgent and important their mission was, if they were up so early.

They didn't deliver the papers on their bikes as they normally did. Instead, their father drove them. Usually if someone helped, it was their mother. But that day Patrick opened the tailgate of the station wagon and drove very slowly through the dark streets of their neighborhood while Percival and Gideon ran back and forth from the car, grabbing papers from the tailgate and flinging them onto porches. They did not see a single other person, and even the dogs were not out yet—even the shaggy English sheepdog that always brought them pinecones and followed them for blocks. Gideon thought that if the sheepdog was asleep, then in all the world just two paperboys and their father must be out just then, under such a black sky.

It was still dark when they finished, and Patrick took them to the Big Boy for breakfast. They almost never went to restaurants. It was too expensive to feed seven boys, and their parents did not think it fair to take just one or two of them. But that morning Patrick said, "Carbohydrate loading," winking at them and ordering stacks of pancakes. Gideon remembered coming out of the Big Boy with his belly full, into a sober gray dawn. Later the rest of the family piled into the station wagon for the two-hour drive to Harford County. He could not remember the details of the actual race or how either of them had done.

This morning, running long slow distance in the too-chilly mountain air of Utah, he'd thought how far away those times seemed, when his performance in a race had not mattered as much as the memory of a long night fading into dawn and the special, heady feeling of delivering papers with Percival and his father in the dark. He hadn't liked thinking that. He had forced himself to think instead about yesterday's race, which was what he intended to do all along.

Yesterday they'd gone to the Idaho State Invitational, a five-mile run on a hilly golf course, up and down. Gideon had felt good, but he'd made some mistakes and—as usual—hadn't beaten Farley. When they got back, his coach was more pleased with Gideon than Gideon was with himself. "You're looking strong," the coach said. "And that's good, because right now is when you should be starting to peak. Big Sky Conference is just a couple of weeks from now—fifteen miles up in those mountains." He pointed to the mountains beyond the campus, just outside of Ogden. "So if you don't feel good now, I don't know when the hell you will."

Gideon couldn't understand the coach's complacency. He hadn't, after all, caught up with Farley. He knew his father wouldn't have been pleased. His father would have expected more.

Typically, Gideon had run just behind Farley almost the whole way yesterday. He'd come in exactly four seconds behind him. It was always like that: He'd run four seconds behind Farley, or eight seconds or five. "You don't want to look too far ahead," his father used to say to Percival. "If you're running seventh, you don't want to think about beating the guy in first. You want to think about picking off number six, and then after that number five—think about picking them off one by one." But Gideon had nobody in front of him but Farley, and he knew his father would expect him to get closer, race by race. And so far, no matter how hard he tried, he had not been able to do it.

He had run easy this morning even as he thought about all that—which seemed odd now, sitting in the airport feeling like he was carrying weights in his arms and legs. This morning there had been a high sky, and the road was smooth under his feet. It had been years since he'd lost the childhood feeling of being able to go on forever without pain, but still his Sunday road work was easier than the Saturday races, and he was relaxed. He knew that later he would go home, shower, eat, study for a while, then lift weights. But again an unexpected memory had intruded when, thinking about weight-training, his mind had turned once more to Percival.

During that same period back in middle school, when Percival had already won several AAU and TAC events, their father spent endless hours helping Percival with his workouts. At first, Gideon just went along to be a part of it, racing when he could and taking in all of his father's advice. Patrick had said to Percival, "At the higher levels of competition, the difference isn't in your legs or your endurance, it's in your upper-body strength." Patrick had bought a bench press for Percival and put it in the basement, along with barbells and a chinning bar. But after a couple of months of working out, Percival decided his arms were as skinny as ever, so he quit. Later he worked out sporadically—every day for a week or two and then not at all for months. He never lifted on a regular basis until he went into the Marines. Gideon understood. The basement was cold, the floor was concrete and forbidding. The weights were in the exact spot where Izzy had once put his pet garter snake, to see if it would hibernate. Gideon never went down to the weight room himself unless Percival was there to keep him company.

Then Percival went into high school in ninth grade and came home with such stories about the cross-country course there that Gideon began to worry. He was a year behind Percival, still in middle school, and wouldn't get to run it for another year.

"The course isn't bad except for this one hill—Killer Mountain," Percival would tell him, holding his hand absolutely vertical to the ground. "Some kids say you can only climb it with a rope, but we have to run up it every day."

Gideon couldn't imagine himself running up Killer Mountain. He hated thinking of Percival running up it every day—a hill steep enough to climb with a rope!—and knowing he was too weak to do such a thing himself. He thought Percival would look down on him for not being able to run it, and his father would hold him in contempt. Of course at the first home meet Gideon saw for himself that the hill wasn't vertical, just very steep, but by then it had become vertical in his mind. He made himself go down to the basement and lift the weights twice a week. His father had taped Percival's weight-lifting schedule to the cinder-block basement wall. Percival ignored the schedule, but Gideon made himself do the whole workout each time. Occasionally Percival came down and did it with him, and then it seemed easier. But later, when Percival didn't want to be in the basement or anywhere else with Gideon, Gideon kept lifting weights anyway. His body was strong, and he could rely on it, and if that was all he was going to have, if Percival were going to hate him, then he would lift as many weights as he had to. But he hated weight-training, even now. He wouldn't think about it until he got back to the apartment; pick them off one at a time.

He had begun sweating. He pulled open the Velcro seams of his RipOff sweatpants and refastened the Velcro around his waist so he could carry the pants until he stopped. Too cold at this time of year to start out with nothing over his shorts. People thought Patrick had designed the RipOffs for Gideon, but that wasn't true. Percival had been the inspiration—not because of Percival's dedication to running, but because of the obnoxious way he acted when it was cold. Either he wouldn't run at all in winter or if he did he'd bundle up like Santa Claus and then get mad because he'd soon be too hot. He'd start sweating and want to be stripped down to shorts and tank top, that moment, right then. "God, I hate having to stop to pull these sweats over my shoes," he'd yell. "First you warm up and then you stop to undress and first thing you know you're freezing your ass."

When the weather got really cold, Percival would stay inside. "Jesus Christ, Percival!" their father would yell. "If you want to be any kind of serious runner, then you have to run all year."

"Yeah, I know," Percival would say, but he wouldn't do it. He'd go once or twice to the indoor track above the gym at the Y, but then he'd quit. The track was banked, it made him dizzy, it made him feel like one of those hamsters on a treadmill. Finally Patrick sat down at the sewing machine and said, "Okay, Percival, after today you're going to have no excuse." He ripped the two outer seams of Percival's sweatpants open from ankle to waist, and replaced the stitching with Velcro. The Velcro held the seams together but was easy to pull apart. You could yank the seams open and take the pants off without pulling them down over your shoes.

His father had stood up at the machine looking as sweaty and red in the face as if he'd just run the mile. "And this, fool," he said, holding the product up for Percival to see, "is why all young men should learn to sew." He reminded everyone that he had fashioned his disposable diaper on this same sewing machine eighteen years ago, to preserve the shitty little butts of his sons. He reminded them that Izzy had been named after Isaac Singer, who had invented the sewing machine in the first place. He shamed Percival into running in the cold all that winter. Later he made pairs of RipOffs for Gideon and the twins and Simon, and still later for the entire high school cross-country team. But by then people had forgotten that Percival was the inspiration.

Gideon did not intend to think about that. Percival had run well his freshman and sophomore years in high school. Then everything began to change. Or rather, it changed all at once, during the race at Brunswick when Percival was a junior. After that he and Percival still ran cross-country and track together for the high school, but Percival hardly spoke to him. For two years, he spent every waking moment with Tim O'Neal. In the spring of his senior year, he even quit the track team. But Gideon kept running. He won the state cross-country championship two years in a row. Sometimes it seemed to him that running was all he had left.

When he was a senior, the *Freestate Sentinel* ran a picture of Gideon holding his trophies, with the rest of the high school team standing behind him. They were all wearing RipOffs. That was when people began assuming the RipOffs had been made for Gideon. Not long afterward, Percival dropped out of the community college to join the Marines, and Gideon decided to come to Utah.

But now, after more than a year here, he usually felt at home. He was a sophomore. He rarely thought about Percival anymore, especially on these Sunday-morning runs. Mostly he thought about Farley and the strategies he would follow to beat him. Or at least that's what he *had* thought about, until his legs started feeling like weights were attached to all the bones.

Yesterday, in his desk drawer, he had come across the slip of paper on which he'd written a quote from Brendan Foster, who received the bronze medal in the 1976 Olympics ten-thousand meter run. It was in his drawer and not on his wall with the other quotes, because he didn't want anybody else to see it. "It seems to me that about six or so athletes at the Olympic starting line have good chances," Foster had said, "but out of those six, one knows he is going to win. And there's a big difference between wanting to win and knowing you will win."

He supposed that before his limbs had gotten heavy, that was the real difference between him and Farley right now. They were both talented, but Farley had the edge. He was older, stronger, and more experienced, and he knew he was going to win. But sometime—Gideon had played this over and over in his mind—all that would change. A day would come when he would pass Farley. His father expected it, and Gideon expected it, too. It might happen when Farley was tired, or Farley tripped; it didn't matter why. Gideon didn't kid himself that it would happen because he was so much faster than Farley. He knew he wasn't; their abilities were very close. It would happen because for one race, for whatever reason, Gideon would get the edge. And afterward Gideon, instead of Farley, would be the one who knew he was going to win.

It wasn't that he didn't like Farley. He did. They ate together, sat on the bus together coming home from meets. He'd liked Percival, too—more—and that didn't stop him from doing what he did at Brunswick. He pushed the thought away. Until today he had not thought there was any way, now that he had been running cross-country with Farley for two years, that he was going to let Farley graduate a year from now without having beaten him.

This morning, he had been sweating hard as he neared the end of his run, but he had not felt tired. He could tell from the strength in his body that the coach had been right when he said Gideon was starting to peak. He knew why the coach had been pleased with him. In spite of his loss the day before, he was getting closer to beating Farley every race. Even his father would have to approve. He turned a final corner, heading back to his apartment. In the distance his roommate, Daniel, was waving at him from the balcony. Normally Daniel would still be asleep. He was the laziest roommate Gideon had ever had. Lazier than any of his brothers. It seemed odd for Daniel to be gesturing with such unaccustomed energy. The high, heady feeling went out of his limbs. There was something urgent and ominous about Daniel's wave. He did not realize how ominous until he heard his father's voice on the phone. He listened to his father tell him about the explosion in Lebanon. He said he would be home as soon as he could get there.

His father told him not to come.

He didn't know why he did what he did next. He didn't say a word to Daniel. He turned and walked out the door and down the stairs and started to run again. It was crazy, because he had just run twelve miles.

He ran a block. His mind was empty at first. When a thought came to him it was a double thought, first of Percival being blown apart and then of his father telling him not to come home. A sinking feeling came over him—not the black dots before the eyes when you're about to pass out, but a more entire feeling, as if someone had painted the inside of him with tar. He couldn't run any farther and could barely walk. His limbs were heavy, on the edge of paralysis. He felt that, in a moment, his limbs would refuse to move at all. Moving fast was all he could ever count on, and at that moment, that simply, it was gone. He forced himself to walk back to the apartment. It was like trying to walk through water. This must be what it felt like to have polio, he thought. He sat in front of the TV watching the news updates. Daniel hovered around, but Gideon could not bring himself to speak. Percival was probably dead. His arms and his legs did not want to move.

"I could drive you to the airport in Salt Lake City," Daniel said finally. "If you want to go home."

"They told me not to come," Gideon said.

"They said that to make it easy for you, probably. It's probably tough being at home right now."

"Yeah, probably."

Daniel dropped him off at the airport. He had not checked airline schedules and had to wait half the day for a plane to Denver. Now he was going to have to wait another hour before he could get from Denver to Chicago. He hoped his arms and legs would hold out. He told himself all he had to do was get on that plane to Chicago. Then his legs would have the whole flight to recover, they wouldn't have to move an inch. He told himself this was exactly like reaching down and going on when you were too tired to finish a race. Once, during some race, Gideon had slowed down and his father had shouted to him, "It's only another two-twenty, Gideon. Anyone can run a two-twenty." Gideon had pictured himself running just halfway around the track, and it did not seem so impossible. In Chicago all he had to do was get off the plane, walk through the airport, and get on another plane to Washington. It was no worse than gutting it out through that last two-twenty. He remembered his father's words. No matter how tired he was, if he concentrated hard enough, he could always finish.

Mag had begun to feel almost numb. A whole day had passed and they still knew nothing. The eleven o'clock news was coming on. Even the phone and the doorbell had finally stopped ringing. Earlier, in her slightly removed state, Mag had concentrated on Percival for hours, sending out tendrils of protective thought as if they might still do some good. But eventually she could not sustain even that. In the enormous commotion, her fear of each caller being the Marines became only an ache somewhere below the skin. There was just too much activity.

In late afternoon, Beth O'Neal called to say that she, too, had heard nothing. The news bulletins became further and further apart. They waited. Simon rubbed his missing ear and kept looking down at the FREESTATE STRIDERS logo on Percival's old shirt he was wearing. Patrick squinted because his headache persisted, but his eyes stayed open. Izzy kept observing Patrick the way Mag imagined he would observe a laboratory specimen, with great interest but also a certain amount of anguish for having to subject his own father to such scrutiny. And just before supper—a meal no one really wanted after the late, aborted lunch, but which Alfred insisted upon in the name of normality—Cynthia arrived.

Mag saw her coming up the walk in the rain, trailed by her boys. She was wearing jeans and a baggy sweatshirt that did not disguise at all the size of her breasts. Her sons, Jason and Joshua—those terrible names, clichés of names, when Mag had named her own sons so much more imaginatively—looked wide-eyed and so frightened that Mag wondered what Cynthia had told them. Stepping into the hall, Cynthia leaned forward as if she were debating whether to hug Mag. In the end she only lifted her hands and shoved something forward, which turned out to be homemade bread. It was very awkward.

The children stood in the hallway in awed silence until Mag said, "Come on in, Alfred's fixing supper in the kitchen. Go say hello to everybody." A wave of relief came into their huge eyes, and they scrambled off so joyfully that Mag realized for the sixth or seventh time since she'd met them that it wasn't the boys she disliked, only Cynthia's crime of foisting them on Alfred. It was Cynthia—not the boys themselves—who had called upon Alfred's sense of responsibility to the point that he asked for

Mag's house. And also, though she tried not to admit this, she would have liked the boys to have had some distant resemblance to Alfred—his high cheekbones, his square chin, *something*—since he was bent on sacrificing himself for them even at the cost of children of his own. But the boys looked exactly like Cynthia.

"That was very sweet of you," Mag said, turning the bread over in her hands. "Did you make it yourself?" Cynthia nodded. *Fat chance.* Here was a woman with two sons, a divorce, a master's degree, and a job with the school system. Why should she spend her day off kneading bread?

"The kids helped. It gave us something to do. I didn't want them running around over here while you were waiting to hear something."

Of course not. The kids could run around here after Mag had moved to the Keys. She was not taken in by the good-mother image of Cynthia cooped up in the rain with small children and a clump of yeast dough.

"Patrick still doing okay, Mag?"

Mag. Patrick. Calling them by their first names ever since their first meeting—just like that—though neither of them had ever said, "Call me Mag" or "Call me Patrick." As simple as moving into the house. What would be better? Mrs. Singer? Mr. Singer? Certainly not Mother or Dad.

They walked through the hallway into the family room and kitchen, where Cynthia kissed Alfred lightly on the mouth—a brisk, businesslike kiss. Mag's sister had told her once, "If Alfred marries Cynthia, then you'll finally have a daughter," but the idea seemed ludicrous. Mag could never view Cynthia as a daughter. Daughters would be like her nieces, who'd sulked their way through adolescence into languid adulthood, guided by a feminine mystique Mag couldn't understand. Cynthia was anything but languid and daughterly. She was a vamp.

Of course she didn't look particularly vampy right now. Mag searched for a better word. Except for her overripe body, the woman wasn't even particularly feminine. The calculated kiss she had given Alfred summed her up perfectly—a gesture preplanned to elicit approval from prospective in-laws, given with the same reasonableness and essential lack of passion that she worried about in Alfred. Conniving, yes. But when you got right down to it, Cynthia was a woman who'd named her sons the names every other mother was choosing that year—names that would never be embarrassing or unusual or even interesting.

A taker: That was the word. Cynthia was a taker.

Alfred was setting the table. Cynthia immediately began to help him. Mag was struck by how quickly the two of them seemed to have settled down to routine. They probably set the table together just this way back in their little apartment. She could envision them clearly a couple of years from now—locked in to dinner at six, Sunday breakfasts, semiannual visits to the dentist. Having ruled out more children, they would have to settle for routine as the sole fruit of their orderly minds. Poor Alfred; he deserved better. Even she herself had had a little excitement over the years. After the children were born, Patrick still went after her with the same hunger he'd had in the backseat of his car, and she'd said once, "For God's sake, what motivates all this?" And he'd replied, "It's your blond hair and white skin and pink nipples. You look more naked than other women." His answer had excited her—spoken to her of his experience with women before he met her, and his continuing lust for her, and the life they had woven of it. Of course it had turned out to be all a trap—a way of getting her well trained. But at the time her bounty of secret sex and unplanned sons had seemed almost daring. Alfred would not have even that. Cynthia, too, might look more naked than other women when she undressed, but Mag suspected she would turn out to be not a great love but only a good roll in the hay, the way piano lessons had turned out to be only a technical exercise. And Alfred would be left with her kids. More than ever, Mag did not want Cynthia living in her house.

— 114 —

"Dinner's served," Alfred said. Looking at the food, Mag felt that only minutes had passed since their disastrous lunch, with Simon digging blood from beneath his fingernails. It was pure wrongness, sitting down to a family meal of good food and laughter. Why did it matter who lived in her house?

After supper, Jason and Joshua fell asleep in front of the TV, with their heads on either side of Simon's lap. Simon remained motionless for over an hour so as not to awaken them. His new-found capacity for stillness disturbed Mag, but she did not say so. At nine, Alfred and Cynthia carried the sleeping boys out to the car to go home. Simon, too, got up and started walking back and forth across the family room. His hours of stillness had revived him to violent energy, though he had been up this morning before five. Occasionally he sat, but then he leaped up after a few minutes and walked some more. Izzy and the twins were sprawled on the carpet near the TV, but Simon didn't stop his pacing, only stepped over them each time as he passed. And now the news was coming on, and Simon was still walking.

The news told them nothing. There was a recap of the day's events. The hotline number. Films of young Marines working under floodlights, trying to pry out other Marines still crushed under smoldering debris. Destruction. Then President Reagan came on, standing under a large black umbrella held by an aide, holding his wife's hand. He had the grace to look pained.

"There are no words," he said, "that can express our outrage and, I think, the outrage of all Americans at the despicable act . . ."

Patrick strode over to the TV set and turned it off. "Let's go to bed," he said. He sounded imperious . . . annoying. No one moved.

"I can't believe last night at this time nothing was wrong," Simon said. He did not stop pacing. He reached the far end of the family room and opened the slider to let Lucifer in.

"None of us can believe this," Izzy said.

It was true: They did not believe it. Even what little they knew . . . it was as if, in a certain sense, they did not believe it.

The cat shook rainwater from its fur and headed to the kitchen. Simon followed, to feed it.

"He's been out all day, why couldn't you just have left him there?" Mag asked.

"He's hungry, Mother," Izzy said, not waiting for Simon to answer.

"Another mouth to feed, just what we need. I could also do without him sleeping on my pillow."

"Mother, it's only a cat," Izzy said.

"Yes, with its whiskers in my face and its tail in your father's every night."

"At least you get the front end," Izzy said.

"If you think it's such a good deal, then *you* sleep with it."

"Okay, I will." Izzy retrieved the animal from the kitchen and held it in his arms. Mag thought it was bizarre the way he defended Lucifer, considering his work.

"Come on. Upstairs," Patrick said. "We're so tired, we're sniping at each other over nothing."

"I don't think I could sleep," Darren said.

"Go," Patrick said. "You'll be surprised."

To Mag's astonishment, the twins got up. He had the whole family trained so well.

In bed, they lay side by side looking at the ceiling. She didn't know if they were both pretending to be asleep or if they just had nothing to say.

"Whatever happens," Patrick told her finally, "I think we should still consider going to the Keys for the winter."

It seemed, at the moment, the most totally selfish thing he could utter. "I would have to quit my job," she said.

"You've quit jobs before. If something happens, I know the routine would be comforting. But there would be other jobs."

"Do you really think I work because the routine is comforting?"

— 116 —

"I want you to have a future to look forward to," he said. "The Keys could be something to look forward to."

"I don't see how." But she sighed. He sounded like he was trying to be kind. Maybe his head was still hurting. She might have weakened toward him except that the cat, which Izzy had taken to the other room, had found its way down the hall and at that moment jumped onto the bed.

"That took exactly ten minutes," Mag said.

"There's no point getting excited over the cat. It isn't the cat that's really bothering you."

"No shit, Patrick."

"It's the uncertainty. It can be worse than knowing almost anything."

"Not necessarily. There are some things I'd rather be uncertain of than know for sure."

Patrick closed his eyes tighter.

"Are you all right?"

"I'm all right. The Valium gives me a hangover. My eyes feel like they've been splattered with sand. Other than that, I'm terrific."

"Well, if it's only that, I won't worry," she said.

The cat found its usual place between their pillows. It was not true that she didn't hate the cat. It was not true that she could look forward to the Keys. She was about to say something on those subjects. It was stupid to lie here looking at the ceiling. Better to have it out. Something. His breathing changed. She couldn't believe it. Right there, in the middle of a conversation, he had fallen asleep.

She lay there like a fool. There was no sound in the house. Percival might be crushed and his own father slept through it. She stayed awake alone.

A long time passed—hours, she thought. She dreamed waking dreams, reruns of what they had already seen on television. Watching TV, she'd kept hoping one of the rescuers' faces would be Percival's, and she'd know he was all right. In the dream she was walking through the rubble, past men with blowtorches, with pneumatic drills. The faces of the men were dim. She knew Percival was among them, but she did not know if he was above the rubble, drilling, or beneath it, being drilled toward.

The doorbell woke her. She could not have been sleeping. But the clock said . . . what? After three.

The sound again, a jarring into consciousness. Then rational thought. No one would ring at this hour of the night. No normal visitor would come now. So it must be the Marines. The rest of them did not even stir, which struck her as odd. She had feared, always, a moment she couldn't take back—one irrevocable moment when a son would be snatched beyond her and there would be nothing she could do. She had not thought it would come in the darkness, or that she would have to face it alone.

She slid out of bed and pulled her robe on, which she had left on her night table, as if she had known she would need it. Her heart hammered in her throat, but she did not cry as she walked down the steps; she would not cry until they told her.

She turned on the porch light and peered through the peephole. She expected to see a khaki uniform, or a formal blue one, out there in the dark. She was prepared for that. A head of curly blond hair shined beneath the porch light, matted down from the rain. There was no cap and no uniform. The curls were wiry and golden. Only one person had hair quite like that. She opened the door.

"Gideon," she said. She'd known he would come.

MONDAY

October 24, 1983

7

Gideon's watch was still on Utah time and he did not know how to adjust it. The first thing he said to his mother was, "What time is it here?" because when he looked at his watch, he could not remember whether to add two hours or subtract them or how to do simple math. His arms and legs weighed a ton. After he got off the plane at Dulles airport, he took the Metro into D.C. and then out to Maryland. He rode two buses. When it got so late the buses stopped running, he hitched a ride and then walked. Each time his feet touched the ground, they were so heavy he did not think he could lift them again. But he did.

"Twenty after three," his mother said, looking up at the family room clock. She was combing her hair with her hands. He had thought she would be awake, conducting a vigil of sorts, but from her hair he could tell she had been sleeping. It seemed wrong. There were wrinkles on her forehead, and her eyes seemed sunken back into their sockets. She was younger than most of his friends' mothers, but now he could see that she was old.

"I guess you haven't heard anything, then," he said. If they'd heard, they would all be up.

"No, but I thought you were the Marines," she told him. "You know, they don't call you if it's bad news. They send a Marine." She stopped talking and smiled in a sad way. "I'm glad you came," she said. He felt as if she were tolerating him but really wishing the doorbell hadn't rung. He had a key somewhere but had forgotten to bring it. He should have brought his key. She was leading him into the family room. "Dad thought it would be easier for you to stay at school, but everyone else is here," she told him. "People kept coming over all day. They kept bringing food. Are you hungry?"

"I don't know," he said. He didn't think she was glad to see him. The weighted-down feeling was strong inside him. The legs had been his main problems, but now it was hard to move his hands.

"Well, you're probably hungry," she said. She walked through the family room to the kitchen, and he followed. The kitchen light flooded on, bright yellow, bringing the room up from dimness: refrigerator, range top, all of it sharp-edged, sudden. With the heaviness inside him, he wanted muted colors; it seemed to him now that the day, the planes, the Metro, the buses, all had been muted. Everything . . . muted, unreal—and now the kitchen was too bright. His mother was taking food out of the refrigerator; she didn't notice him squinting. She piled some macaroni and cheese onto a paper plate and put it into the microwave. She was always feeding them, but never what they liked. He had always hated macaroni.

"I don't think I can eat anything," he said. "I feel like I'm still moving."

She smiled then. "*That* shouldn't bother you."

"I mean still in a plane or car or something. Maybe I'll just take a shower and try to sleep."

"Everyone else is sleeping. They're all sleeping like babies." She sounded a little dazed. "When the doorbell rang, nobody heard it but me. You could've been the Marines."

"Yeah," Gideon said. He started to pick up his gear, to carry it to his room.

"Didn't you have a race the other day?"

"Yesterday. No . . . Saturday." Was it Sunday now, or Monday? If it was Monday, his physics lecture would begin in a few hours. He hadn't brought his book.

"Where was it? How'd you do?"

"Huh?"

"Your race," she said.

"Oh . . . the Idaho State Invitational. I came in second. Farley won."

"We didn't even ask you about the race on the phone. Dad felt bad about that afterward."

"It didn't matter," Gideon said. The race seemed a long time ago. She didn't seem to notice that he could barely walk.

"How much did he beat you by?"

"Four seconds. No—five, I think. I can't remember."

She got a knowing look on her face. "Only five seconds, huh?"

Upstairs, Gideon showered and then went into the room he used to share with Izzy and Percival. Izzy was out cold. Gideon turned on the little reading lamp, figuring it wouldn't bother him. He was sure he wasn't going to be able to sleep, himself; it seemed to him somebody ought not to sleep.

The room was pretty much the way it had always been, though maybe less of a slop heap. It had never been big enough for three kids, but Izzy had always managed to keep his area more or less separate—an old desk shoved against his bed, where he did his science fair projects when they were younger and later kept his books. Gideon's bed and Percival's were along the opposite wall, with a chest of drawers between them. There wasn't enough space for trophy cases, so all the running medals from high school, his and Percival's both, were in an open bookcase, jumbled together. You couldn't tell whose were whose.

When they were younger, he and Percival used to like running in races where the prize was a trophy instead of a medal. Trophies took up more room on the shelf and looked more impressive. Some were lightweight, made of synthetic marble and ersatz silver, but others felt heavy in the hand, solid and expensive. Their father used to point out that the prize had nothing to do with the importance of the race, but still in the early years they had liked having trophies. One of them—he or Percival, he couldn't remember which—once had a trophy that fell apart entirely, cracked in what was supposed to be the marble base, revealing itself to be plastic weighted by sand in the middle, which trickled slowly to the floor. They had watched it empty its insides and laughed.

"Sand. Do you believe that? Talk about tacky!"

He'd won some of the trophies and Percival had won some, and at first all they'd cared about was that their case was getting so full. It was a lot more impressive than Izzy's science certificates all over the wall. But the main thing was that the trophy shelf was a team effort.

Even in high school, Gideon and Percival were a team at first. Percival beat Gideon in every cross-country race Gideon's freshman year, but it was only what everybody expected an older brother to do. Together, the two of them helped the high school record a lot. In the spring, during track season, they ran in different events. Percival ran the three-thousand meter and almost always won. Gideon, because the coach insisted on it, ran the mile.

It wasn't one of his shining efforts. The first time Gideon ran the mile in an actual race, not a workout, his mouth went completely dry after the first quarter. His father had once said to Percival, "Whatever you do in a race, don't stop and don't walk."

Gideon had heard that, even though his father had been talking to his brother. So in that race, he didn't stop. He ran, touching his dry tongue to the top of his mouth, trying to conjure up some spit. Nothing came. His tongue and the roof of his mouth wanted to stick together. Someone passed him, but he didn't care. His tongue felt like it was swelling. He was not sure if he was still sweating. In heat stroke you stopped sweating, and maybe the first sign of heat stroke was that your tongue went dry.

He was running in last place. The dryness filled his whole mind; if his tongue got any bigger, he would choke.

Percival ran up beside the track and said, "What's the matter?" It was against the rules to run alongside another runner on the track.

"Mouth's dry."

"I've had that happen. It comes back."

"When you stop?"

"Even while you're running."

"Get the hell away from him!" the coach yelled at Percival. Percival ran back to the sidelines. The water did not come back into Gideon's mouth, but he was able to pass one other runner and not come in last. When he finished the race, he bent over and put his hands on his knees to get his breath. A great swell of nausea overcame him. He puked in front of everybody.

After that Gideon managed to walk away from the stands before he threw up after running the mile. His mouth went dry every single race. But because of Percival's help that first day, he never stopped and he never walked. The next year the coach would let him run the two-mile, where the pace was slower, and he would feel all right.

Mostly, during Gideon's first year of high school, he and Percival were kind to each other. Once Percival missed winning a race by half a step, and Gideon said, "You got beat by a guy who had a beard. Wait till you grow your own beard and see what happens."

Percival slapped hands with him, but the joke about the beard was really no joke. Other guys had whiskers and looked like men. Percival looked like a toothpick. But that day, even though Percival only came in second, the important thing was that they got a nice trophy to put in their case.

The summer after Gideon's freshman year, just before he turned fifteen, he suddenly grew six inches and filled out. Percival, a year older, did not. That fall, everything between them changed. It changed the day they ran their cross-country race in a little mountain town called Brunswick.

They had both run at Brunswick High School before; they did it every year. The course was pretty standard. You started out in the stadium, then ran around the school and into a wooded area on the school grounds. There was one bad hill leading out of the stadium, but after that, just rolling ground and then a narrow path leading through the trees. You ran the circle twice. The finish line was inside the stadium gates, right in front of the bleachers where everybody could see you.

It was a cool day with an overcast sky—purplish clouds, and a breeze coming down from the mountains, but no wind on the ground. It was the weather Gideon liked best: gray, sunless weather. He never liked to run in heat. On the second time around—he could not remember now how this had happened— he had been looking at the sky and at the back of the runner in front of him. He was running sixth or seventh just then. He picked up his pace to pass the man in front of him. "If you're going to pass, you have to blow around him so he won't repass you—so you'll break his heart and he won't have the will to catch up with you again," his father often said.

He passed the other runner with no effort at all. It was as if he were a spectator watching himself do it. It was that easy. Another runner was in front of him, and he set his sights on him. As he picked up his pace to narrow the gap, he seemed to be an observer and a participant at the same time, aware of his breathing, aware that the increased effort didn't hurt, but also as detached as a bird in that purple-gray sky, looking on as he passed the next runner and the next. He was fast. Strong. Picking them off one by one.

In the trees the path was wet from a recent rain, a slick yellowish clay. His footing held, his pace didn't slacken. When he came out of the woods, he immediately sprinted past several more runners. He did not realize one of them must have been Percival; he did not look at them individually and was not thinking that at all. He was outside himself, watching himself head toward the stadium and into the gate, across the finish line.

Afterward, winded, he no longer felt the sense of detachment from himself, but the strength stayed with him. It was his first cross-country win in high school. He could have run the course again.

When Percival came up to him afterward, he was smiling with his mouth but not his eyes. "All *right*." He slapped Gideon's hands. But Percival's eyes didn't smile.

His father said to him, "Some run, Gideon." But his eyes, too, were serious, and Gideon knew he'd hoped that Percival would win.

After that, Gideon won most of the races. After that, his father expected it. But for the rest of high school, Percival was not his friend. He spent his time with Tim O'Neal and ignored Gideon almost completely.

If he had been younger, it would have broken his heart. But it didn't. Sometimes he still thought: I couldn't help winning that day. When they were younger, he couldn't help letting Percival get the better of him in a fight, and on that day he couldn't help winning.

The Brunswick trophy was still on the shelf. Funny, Percival might have hidden it or disposed of it, considering. But there it was—tacky, as anonymous as the others. He supposed Percival didn't care about it so much anymore. Last summer, when he was home on leave, he hadn't seemed to. But he couldn't be sure. Maybe even now Percival held it against him that he had won at Brunswick and kept winning afterward, while Percival did not.

Or maybe he was dead, and didn't care about anything.

Gideon moved his hand toward the trophy shelf, but his fingers were heavy and did not want to go. This morning, when he had not been able to run anymore, he had thought: This is just from the shock. But all day and all night, traveling in planes and cars and buses, it had only grown worse. On the last stretch, when he had to walk, the paralysis had been like a great cat poised above him, ready to pounce. It was like the end of a bad race when you hang on through the finish and then collapse. And now it was as if the race had ended. He did not know if he would be able to run again. He did not know how long he would be able to walk or lift his hands. In the light from the reading lamp it was impossible to tell whose trophies were whose. It was as if they were a history of him and Percival, as if the two of them were the same, jumbled together, Percival in Lebanon and Gideon in Maryland, and as if both of them might be dead.

Mag turned out all but one of the lights in the family room, but she was wide awake. Here is another truth, she thought: She loved them best when they were winning. Another strike against her: never to achieve any great heights herself, but to expect them from her children. She had felt trapped when they were little, but when Percival won the Junior Olympics at the age of twelve, she had ridden on a streak of pure joy for days . . . and when Alfred was elected student council president, when Izzy got his scholarships . . . and especially when Gideon started winning—year after year, race after race—she felt, truly, that she was capable of producing champions. Yet tonight something seemed wrong with Gideon, even more than his distress over Percival or his exhaustion after his trip. It was not like him to look so unconcerned when she asked about his race and not like him (even at a time like this) to pretend he couldn't remember how many seconds Farley had beaten him by. It was as if losing made him ashamed. She'd never thought of the price to any of them.

Ultimately, the only important thing—wasn't it?—was the price.

Alfred's cold heart, Gideon's obsession with running, Izzy's brooding, Simon's silent fingers. It seemed to her they were all the result of trying too hard to win. And wasn't a mother who condoned that somehow to blame? In the dim room Mag stared out the sliding glass door exactly as she had twenty-four hours ago, into the predawn darkness that told her no more now than it had then. The rain had stopped. Gideon had come and they were complete except for Percival. She did not care about their winning. Only let them all come home.

But how could she expect it? She'd given them the names of champions right from the start—Alfred the Great, responsible for a kingdom. Isaac Singer, the intellectual. She had never considered that golden-haired Gideon might end up as he was tonight, dragging his bag upstairs as if the legs that carried him to victory were made of putty. And Percival—the knight . . . Didn't knights always go to battle? Wasn't he one of the ones looking for the Holy Grail? And wasn't it someone else who found it?

Gideon's shower stopped running. She heard him walking around the bedroom, and then silence. The idea of all of them sleeping, dreaming, as if life were the same as it had been before, seemed absurd.

Outside a car came down the street, braked, and stopped. It was the delivery man with the *Freestate Sentinel*, dropping Simon's papers in a bundle in the driveway, for him to roll when he got up. She heard the car drive off. She should go out there; she should look at the headlines. She should read about Beirut. There would be some mention of Percival and Tim O'Neal: Local boys stationed at bombed-out airport; fate uncertain. She could not make herself do it. She turned out the light and went up the stairs.

Down the hall, in Percival's room—the room where Izzy and

Gideon were sleeping—a small reading lamp was shining. She thought maybe Gideon was still up. A small comfort bloomed in her chest, though she knew Gideon was tired. She wanted someone else to be awake.

Peering in, she saw Izzy first, snoring the way Patrick snored, hair tangled, clutching the pillow for dear life. All day he had been observing Patrick's blind spell and recovery with what she assumed was scientific interest, absorbed and yet apparently pained by his need to examine his own father that way. And now—if she knew Izzy—he was having nightmares about it. But Gideon looked even stranger. He had fallen asleep sitting on the floor in the corner, next to the bookcase with the trophies. His knees were bent to his chest, his head had drooped onto his shoulder, and one of the trophies was lying by his foot, as if he had drifted off studying past triumphs. For a moment she wondered if he had come home so solemn because the waiting and the possible mourning would keep him from running just when he needed to the most—when he needed to intensify his training because conference championships were coming up.

Maybe he was simply afraid to tell her. He was afraid because she expected him to win no matter what. But in that case, after they had urged him to stay in Utah . . . in that case, why did he come?

His face was pale and strained-looking. She realized he had not been gloating over old victories or future races, either one. The trophies on that shelf were not just his, but Percival's too. A wave of sadness filled her. She started toward him, to shake him awake, get him into bed. He would be sore and stiff when he woke up in that position. But before she could touch him she remembered something. She remembered what he had tried to do for Percival the night Darren got arrested.

It had not happened because of any terrible crime. All the Singer boys after Alfred had learned to drive before they were old enough. As soon as Izzy got his license he taught Percival (who was thirteen at the time), and Percival taught Simon when Simon was twelve. Discovering this, Mag and Patrick issued an ultimatum: "If we ever hear of any of you driving without a license again, you can rest assured you'll never *get* a license and the one who taught you doesn't drive for a year." But once they paid the matter lip service, it was largely ignored. Mag and Patrick were both at work all day and felt it unwise to make too many rules they couldn't enforce. The older boys were careful about the cars because they needed them to get to part-time jobs and track practice. Also, Mag had visions of catastrophe striking while she was away—another broken ankle like Izzy's, or an illness that required a trip to the emergency room—and was relieved that even Simon could drive his brothers to the rescue if necessary. It did not occur to her that Darren, fifteen years old, would decide to go pick up Merle one night because the house was momentarily empty and Merle was stranded at a friend's. Or that, on the way home, they would be pulled over by the police.

Darren was not stopped for speeding or weaving down the road, but rather for going too slowly. He had never driven at night before and was disoriented by the headlights and the difficulty of seeing where his lane was on the road. The twins rarely thought before reacting to each other, so in his haste to get his brother, Darren had left even his learner's permit at home.

Mag suspected he might have gotten off with just a warning had he been somebody else. But his pale hair and skin made him look younger than he was—an effect accentuated by an identical brother in the passenger seat—and Mag could well imagine him trying to explain about his learner's permit in such a thin, shaky voice that Merle finally got upset, too, and the policeman decided from the sound that they must be guilty of something. Though she had always loved the attention the twins attracted—girls vying for them even though they were so homely, and people watching them run because they stayed in stride with each other (a kind of victory, she supposed, though they never won the races)—there were times when their doubleness caught up with them. When Merle got pneumonia, Darren complained so bitterly of pains in his lungs that he had to go to the doctor, too. And when fifteen-year-old Darren took the car to pick up his brother, their twinness got him arrested.

The police called the house to notify the family but were told that Mr. and Mrs. Singer were out of town. This was not true; they were only at meetings. But Gideon, who'd answered the phone, reasoned it would be wise to keep his parents out of it. Perhaps he also wanted to make Percival a hero in the eyes of the twins, who usually looked up only to Gideon. He told the police that Percival, who was eighteen and therefore of age, would come to the station to get his brother.

This was during that period when Percival spoke to Gideon only under duress. It was also a time when Percival went to as few classes as possible but spent most of his weekday evenings home by parental decree. Mag insisted he could be grounded as long as he lived at home and believed he might do some home-work if he had no other choice. Gideon had just come in when the police called. He didn't realize until later that Percival was not in their room as expected, but out taking advantage of their parents' absence, probably raising hell somewhere with Tim O'Neal.

Mag and Patrick learned the rest of the story later. For the next two hours, Gideon looked for his brother. He called Tim O'Neal's house and the homes of several of Tim's friends. He went to a spot where Percival and his girlfriend were known to park. He searched in several high school hangouts. He finally found him eating a barbecue sandwich with Tim in a restaurant called Flip's. Gideon, Percival, and Tim arrived at the police station not long after Mag and Patrick did (having been noti-fied, after all, by Merle). They stood under the too-bright flu-orescent lights of the precinct house, Percival and Tim looking a little sheepish and Gideon appearing to be in real agony.

"We managed to find our way back into town," Patrick said sarcastically to Gideon, having learned of Gideon's deception. "I didn't know where you were," Gideon said, which was true.

"It's okay," Mag told him. She had assumed Gideon's pain

was from anticipated parental anger, but her letting him off did not seem to deflect it. Tim O'Neal excused himself and went home. Percival walked as far away from Gideon as he could. Gideon looked even more desolate. Mag knew then he regretted entangling Percival in a situation he might have avoided otherwise, on a night when everyone might have believed him safely grounded at home. Gideon's discomfort surprised her, because Percival was bestowing no kindnesses on him in those days, and she hadn't thought Gideon would care. But that night—and again now, looking at his crouched form on the floor—she understood the panic that must have possessed him, to keep him driving from place to place trying to find his brother, so Percival could rescue the twins and be the hero . . . and the distress of realizing finally that his gesture was only going to get Percival in more trouble.

"Gideon!" she whispered. He didn't move until she said it a second time. Then he woke up so slowly—a lazy opening of an eye—that it was as if he were moving in slow motion. She knew there must be something terribly wrong with him. Odd . . . she'd once thought that because Percival tormented him and beat on him during the early years and finally stopped speaking to him, a rage had grown in Gideon and killed his attachment. She'd even thought his anger was what made him run so fast. But it was not true at all. The night he tried to let Percival bail out Darren, and today when he flew home from Utah, he did it out of love. Mag kneeled down so he could hear her, but spoke low enough not to wake him all the way up. "Get in bed," she said.

With labored, robotlike movements, he stood up, walked the few steps to his bed, and fell clumsily onto his mattress. He pulled the cover to his chest. She switched off the light. She wanted to bend over and kiss him the way she'd done when he was little, but she only touched his hair on her way out of the room.

There was no point in trying to sleep. The night was almost

over. She walked into Simon's bedroom and turned off his alarm. She did not want him out there this morning under the dark sky. She didn't want him cold or fleeing from vicious dogs. It was bad enough that he was ready to sacrifice himself to a surgeon's knife. She would deliver the papers herself.

She put on a pair of RipOffs and another sweatshirt on top of it and running shoes that one of the boys had grown out of. Patrick turned over and groaned while she dressed in the darkness, but he didn't wake up. Even Lucifer, curled between Patrick's face and Mag's pillow, gazed up at her but didn't stir. Who said cats were nocturnal animals?

Downstairs, she found two sets of cotton work gloves in the closet. Patrick had taught the boys to layer themselves with clothes. She didn't bring the papers into the garage. She didn't want to see them that clearly. Even where they lay stacked in the driveway under the porch light, their copy was all too visible. She caught a glimpse of a headline and a picture of the ruined building beneath. She didn't look at it, wouldn't. It wouldn't tell her anything new. She turned the stacks of papers upside down, so the headlines didn't show.

The temperature was not below freezing, but the darkness felt damp and bitter. She pulled up the hood of one of her sweatshirts and sat on the driveway, rolling the papers. She was not as fast as the boys, but she was steady. She folded, she snapped rubber bands into place. In time she wasn't even cold.

Was Percival cold?

Simon would warm him by having his ear fixed. He would buy his brother life. Let Simon sleep, she thought. Everything was topsy-turvy. Before yesterday, she'd demanded the ear operation from him as surely as she'd demanded victory from the others. Why did she think she needed perfection? Just let them all come home. She dragged out what *Freestate Sentinel* bags the boys had managed to accumulate over the years and stuffed the papers in. She loaded them into the station wagon and drove off.

She could not remember doing the papers by herself before.

Whenever she helped Simon, she always did certain houses and he did others; she did not know his part of the route well. She improvised. Whenever she was not sure if a house got a paper or not, she gave them one. If she ran out, it would happen on the section she knew. Then she would call the office and say she was short. The *Freestate Sentinel* could afford to give away a few extra papers. Simon must sleep; he must have time for his head to clear. There was a sort of missionary zeal about her task. She felt sluggish from being awake most of the night, but she made herself concentrate. Trying to figure out which houses got papers and which didn't, she was briefly so absorbed that for a moment there was only that. It was not until she drove over onto Trevor Circle that she remembered Monster. She had a vision of the bruise on Simon's leg. A fury filled her. It seemed that she'd been gearing up all along to face the dog this morning.

She delivered to the first few houses cautiously, but there was no sign of the animal. She carried a full load in her pack, ready to swing it at him, use it in her defense. Adrenaline coursed through her; she was wide awake. Four houses, five. No dog came charging at her, there was not even any sound.

She approached Monster's driveway. A fierce, rapid barking began. It was almost a relief. She moved closer, walking at her usual pace. Then she saw that the beast was inside, facing her from behind a living room window, perched on the back of a couch. She was disappointed. As she approached the porch, the dog bared its teeth at her, snarled, then resumed its quick, frenzied yapping. She bared her own teeth back. Retreating a little, she tossed the paper at the window, letting it hit the glass right in front of Monster's teeth. He made as if to catch it—stupid— and then realized the paper was on the other side of glass, out of reach. Angry, he snarled again, watching the paper drop onto the porch. It was satisfying, giving the beast a taste of its own impotence. Mag wanted something more. She wanted to vanquish it utterly. But the owners had been responsible for once, kept the dog inside—and she felt cheated.

8

A cloudy light had sheared away the darkness by the time Izzy woke up. He hadn't thought he'd be able to sleep so long, with everything that was on his mind. Rubbing the fuzziness out of his eyes, he gazed around and could see even without his glasses that Gideon was in one of the other beds. He wasn't surprised. For years when they were younger, Percival and Gideon had been practically glued to each other, doing everything together and keeping him up half the night with their talking. They were worse than the twins. Later the talking stopped except for formalities—"I think those're my socks you've got on, Gideon." "Oh, yeah." A stripping off of socks. Absolute politeness. But Izzy thought they were pretty attached even through their silence. Now Gideon looked a little sick. That was probably normal, considering what time he must have gotten in. Izzy supposed the only one who'd really thought Gideon would stay at school was his father.

He remembered now that he'd dreamed about his father. He'd dreamed his father was in a cage, like one of the laboratory dogs at school. God. He'd watched his father the whole damned day yesterday and had no more clue to what was wrong with him now than he did before. He reached for his glasses on the night table and cleaned them with the sleeve of his shirt that was lying on the floor. When he put them on, the room came clear, but the reason for the blind spells didn't, and it was driving him nuts.

He dressed quietly and went downstairs. His mother was sitting at the kitchen table drinking tea. She had made a whole pot of tea, as if they were in for a long siege, but nobody else seemed to be up. The TV was not on, and the morning paper was lying on the table untouched.

"Izzy," she said, as if it had taken her a minute to figure out which one he was. She looked awful. She had on a pair of those baggy old RipOffs his father had made when he was still experimenting with the design, and her hair looked like she'd been out in the wind. She didn't have on any makeup.

He was going to ask her if she'd heard anything, but she spoke first. "Are you still living with that same girl?" she asked. He was surprised she'd think about that right now. He never told her when he was living with a girl, but since the twins had come to College Park to school this year, they always filled her in. It embarrassed him that she knew about his various girlfriends, because they made him look so unreliable. Izzy knew that in no other sense had he ever been an irresponsible person.

"She moved out last week," he said. It was odd, but he hadn't thought about Jocelyn from the moment she left until now. It was odd that a person could live in the same apartment with someone for eleven weeks, sleep with her every night, eat dinner with her, talk to her for hours every day, and when she left not think about her at all.

"Well, if one of them ever lasts over three or four months, bring her home to meet us," his mother said.

"Snide, Mother."

"You're very nice-looking, Izzy. It must be hard on the girls." She sounded tired. He figured she hadn't slept. "Want some tea?" she asked.

"I'll get it." He went to the cabinet for a cup. He wondered what his mother would say if he told her he'd picked the fight with Jocelyn on purpose. He couldn't exactly tell her the whole story, considering the circumstances. Jocelyn had been running around his apartment in her underwear at the time. But the point was, Izzy was annoyed by it. He had been trying to get her to be serious. He wanted Jocelyn to think of someone to take one of his laboratory dogs, Rusty. Rusty was half Labrador, half golden retriever, a gentle, playful dog that would make the perfect pet. The trouble was, he was four months old and growing out of his cage in the lab. Izzy didn't want to take him to the pound with the rest of the dogs because he was pretty sure nobody would get far enough past Rusty's size to appreciate his temperament. They'd decide on a smaller puppy, and three days later Rusty would be gassed.

But Jocelyn hadn't been in the mood for thinking about laboratory animals just then. She was wearing red and black string bikini underpants and a little red bra, drinking Michelob from a bottle—not her first Michelob, either. Normally there was nothing Izzy would have liked better. But he wanted her to concentrate on Rusty. Every time a dog like Rusty came along, Izzy thought how taking the dogs to the pound was no better than killing them with pentobarb, which was what he'd done working on an experiment at Biolab two years ago. God, he'd hated that. And Jocelyn knew it, too.

"I don't mind the killing when it's necessary," he'd told her, making it clear that killing *had* been necessary at Biolab, in order to study the kidneys and adrenal glands afterward. "But it tears me up to be involved in it." He hadn't the heart for it, he'd said; he liked his animals to live. At the time, Izzy's story had moved Jocelyn almost to tears. She'd made love to him for an hour without him having to do any of the work—which he'd more or less expected, because Debbie and Traci had done the same thing. But that night she was waving the Michelob bottle at him and looking at him sideways, showing off her eyelashes to good effect. "Want one?" she asked, pointing to the beer.

He shook his head no. She didn't take his concerns seriously. He was running a simple behavioral study, and Jocelyn's attitude was, as she put it: "For God's sake, Izzy, what do you get so worked up about? None of the dogs are even killed or hurt." She didn't see, as Izzy did, how much the dogs hated being caged up. The spirited ones like Rusty came running up to the bars of their cages as soon as he walked into the lab—running as best they could with their paws getting stuck in the metal flooring—whining for his attention, licking his fingers, playing. He couldn't take them outside and roughhouse with them as he would have liked because it would skew the test results, but he felt for them. The only thing that kept him going was knowing these experiments might mean a breakthrough in cancer research someday—or, as Jocelyn pointed out, "It might not mean a damned thing." But in any case he liked to find homes for his dogs when he was finished with them, especially ones like Rusty.

Jocelyn took another swig of her beer and slithered over to him. She read too much literature, which made her feel she had to do things dramatically. This was not her normal walk at all. Watching her move made Izzy think of a snake he once had—Henry. He had liked the snake a lot. Henry had no choice but to slither, but on Jocelyn it looked ridiculous. Izzy was in a poor frame of mind before Jocelyn even touched him. She pulled his glasses off. "You and your poor bleeding heart," she murmured. She placed his hand on her rear end. "My sweet Izzy, who puts a dozen dogs in little metal cages and then tries to find them a home." She was being Scarlett O'Hara—seductive but heartless. Part of her attraction for him was that she was in the English department, with a whole different set of friends who might take his dogs. But he hated the dramatics. And besides, what good was she doing him now?

She put her hands under his shirt. She was drunk. He didn't like drunk women when he was trying to think.

"Izzy the Vivisectionist," she said. "Izzy the Vivi, trying to soothe his conscience."

That did it. The opaque feeling started inside him, of not caring anymore. Exactly that feeling had come over him when he broke up with Debbie and Traci and Arlene. Jocelyn did not sense his distance; she was too drunk. She kept rubbing against him. He took his hand off her underpants.

He poured tea into his cup. Obviously this was not a story he could tell his mother. But a sudden idea occurred to him.

"Mother, how would you like one of the world's nicest watchdogs?" he asked.

Mag, who had been staring at the unopened newspaper, looked up. "Lord, no," she said. "Unless maybe he'd eat Lucifer."

There was no sugar on the table. She sometimes hid it on the theory that if she made it difficult to find, her sons would learn to eat cereal and drink tea without it. His father had given up sugar entirely when the blind spells started, so maybe her campaign had done some good.

She watched him rummage through the cabinets for sugar but didn't tell him where it was. He finally found it behind a box of spaghetti in the pantry. His mother sighed.

"You're still killing dogs, aren't you?" she asked.

"We give them to the pound," he said. "*They* kill them."

"Maybe you should find another line of work."

"I couldn't," he said. Of course his mother, of all people, ought to know that, and her suggesting otherwise made him feel desolate. She knew he expected someday to come up with a breakthrough, which would vindicate him for whatever pain he had inflicted on the animals thus far. The trouble was, more and more lately, he didn't believe he was capable of a breakthrough. Even when it came to his father's eyes . . . he ought to have some hint by now, but he'd watched him every time he'd been home for the past year, and he didn't have a clue.

"Izzy . . . you still get those migraines?" his mother asked.

"I only had them that one summer two years ago," he said. He rarely told anyone about those migraines. He didn't mind Jocelyn and the others knowing he had no heart for killing dogs, but he thought mentioning the migraines might sound un-manly. It was an honor to be hired by Biolab for the summer— Dr. McMillan hired only one graduating senior each year; Izzy wouldn't have wanted anyone to think he couldn't handle it. Izzy had read all of Dr. McMillan's papers before he started work. He knew Dr. McMillan was not a man who believed in letting technicians run his experiments. He did everything him-self, down to cleaning out the cages, and Izzy assisted. There were a dozen puppies at a time. Izzy helped with the feedings, the injections, the keeping of records. When the dogs were ten weeks old, they were killed—painlessly, Dr. McMillan said— with a single shot of sodium pentobarbital. Izzy was expected to help with that, too. Afterward Dr. McMillan cut the corpses apart, to take out the kidneys and the adrenal glands.

It was an important experiment, and the puppies had to be killed. But there were two bad things about the killings. One was the individual deaths. He'd expected that. The puppies were not healthy and would not have lived long anyway. They were from a strain bred to be allergic to just about everything they ate. Their eyes watered, and they did not gain weight. But they were small and ("like any baby creature," Dr. McMillan had warned) they were cute.

The second difficult part was knowing that the other lab an-imals were watching while the puppy in question was being killed. Izzy had not anticipated that. It seemed childish and womanish to care that a dozen dumb animals were observing, but it preyed on his mind all the same. The cages lined three walls of the lab, and the examining table was in the middle. The other puppies watched while one of them was laid out on that stainless-steel table, held fast by Izzy's hands, and looked up with that sideways look of helplessness and fear. The others were watching while the puppy in question squirmed, as they invariably did unless they were one of the mute, trusting ones. They heard the puppy squeal as the needle went in . . . and listened as the squealing turned into more of a sigh, drawn out and lower-pitched, and the jerking limbs went still.

A phobia over such things would be anathema to a research scientist. Izzy had known he would be a research scientist ever since he put the snake, Henry, down in the cold basement for a science fair project, to see if it would hibernate.

In the lab, on the stainless-steel table, his hands had been steady, because if he faltered he would cause pain. An odd concern, considering. And from the cages a dense stillness while the killing and the cutting went on. "Animals can't reason," Dr. McMillan said, hearing it too. Izzy kept repeating to himself: Puppies don't think, they're not over there thinking, "Next time it will be me." But he left the lab with grinding headaches. He took aspirin and closed his eyes, but neither measure helped. "You're hungry," his mother said, dishing out plates of meat and potatoes. If he ate, he only felt worse. Sleep dulled the headaches, but sometimes they lasted for days. The pain was like a thing outside himself. The killings went on. He stopped trying to numb it and defied it instead. He went out almost every night with Arlene.

She was a redhead with apricot skin. Her eyelashes were black. She was the first girl he had actually loved—the girl he had loved since high school. He said to himself: *Set me as a seal upon your heart, a seal upon your hand. Love is as strong as death.* He had read this in a Philosophy from the Bible course, and the words kept coming back to him. Love was as strong as death. He did not tell Arlene about the headaches. He only expected her to cure him.

This seemed reasonable because their love had already survived quite a lot. It was Arlene's porch roof he'd jumped from
the morning he'd broken his ankle in high school. For weeks he'd
been spending a half hour in her bedroom every morning during his paper route, although at that time she wouldn't let him
actually have sex with her. But they spent half an hour in each
other's arms before he climbed out of her bedroom window,
tiptoed over her porch roof, and leaped over high shrubbery to
her yard and his waiting bike. Her parents slept at the opposite
end of the house and didn't suspect. But that morning Izzy
didn't clear the junipers. He lost his balance and landed full on
his ankle. The pain was so immediate and so searing that at first
he did not think he could get up. Finally he managed to crawl
back to his bike, so as not to implicate Arlene. He would rather
die from the pain in his leg than be banished from Arlene's bed.
Fortunately, Izzy's mother came looking for him a few minutes
later—he could never understand why—and drove him to the
emergency room. His family had always believed the accident
happened because his bike jumped the curb.

Later, Arlene had gone away to college in New York. But
every summer she came home, and every summer they realized
anew that they were in love.

Looking at Arlene the year he worked at Biolab, Izzy did not
feel just desire at the sight of her apricot skin, but also a thick
sweetness at the back of his throat, like a permanent coating of
honey. It sounded bizarre when he described it, but he didn't
really mind. He liked the sense of something permanent. He
believed that after his first two years of graduate school, they
would marry. He believed his headaches would respond to her
presence. Her love would be stronger than the deaths of those
lab animals. So they went out every night, and she had no effect on his headaches at all.

One humid night in late July, lying next to her after they had
made love, his head began to throb. Usually it did not do that
so soon after orgasm. Arlene was half asleep in the crook of his
arm. He looked at her. Instead of being overcome by tender-

ness, he felt an opaque and absolute cessation of emotion descend on him. It was almost as if someone had cast a blanket over his body, except that it was cold instead of warm. He felt no heat, no love, no anger. Arlene's black eyelashes cast a shadow on her cheek. Her hair was curled against her forehead, and her skin gave off its golden glow. He could not understand why he had wanted Arlene so much for so many years; why he had dreamed about her during those nights when he was at the University of Maryland and she in New York, why he had wanted her so absolutely even when other girls pursued him, even when (as happened sometimes) he had spent the evening in someone else's bed. His need for her—if she could not cure his headaches—seemed suddenly absurd. His head pounded, and the most compelling exhaustion filled him. He told her he was ill and he fled, wanting only to go home and sleep. She called the following evening to check on his health. He picked a fight with her—did it, he remembered, in the cruelest and most unfeeling way. He was not proud of that. Since then he had lived with three different women. His relationship with each of them had begun with the same sweetness he had felt for Arlene—and at some point the curtain of uncaring, even of revulsion, had descended exactly as it had with her. And each time, the incident precipitating it had something to do with his laboratory dogs.

After each killing at Biolab, in another section of the building, the kidneys and adrenals had been fixed in paraffin. The paraffin was sliced into fine strips, to be studied under the microscope. Izzy recorded the changes he saw, and Dr. McMillan recorded his own observations, slide after slide. For days there was nothing but that dry, clean peering under the microscope. In August, after he broke up with Arlene, there was a string of such days away from the dogs, and it was then that Izzy's headaches went away.

Izzy believed this happened because when you brought an experiment down to the microscopic level—or at least down to the smallest level you could detect—it would begin to yield its sense. You could see in a very clear way what effect a certain diet would have on a certain species, and the individual creatures became less important. This had happened even when he was a child watching Moanin' convulse from distemper every day after school—convulsions that were the price of the dog's surviving the disease at all—and later when poor old Henry the snake had curled up like a dead thing and hibernated on the basement floor. He'd hated seeing it, but the records he kept showed that Moanin's fits occurred at the same hours each day, and Henry hibernated in the basement just like every other snake hibernated in the wild. He still struggled between wanting to complete his science fair project and wanting to carry Henry upstairs to the stripe of morning sun that fell into his bedroom. But he always managed to go on because there was some comfort in discovering the pattern.

At Biolab, after his headaches went away, Izzy told himself that at the cellular level there was no noisy death, just order. It was not that the slides he observed under the microscope justified the killings or rendered the suffering of the puppies less— only that they revealed some sense behind the nastiness. Ultimately, the experiments could save human lives. When he made his own scientific breakthrough someday—because surely all this would eventually lead to that—then the end would finally justify the means. But when he caught himself thinking that way lately, he sounded like something out of Nazi Germany.

"Well, if you're going to have symptoms, I'm glad it's only a Don Juan complex and not headaches," his mother said. She was being flip, but the truth was, now that he doubted he'd make his breakthrough, he was afraid his Don Juan complex might become a permanent thing. It was as if, considering his work, he had no right to such luxuries as a lasting relationship. It did not cheer him that he had analyzed himself so well.

His father was coming down the stairs. Izzy could not see him from here, but he could hear him walking. He knew his father was all right by the cadence of his steps. They were even and not tentative, as they were during the blind spells. But his father was holding Lucifer in his arms as he rounded the corner into the kitchen, and for a moment he looked to Izzy like a child clutching a rag doll in his hands.

Then the cat jumped down when it caught sight of its dish, and his father seemed normal again.

"Everyone's up early," Patrick said.

"Gideon's here," Mag told him.

If Izzy hadn't known his father better, he would have thought he was about to sigh. "This is going to be doubly hard for Gideon," he said. Then, noticing his mother, he said, "Not watching TV? Not reading the paper?"

"You think they're really going to tell us anything new?"

"No. I think one way or another, at this point we'll probably hear whatever we hear directly from the Marines." His father said that matter-of-factly, but as he spoke he poured himself a cup of barely tepid tea from the pot on the table and started drinking it. He never drank tea that wasn't steaming. Opening the paper, he sipped tea and looked at the picture of the collapsed headquarters building. He scanned the headlines and then the articles. He did not change expression. Then he said, uncharacteristically, "Oh, shit."

"What's in the paper?" his mother shouted. "What did you see?"

She jumped up and went around to look at the paper. Her face was the color of chalk. But when his father looked up, they could see that it was not some news about Percival he was reacting to but his eyes. Quite suddenly, they had closed to pinpoints, leaving his irises round and opaque as buttons.

"Izzy, how about bringing me my medicine?" he asked.

Izzy did as he was told, but he felt blank and empty. Why a blind spell now? The stress of a new day of waiting? Of waking to the recounting of the news in the paper? He just didn't know. He felt almost nauseated with helplessness. This is what it would come to, he thought: a crisis, suffering—and he, who had caused so much suffering, powerless to help.

The phone began to ring. His instinct was to stay exactly where he was, observing his father, in case something occurred to him. But when his father turned, he was slow because of his eyes, and his mother did not get up from the table. He went into the phone room and answered.

"Oh . . . is that Alfred?" the voice said.

"Izzy."

It was Beth O'Neal. "Tim just called," she blurted out. "It turns out they *were* billeted there in the headquarters. He was out on a detail at the perimeter of the airport when it happened. They're just now bringing them back in."

"That's good news."

"Yes, but I don't know how to tell you the rest. The thing is . . . Percival wasn't with him. The last time they were together was a few days ago. Tim says he doesn't know what's happened since, but the last time he saw him—oh, Izzy—Percival was still in that building that got blown up."

Mag knew even before Izzy got off the phone. She felt she knew absolutely. She sat at the table, unable to move, while Izzy and Patrick hovered around her, telling her it wasn't necessarily as bad as it sounded. It was as if they were deliberately trying to preserve a lie.

"Listen, Mag. Normally those Amtrac vehicles are attached to headquarters, but with all the activity going on, they'd been moving them out to the line companies pretty regularly. So the fact that Percival was still there when Tim was detailed out doesn't mean anything."

"You're the one who always says to be realistic," she told him. "Be realistic, Patrick." It seemed completely heartless for him to be denying the seriousness right now—*especially now*—while he was blind.

"It's true that it might not mean anything, Mother," Izzy said.

"Tim went to Charlie company at the south end of the airport, but he's pretty sure Percival went with some guys who were moved to Alpha or Bravo company later that day. Beth says he's pretty sure."

Mag said nothing.

"Or he could have been on leave," Izzy said. "There were thirty or forty guys away on leave. Apparently Tim and Percival were both due for a leave, and maybe Percival got one."

"Mag, are you even listening?" Patrick asked.

"I hear you," she said. She heard, but she didn't understand. She didn't understand Charlie and Bravo and all that alphabet soup; she didn't know what a line company was. Until a month ago she'd thought Amtrak meant trains until Alfred explained it was spelled Amtrac with a *c* on the end, and it was an armored vehicle like a big box on treads. She still couldn't picture Percival driving one. What difference did it make? Percival was dead.

"Tim is going to call back as soon as he hears anything. At least we have that." Patrick was saying that because the Marine Corps hotline still didn't have its first list of survivors. It was expected sometime today. But Mag knew: Tim would be on the list—they already knew that from his call—and Percival wouldn't. Beth O'Neal deserved it; Mag didn't. Death was running in her blood.

Patrick touched her shoulder. "Mag, don't write an end to the story before you know for sure."

She shook his hand away. "It seems to me the end has already been written." He touched her again, but she could not bear it. "Leave me alone," she said under her breath.

"Where are you going?"

"Upstairs to get out of these sweatpants. Then I'm going to work."

"You couldn't," Izzy said.

"I could," she said.

She ignored the twins, who greeted her at the top of the stairs.

She dressed, found a coat, went out the door. She was on her way to work, and it would save her.

She felt strangely detached as she drove. It was like the feeling she had yesterday when she seemed to be watching the scene from a distance, only stronger. She'd worked full-time since Simon went to school. Since Simon's lungs filled up from antibiotics. Working had insulated her then from what she might feel if something happened to her sons while she was home tending them, and it would insulate her now. It had been nine years and half a dozen jobs since that first one, but she would not think of that. She watched the road. She might have been floating. She remembered one particular job with the Department of Social Services, just after she'd finally finished school. It had taken her eleven years to get her degree, going part time, and without a master's she should have remained doing the paperwork, but a visiting caseworker had quit. She steered the station wagon into the traffic. She could almost believe it wasn't today and Percival wasn't dead. She could almost believe she was still a social worker, all those years ago.

Back then, she'd spent her time driving around, visiting cases. There were women whose husbands had left and a man who had been released from a mental hospital, but mostly old people. Mrs. Cohen made her *rugelach* with gnarled arthritic hands, which she'd learned to do as a child in Russia. Mrs. McClune told stories in a smoky Irish accent, of failed potato crops and ocean crossings and a schoolteacher who'd sidled his hand up her leg more than seventy years ago, while the rest of the class was reading a lesson. Listening, Mag often forgot the time. The only one she didn't like was Mr. Carney, who lived in a dark apartment fashioned from the back room of his son-in-law's grocery store. The place smelled of mildew, and he dwelled on his ailments.

One day, she was on her way to his house and had stopped near the one-lane bridge over the creek, waiting for an approaching car to cross. On the drive over she'd been trying to remember how to pitch her voice so Mr. Carney wouldn't yell at her from his denture-sour mouth, "Young lady, I'm eighty-two years old and I can't hear a damned thing you're saying." And then she stepped on her brakes and lost the old man in the winter-dull of her mind, because outside it had suddenly become spring. Green just beginning to show on the trees, the creek swollen from rain. Sky pale blue, air shot through with a golden heat. She stretched her arm out the window, as if she might catch the season in her hand. Below her, on the bank, was a pleasant-looking boy fishing with a makeshift rod. He should have been in school, but the sight of him free in the sunshine was pleasant. He reminded her of someone. She thought of Tom Sawyer and Huckleberry Finn. It wasn't until she began to step on the gas again that she realized it was Percival.

She pulled over and left the car on the grass by the road. Percival had not noticed her. He sat by the creek, looking content for once, a sweet-faced boy. He was in the ninth grade then—fourteen, the same age Simon was now, but so small that waitresses in restaurants still wanted to give him the children's menu. He pretended it didn't matter, but a mute fury had grown in him all year. At home he wrapped himself in towels after showers instead of running naked through the upstairs like the younger boys, feigning modesty with the twins and Gideon because "I don't want you to see my hairy dinger." But everyone knew. "Yeah, about as much hair as on the palm of my hand." The previous fall, running high-school cross country for the first time, Percival had won only a single meet. The other runners were all bigger and stronger than he was, better in the final sprint. Patrick said not to worry, it was unusual for a freshman Percival's size to win at all; eventually he would mature. But Percival became restless, and during second semester started having trouble with some of his teachers. Now, with track season approaching, he had begun to cut school. Mag intended to lecture him and take him back to class. She felt that throwing him out of the car farther and farther from home when he was younger had made him willing to venture wherever he pleased, had increased his confidence in hoofing it. She meant to be firm with him. Besides, she had to go see Mr. Carney. She did not mean to call down the hill in a cheerful voice: "What're you using for bait?"

Percival did not seem surprised to see her. He pulled his string out of the water, grinning. On his hook was a water-logged piece of bologna from the sandwich she had packed him. She'd acquiesced to his queasiness over the school cafeteria and packed him lunches every day, but now she realized he could also leave the premises more easily with a bag of food. She should have been angry, but she was not. Percival was smiling, and it reminded her of the joyfulness of all her sons—of Simon when he was snapping his fingers, and of Gideon with his face full of color while he was running. Her feeling for them surrounded her, and the sun made a warm spot on her back.

"You'll never catch anything with lunch meat," she said.

Percival shrugged.

"Did you eat anything, or use it all for the fish?"

"I ate the cookies."

"Yes, and three hours from now you'll be moaning on the floor with low blood sugar thinking you're going to die."

"I doubt it."

She waited for the anger to come. What came was her memory of stopping at the supermarket before she went to work. She had promised to bring bagels and yogurt to Mrs. Cohen; she'd also picked up a few groceries for herself. She went back to the car and got out strawberries and Doritos and a bottle of grapefruit juice. They had a picnic on the bank of the creek. The sun was almost hot; it burned the winter out of her. Her anger never came.

"What excuse were you going to write for your absence?" she asked. Percival could forge both her signature and Patrick's better than any of the other children. He did it for his brothers when they had papers to be signed and she had already left for work. Sometimes Mag felt guilty, but mostly she was grateful to Percival for handling all those tiresome papers for her, leaving her free. Of course that was a mistake.

"They think I'm having root-canal work done," he said. Patrick had made several trips to the dentist recently to have a root canal made in one of his molars.

"Are you having root-canal work because of the nice weather, or because of English?"

"Both," he said.

Percival hated his English teacher. He had gotten a 97 the first marking period, but then he'd acted up in class until the teacher made him write a certain sentence twenty-five times. He wrote it in an illegible chicken scratch. He did not believe a high school student should be subjected to writing sentences. There was no further punishment the teacher could inflict, except make sure he never got another high grade in her class. Percival did better than almost anyone on the standardized English tests, so she could not flunk him as she would have liked, but she marked him down. "She's not being fair!" Percival often screamed.

"So she's not fair. Life is not fair. You think every boss you have when you take a job will be fair?" Patrick said. "You have to learn to cope in life even with unpleasant English teachers."

Percival's way of coping was to cut the class.

"I didn't cut the whole day," he told Mag. "I didn't leave till after math." He was getting an A in geometry; why should he cut math?

"That was noble of you."

"I thought so."

"What period was English?"

"Third."

"Is it over now?"

"Of course. It's after lunch, what do you think?"

"Then you don't mind my taking you back."

"For what? For gym and history? I don't care." His eyes narrowed. "What're you going to tell them?"

"I'll tell them the dentist appointment took longer than we thought it would. That happens sometimes with root-canal work."

So she dropped him at school, but it was too late to visit Mr. Carney. She went to her next appointment with Betsy Palmer, a twenty-year-old unmarried mother of two, pregnant with a third. Mag liked her. No one had told Betsy the facts of life early on and she still hadn't quite figured them out. Mag referred her to Planned Parenthood. She never admitted she had seven sons of her own or said that birth control didn't always work. She never told Betsy how sick the Pill had made her, never said that Percival had been conceived on Emko foam or that the twins were the result of a diaphragm that fit poorly, as such devices did on women who had given birth three or four times. Betsy never asked her. She was the caseworker and Betsy was the client; Betsy was trapped and Mag was free. Betsy's two-year-old climbed on Mag's lap and pulled at her beads. Betsy was grateful that Mag allowed it, but kindness was easy when escape was an hour away. Mag did not have to cook for those children or do their laundry. She was at work. She accepted a cookie and forgot about Percival and Mr. Carney. When she left, the sun was still warm outside Betsy Palmer's housing project, and Mag's mind was empty as the sky.

Mr. Carney was dead. They told her the next morning when she got to the office. He had fallen in his kitchen about the time Mag would have visited. His son-in-law found him, still warm, when he brought him a carton of eggs from the store at closing time.

Mag really would not have needed to quit. She learned later it was almost impossible to be fired from a government agency, even for killing a client. She had not actually killed him, of course; the supervisors assured her she had not done that. He was old, ill; he soon would have gone into a nursing home. She quit all the same. She claimed responsibility—nobly, she thought—but she was never sorry. Percival, subdued by the idea that his mother had caused a death because she had picnicked with him, did not cut school again for the rest of the year. He ended up with a C in English and had a better track season than they expected. She thought of Mr. Carney sometimes with the same detachment she felt when she remembered Mrs. Cohen or Mrs. McClune or Betsy Palmer. Two years later when Gideon ran faster than Percival at the cross-country meet in Brunswick, when Gideon came in first and Percival came in fifth, Mag looked at Percival's ragged, defeated face and, remembering his grin that day at the creek and the good months that had followed it, was not sorry then, either, that Mr. Carney had died.

A light in front of her turned red. She slammed on the brakes and barely managed to avoid hitting the car in front of her. For a moment her heart leapt to her throat, but then an awful calm descended upon her. She was not going to have an accident. She had almost had an accident once before, but it would not happen again today. She was perfectly safe. She knew it absolutely.

After Mr. Carney died, she hadn't known it would be so easy for a cold-blooded murderer to get other jobs. The hospital hired her to help check out Medicaid patients. She did that until the day Izzy broke his ankle and then she never went back. Later she worked for the county's parks and recreation program, signing people up to use pavilions on summer weekends and take tennis classes in the park. The older boys learned to drive, and she thought: I can concentrate on working now; they will drive away from me. But they did not drive away, they only used gallons of gas and came home when the tank read empty. The younger boys stampeded the house, left shoes in the family room, ate crackers on the rug, yelled in front of company, "Tell Darren to stop farting!" until civilizing them was all she could do. She counseled displaced housewives; helped organize a shelter for the abused. Her sons contracted pneumonia, tore ligaments, got drunk, dented cars; there was always some reason to quit. She said to herself: These jobs are markers, I am laying the base; and waited, biding her time, for her career. When Simon was ten her opportunity finally came. She was called to an interview in Washington, an hour away, with a nonprofit women's agency that needed an administrator.

So there she was, driving home from Washington after spending a full two hours talking to the agency's director, knowing she would be made an offer because she had presented herself so well. She was driving along I-270 north of the beltway, ready to pull out to pass. A horn honked at her from her left, from a car that had been coming up beside her in her blind spot. She jerked the wheel hard to the right. Her car headed for the shoulder, toward a hill, a great bank of trees. She jerked back to the left. She oversteered again. The car began to zigzag, out of control. She couldn't believe it. She moved the wheel, and the car did not respond. It was going in its own direction. It couldn't be happening, but of course it was. She did not have time to be frightened. The car hurtled ahead. Careened. Turned. *I am dead*, she thought. She waited for the impact, but the other vehicles on the highway had stopped. Her car skidded across an empty lane, slowed, and came to a halt on the grassy median strip. She had not hit anything. People pulled over, asking if she was all right. She nodded, smiling, thinking, *I should be dead*. She sat there shaking, and after a while she drove away. She had not even bumped her head on the headrest. It was a warning.

"What? You think it's an omen?" Patrick roared at her. "You think God is interested in whether you work in the city or not? That He wants you to stay home and take care of your kids? What an arrogant, racist attitude. You think God is more interested in you than those refugees trying to get out of Vietnam?"

He had a point, of course, but two days later when they called to offer her the job in Washington, she turned it down.

She did not choose her life. She did laundry and ran errands and took jobs that were always jobs, never careers—even the present one—but it was not her choice. She had floated into it and it carried her, an undertow, and she couldn't get out. It was not what she chose. So she did none of it very well, only told herself it would soon be over, the boys grown, Patrick successful. And this was her punishment.

But why hadn't it happened before? Why now, when she was almost finished raising them, when they were finally coming into their own?

She would not have an accident however badly she drove today because of the irony. She would need to be alive and well to savor the death of her son.

She pulled off the road. It was not possible even for her to go to work. Nothing would save her. She made a U-turn and headed home.

A Radio-93 car was in the driveway, and a pretty reporter was standing at the front door, neat in a burgundy suit, with a box of sound equipment belted to her waist and a microphone in her hand. Darren was in the entryway with no coat on, trying to get rid of her, Mag supposed, but it was the reporter who was talking.

". . . understand that your brother and the O'Neal boy were in the same unit. Now that the O'Neal boy has been located, what does this do to your hopes?"

Darren's pale face blanched, and his limp blond hair fell down his forehead into his eyes. "You can't expect us to . . ." he said before his voice rose into a squeak. He cleared his throat. Merle appeared in the doorway behind him, with his ludicrous scraggly mustache.

"You don't just give up hope," he said in a whine almost as unforgiving as Darren's. The reporter inched closer.

"And yet this must be a terrible time for you . . ." Her voice dripped drama. Mag came up behind her on the walk. The woman turned and began to point the microphone in her direction.

"Fuck off," Mag said. She swept by the other woman and

pulled the door closed behind her, bringing the twins inside with her and leaving the reporter on the stoop. For twenty-four years she had refused to use F-words in front of her sons, no matter how angry she got, and now the twins were staring at her as if she'd lost her mind.

"It's not something they can say on the radio," she explained. "They couldn't use the tape." The twins didn't change their expression. Why were they trying to be the media contact, anyway? It was Gideon they loved, not Percival. Why did their voices betray them as if they cared?

"She went away, didn't she?" Mag asked. The twins looked pathetic. "Didn't she?" she whispered. In unison, both of them nodded and shuffled down the hall. Mag went into the living room and turned the stereo up as loud as she could.

9

All night, Alfred's sleep had been interrupted by troubling dreams that vanished from memory the moment he startled awake. Five or six times he found himself sitting in bed, feeling as if some urgent responsibility had been presented to him in his dream and was hanging over him now, if only he could remember what it was. For long moments he stared into the darkness, the sound of his heartbeat drumming in his ears. And then, exhausted but still without knowing what was expected of him, he fell back to sleep. Toward morning, in the half-light, Cynthia touched his shoulder. "I'll take off of work today, too," she said. "We can take the boys to your mother's if you want, or leave them with the sitter, it doesn't matter. I wouldn't feel right going in to work."

He had been dozing when she said that. For a moment he was disoriented . . . his dream lingering on the edge of consciousness, the cold morning air against his face. Then her voice began to soothe him. She was not going to work. She would be with him all day, whatever happened, whatever news . . . He did not think beyond that. He was touching her, taking her breasts in his hands, feeling the nipples grow hard, rubbing her belly, her thighs. She moved against him, allowing it. He buried his head in her breasts. She was caressing him—not in a lewd, stolen way but freely, softly, like the wiping away of tears. A swelling, exultation; and then he was inside her. Afterward she fell asleep but he lay awake beside her, watching. He had not thought he would make love to her until the waiting was over. But now he felt no guilt, no regret.

It was a great relief, and not just physical. He had always believed in abstinence before—something his internal sense of justice demanded, he supposed. At Grandmother Singer's, he had never eaten the Lifesavers he brought, knowing his brothers were existing on stewed chicken and lettuce. And once, when Simon had an allergic reaction after his tonsillectomy and seemed likely to choke to death, Alfred managed to go several days without eating at all. He'd thought it wrong to enjoy his health and his pleasures while someone he cared for was suffering. But lying in bed with Cynthia, those gestures seemed as childish as Simon's deciding to have his ear fixed if Percival would live—the sort of mute, meaningless sacrifice you make only when there is nothing else you can do. It no longer seemed necessary. What was necessary was to handle the crisis. And it seemed to him that if Cynthia would take off work today to stay with him, then he could handle anything the Singer household could dish out—his mother's behavior, his father's blindness, even his brother's death.

He moved against Cynthia for warmth, intending to get up in a moment, but instead he slept again, deep and dreamless. When he awakened, it was almost noon. He had not done that since he was a teenager. He heard Cynthia making lunch in the kitchen, talking to the boys.

"You should have gotten me up," he said, after dressing quickly and joining them. "I never sleep like that."

"I figured if you did, you must need it. I called over to your house. Tim O'Neal called his family, but they still don't have word on Percival. There's nothing you can do. Your father's having trouble with his eyes, but everyone else is there."

"He's never had blind spells two days in a row before," Alfred said. "They say it isn't stress, but it probably is."

"You hungry?" Cynthia asked.

He was. Another time, he might have felt ashamed for wanting food at such a time, but not now. "After lunch we can all go over there," he said. "The kids can't make it any worse. Actually it might be nice to have them around."

If Tim O'Neal had called home, that meant they would probably get the news today, one way or the other. It would be easier to have Cynthia and the boys with him when it came. Cynthia handed him a sandwich and smiled. He noticed that she was wearing the same blouse she'd worn the day they met, and though it had been eight months since then, her appearance struck him even now as remarkable.

She'd been standing by the coffee machine in the teacher's lounge that first day, much as she was standing in the kitchen now. She'd just finished counseling a student from his homeroom and was ready to tell him her impressions. *His* first impression was of the blouse—a bright, almost violent purple favored by students but never worn by teachers because very few women over twenty-one could get away with it. But on Cynthia it looked fine, a measure of her attractiveness.

Of course, it was not only the blouse but what was under it that impressed him, though at the time he'd tried not to think about that. He never involved himself with women he met at work. Still, he'd observed that Cynthia's skin seemed luminous against the purple blouse, and that her ordinary brown hair—

short and brushed back from her face in a modest, businesslike way—had a particular sheen to it. Her face was round but with sharply defined features—not at all pixieish—and her eyes were an alert greenish gray. Having noticed those things, he tried to focus on her not as a woman but as a psychologist, a professional. Her manner was confident. He tried to listen but could not remember what she said. All through the conference his attention kept wandering away from the plight of his student to the enormous—even under the loose blouse—size of Cynthia's breasts.

He became acutely conscious of trying not to stare. Still reminding himself that she was a colleague, not an accessible woman, he asked her to dinner. He stared at her breasts in the restaurant. "When you work with teenagers," she said later, "you get used to getting the eye from the students and the teachers both. It's the first thing they deal with." He watched her being aware of his staring and was terrified that, when he took her back to his apartment as he planned to do as soon as they finished eating, she was not going to let him touch her.

What actually happened was that she refused to go back to his apartment at all, because she had to get home to her babysitter.

"Your babysitter?" When he picked her up, he had assumed the other woman in her apartment was a roommate.

"I have two little boys." He felt slightly sick at the idea of her having children, but his desire for her did not diminish.

Later she said, "I managed to accumulate a marriage certificate, a graduate degree, two babies, and a divorce all in a three-year span."

She was two years older than he was. He had never dated an older woman. He had never dated a woman with even one child, much less two.

He expected to forget her.

He could not stop thinking about getting his hands on her breasts.

It made no sense. He was not a casual person. He had been

in love once before and anticipated that there would be consequences when it happened again. He wanted to place his affection appropriately.

He thought about her—he had never done this with any woman before—during his classes.

It was unlike him to become obsessed with a woman's body, especially a woman who was—he knew this was uncharitable—disproportionate. He preferred ordinary, clean-cut good looks, though he was not averse to hidden treasure underneath. His first great love in college had seemed perfectly unexceptional clothed, but naked turned out to have voluptuous hips not nearly as narrow or fleshless as they appeared in jeans. He liked that well enough but had never been attracted to outward shows of cleavage or curve.

He could not get Cynthia out of his mind. They went to dinner and to movies; they chaperoned several dances at his school. Touching her breasts and later touching all the rest of her did not quench his craving. He felt as if he were diving into a lake with buried treasure at the bottom, aware of the potential reward but unable to hold his breath long enough to reach it and be satisfied. He came up for air and no sooner caught his breath than he was ready to dive again. When he was younger, he had sometimes felt this way about music. There were pieces he could not get enough of. He played the records over and over again while his parents were at work. When they came home he avoided that, not wanting them to think he was crazy, but he was restless, unhappy, until they left again and he could have the stereo to himself. Then finally, after days or weeks, his ear would grow weary, satisfied, and he would not need that particular melody so much anymore. But with Cynthia . . . there seemed to be no end to her. After a time he realized it had nothing to do with the size of her breasts.

Winter passed and by spring they were spending entire weekends together. Sundays they took her boys to Wheaton Regional Park or the Smithsonian or the National Zoo. Both boys liked to ride the Metro. Alfred felt comfortable enough with Jason and Joshua, having grown up accustomed to little brothers whose hands had to be held and noses wiped. At the Smithsonian he pointed out dinosaur bones and Iron Age tools. At the zoo he told them everything he knew about polar bears and poisonous snakes, lifting their small bodies over the crowd so they could see. When they grew tired, he bought them frozen custard cones at the refreshment stand, then sat with Cynthia while they ate and, revived, ran free on the grass. The boys made him feel useful and content. Yet sometimes on these outings he found himself walking as close as he could to Cynthia, away from the boys, touching her shoulder and her hair while restlessness and desire grew in him. He knew that his voice remained steady as he explained why bears liked cold weather or the Wright brothers had so much trouble learning to fly, but his mind was far away at those times. He yearned to be finished with respectable activity, yearned for Jason and Joshua to be fed and tucked into their beds, and for Cynthia to be beside him, alone, in her living room, so he could touch her wherever he wanted to touch.

She told him that she never worked in summer, because she liked having the time to spend with her sons. The Board of Education offered psychologists either a nine-month or a twelve-month contract, and she always chose the shorter one. It occurred to Alfred that during the summer she could use some help paying her rent. Between classes, during breaks in his work, he began to toy with the idea of moving in with her. The little boys liked him; Cynthia's ex-husband lived in Ohio and didn't see them much. It would be pleasant enough to father Jason and Joshua in the daytime and spend nights making love to their mother. Cynthia said she wouldn't let any man move in with her unless there was some sort of commitment; she wanted no more confusion for her sons. He surprised himself by offering to marry her right away. She said no, it was a good idea to live together first, as long as they had the commitment. He moved in. They planned to marry next summer, because Gideon would be home from Utah and Percival would be back from Lebanon. Cynthia had little family and liked the idea that all the Singer brothers would be able to attend.

The thought of a wedding with Percival dead drained the joy from their plan. But now, sitting in the kitchen eating his sandwich, with the memory of their lovemaking and his sudden sleep afterward in his mind, he knew even the death of his brother would not drain his joy in her. It would not drain his joy any more than his mother's disapproval had. Even the death of a brother. God forgive him, but it would not.

He finished the sandwich and helped Cynthia clean the kitchen. Together, they readied the boys. As they drove to his parents' house, he steeled himself to his father's blindness and the possibility of bad news. There was nothing more he could do. But when they pulled up, music from the stereo boomed out onto the driveway—opera distorted by sheer volume—and he knew he should have come earlier.

Inside, Darren had put on old earmuffs to shield himself against the noise, and Merle had covered his ears with a pair of stereo headphones. Izzy, lost in thought in the family room, seemed to be oblivious to it. Simon had the TV on but couldn't hear and didn't seem to care. Alfred wanted to take the twins aside and point out that it was in bad taste to parody life in the Singer household before the crisis, but he could see they were too upset for an etiquette lesson, and the music was too loud to allow normal talk. He found his mother in the living room, sitting on a chair in the same fetal position she'd assumed the day before, looking out of the window.

"I see we're testing *Mefistofele* for its ability to deaden the auditory nerves," Alfred said, lowering the volume.

"Tim and Percival were in the same unit," she told him. "Tim was out someplace when it happened. The last time he saw Percival, Percival was in the building."

The music grew louder. A passionate whistling marked the

final scene of the opera, in which Mephistopheles made his last-ditch pitch for Faust's soul, while the choir of angels prepared to sing him into heaven.

"You can't draw conclusions," Alfred said. He felt trapped, as if she would go on in this vein forever.

"Where's Dad?" he asked.

"Upstairs. Blind. I think he's taking a nap." She sounded bitter.

Voices drifted in from the other room. Simon was saying to Cynthia, "You think all this noise is going to blow the kids' ears out?"

"I don't know about Joshua," she told him, "but it would take more than this to damage Jason."

"We don't want any permanent hearing loss here," Darren said. "Joshua, take my earmuffs."

"Jason gets the headphones," Merle put in.

Cynthia laughed; the little boys giggled. The sound was better than the music. Alfred felt calmer, knowing they were there. A way occurred to him to distract his mother from thinking about Percival.

"Ah, *Mefistofele*," he said. "I got my religious education from *Mefistofele*."

She looked surprised. "Oh, Alfred. You had no religious education."

"I did, really."

Even turned low, the music had its power. Alfred remembered his mother listening to *Mefistofele* during her pregnancies. She favored violent, troubled music then. Eventually she had told him the entire story of Goethe's *Faust*, on which the opera was based—the deal between God and the Devil to see who could win Faust's soul, the temptations Mephistopheles offered, which included Faust's love affair with Margaret. Alfred had especially liked the part where Margaret, mad like Ophelia after Faust betrays her, goes to jail for drowning her illegitimate baby. He liked her refusal to let Faust rescue her, her decision to die and be saved rather than live and be damned. As a child, he had always believed he would have done the same. But then again, in those days he had been capable of starving himself for the sake of his younger brothers.

"We used to have long discussions about this. Don't you remember?"

"I only remember being pregnant," she said. "I always hated finding out I was pregnant—except not so much with you, since you were the first. That's a terrible thing, don't you think?"

"I used to ask you if you believed all that stuff about angels and devils battling over your soul," Alfred said.

"And did I?"

"You always put it off on Dad. You said, 'I don't know if I do or not, but I'll tell you what Dad would say—he'd say it was nonsense.'"

If there had been nothing more to this argument than words and logic, Alfred might have sided with Patrick. But Alfred was ten at the time, and the music spoke of the forces of good and evil in a tongue more compelling than speech. Listening to the wild orchestra, to Mephistopheles whistling across the stage (there was a picture of this on the album cover) in his fury at possibly losing Faust's soul, hearing the chorus of angels come in, singing "Ave Signor" in a sweet melody he hummed sometimes even now—at ten Alfred had been a believer. Years later, when he read Goethe in sophomore world literature—in a poor translation, he supposed—it seemed pale, thin stuff compared to Boito's music.

"I never thought it was nonsense, exactly," Mag said. "I suppose I should have told you that. I would have liked you to have some religion, I guess. So you wouldn't end up—so bloodless."

"I never thought of myself as bloodless," Alfred said.

"I should have taken all of you to church," Mag told him. "I never did because I didn't have the energy. I don't mean just fighting Dad about it—I mean the idea of getting up on Sunday morning and going anywhere."

"You did other things for us."

"I did a lot of laundry."

"You took me to piano lessons."

"Oh . . . that."

"I liked the piano lessons." He had listened to Mag's records and wanted to imitate them, so he had practiced diligently. It always distressed him that his fingers would not do what his mind commanded, but he certainly tried. Then Mrs. Wellman retired and they couldn't settle on another piano teacher, so that phase of his education ended. Afterward, he missed it for years.

Unwilling to let his mother's mood plunge again, he searched for some way to keep the conversation on piano lessons going just a little longer. "I liked having you take me and pick me up from piano," he said. "It was the only time we were together, just the two of us. I liked the way we used to talk in English accents when you dropped me off."

"We did?"

"I'd get out of the car and you'd say, 'Well, see you in hawf an hour, then,' in your accent, and I'd say, 'Jolly good, then . . . hawf an hour.'"

"We talked in English accents?" She seemed a little disoriented. "Oh yes . . . when you were little. That's what you remember about piano lessons?"

"Well . . . one of the things."

His mother looked no happier than she had when he'd offered to watch her house for the winter.

His father had come downstairs. It was clear that he had not been napping but showering, because his hair was still wet. His irises were beginning to be visible, so his sight must be returning. He looked as if he were in pain. Alfred did not know what he could do. Then Cynthia walked in, smiling and getting ready to speak, and Alfred felt—truly—as if he had been rescued.

Mag watched Cynthia and Patrick come through the archway between the hall and the living room. Cynthia was smiling and Patrick was squinting, and they both looked false.

"It's coming back, finally," Patrick said. Sure enough, his

pupils were reappearing, a cold light was glittering from his eyes. Percival was dead, and on Patrick's face was the frank relief of returning sight, the same as yesterday.

"I'll get you some aspirin," Alfred said.

"I already took a couple."

Oh, yes: aspirin to soothe him, everything to soothe him. How, at a time like this, could he be soothed? There was aspirin in the kitchen cabinet, aspirin in each bathroom, in his night table by the bed. Even if he was blind, he would be able to find it. But if he went blind, she'd have to help him anyway, subtly—the way she'd once helped Alfred cook French toast at the age of five, pretending she was doing other things, behaving as if he were perfectly capable of operating the stove. They would have raised seven sons and perhaps buried one, but instead of freedom they would return to those days when all her time was occupied by performing small personal services— chauffering Patrick to doctor's appointments the way she'd once taken the children to lessons and scouts, selecting his clothes. And he would pretend it was nothing, just as he was pretending today that Tim O'Neal's safety did not foretell Percival's death. She would do it because she was well trained. All her energies sucked up into his demands . . . and the possibility of a career, deferred for twenty-five years, snuffed out entirely. Watching his swimming-pool blue eyes open up, and his pretense that his son was still alive, she didn't love him, didn't care if he went forever blind, didn't care at all.

"When we finally get some news," she said coldly, "it's going to come just like that reporter showing up on the doorstep before. All of a sudden there'll be a khaki uniform instead of newspaper people or the neighbors. That's how it's going to happen. It's not going to be . . ." She thought of something. "Or do they wear blues for a death?"

"How many times are you going to say that? Or some version of it?" Patrick asked. "Don't have him dead and buried before you have to."

Oh, he was very noble. Very independent. Capable of grand thoughts but not of finding his shoes, blind, in the closet. Cynthia, beside him, smiled more brightly. What was there to smile about? Was Cynthia trying to soothe her, or were school psychologists just taught to smile when marital tension surfaced among the parents of their students? "What you two need," she told them, "is a drink. I didn't want to tell you this, but one of my great skills is bartending."

It was not yet evening, but the idea of a drink appealed to her. Patrick had not been able to drink for almost ten years because alcohol made him sneeze. But she could get smashing drunk if she felt like it, wipe herself out. Maybe she would. She had always thought Patrick's allergy to liquor was poetic justice—a penalty for the drunken nights he had spent during the years when she was cooped up with small children. And it seemed fitting that alcohol should offer him no escape today, when again he was pretending there was nothing important to attend to at home, even though Tim O'Neal had been found and Percival had not.

Years before, when the boys were very little, Patrick had started getting drunk regularly with another man from work. She thought in part he did it as revenge against her for expecting him to babysit while she took her classes. He believed tending children was her role in life, not his, and he watched them sulkily, angrily . . . and even when he invented the disposable diapers, it was to keep her from complaining and not because he cared enough to spend his time supervising babies. So once a month or so (never on the night she had class; he was careful about that), he went off to drink with his friend from work— deliberately went off without calling, never on the same night twice, in no pattern.

She usually didn't realize he wasn't coming home until it was too late. She would look at her overcooked dinner and redden as understanding dawned on her, anger rose in her throat. It was then that she most wanted to walk out, claim her own freedom as he had claimed his—alone, without responsibilities, carrying all she needed in her backpack. At the same time, though, her sons were there; she could not have left them. She even felt obligated to feign some semblance of normality in front of the older ones.

"Where's Daddy?"

"He had to go somewhere with a friend. He'll have supper later; go ahead now. Eat your beans."

Then the fury would wash over her—not that Patrick was gone, but that he would leave her alone, with three or four young sons, helpless against the obligation, without a car, without a sitter, enslaved.

Ten o'clock came, and eleven, and after the children went to sleep she cleaned house with an energy born of rage, too angry to study or even watch the evening news. She vacuumed, mopped, folded laundry, showered—then dropped, exhausted finally, into bed. She never fell asleep. She lay there and imagined revenge: Patrick drunk and lying on the street, mugged by some teenager, hit by a taxi, rolled by a whore. Ha! He *better* be dead. Midnight came, a moonless dark, and the house made strange noises in the stillness. Patrick was with a woman—a woman quite different from Mag, with smooth tan skin, dark hair, slim hips that brushed Patrick's, not accidentally, as they talked and sipped drinks at the bar. A childless woman, single, free. Mag startled awake, not yet thirty, mother of however many babies (it varied from year to year), not even finished with school.

A sound outside, a car, perhaps. She closed her eyes, hating him, biding her time until he should come in, take over, so that she could walk away from him, be done with wifehood and motherhood and enslavement, go out into the night with her backpack, free. But the car passed . . . and it was one o'clock, two. What if he was really dead? What if he had suffered?

Then, just as she was feeling a little sorry for him, he always showed up. She held her breath as he came up the stairs—al-

ways held her breath—because she believed that with air growing stale in her lungs and Patrick still on the other side of the
bedroom door, she should still have the power to choose him.
Or not.

"You bastard," she said when he tiptoed into the room.

He did not smoke, but the odor of cigarettes clung to his
jacket, and the smell of liquor was on his breath and his skin.
"Mag, honey, don't be mad at me. I'm too sick. I'll be hung over
tomorrow all day." He draped the jacket over the chair and took
off the shirt and got into bed with her, half-clothed.

"Get away from me, Patrick. I mean it." He was pulling up
her nightgown. "What the hell are you doing?" She pulled the
nightgown down.

"I'm sorry. Really. I should have called. I was going to, but
then I got to drinking." He left the nightgown alone and concentrated on stroking her back, easing his hands around to her
breasts. She took them away.

"You know how I lose all track of time when I drink. Do you
hate your husband? Do you really?"

"Yes."

He sighed and got out of bed, pulled his pants off, dropped
them on the floor. Back under the covers he began to rub her
back again—"Don't hate me, Maggie"—and eased his hands
forward until she pulled away. Undaunted, he edged his fingers
toward her breasts, and she evaded him until she was at the very
edge of the bed, feeling ridiculous, engaged in a tug-of-war over
her bosom.

"For God's sake, Patrick, get off. Only a complete shit would
leave me here with four"—six, three—"kids after I've been with
them all day, and not call, just let me think you were lying dead
somewhere. And then come home trying to play lovey-dovey."
But he ignored her, abandoning her breasts and stroking her leg
instead, higher, the soft part of her thigh, and she thought: Well,
if he wants to do *this*, at least he probably hasn't been with a
woman.

"I'm sorry, Mag, I really am." His fingers were inside her, gentle, stroking, and she was wet, she couldn't help it, what with the patient movement and his body pressed against her so she could feel his erection. She smelled the liquor and the smoke on him, exotic smells after talcum and diapers; smelled a life of cigars, three-piece suits, not her own drip-dry cotton life, not at all . . . and his lips and hands finally made her forget herself, because he always made love most skillfully when he was drunk.

Afterward, in the morning, baggy-eyed from lack of sleep, she was always furious. He had been free, and she had been trapped, and he had tricked her, once more, into accepting that. She came to see that he wasn't going to help her with the children—at least not then—but only participate in making more of them, and she hated his drinking and his friend from work. Then just before Simon had his tonsils out, he came home one night sneezing and miserable as if he'd contracted the flu. But it wasn't the flu, it was whatever he'd been drinking. After that, every time he had so much as half a glass of beer, he started sneezing again and again in rapid succession, like someone in the grip of violent hayfever, and he had to stop drinking for good. Whenever she was angry with him she conjured up the image of him helpless, sneezing, punished for his drinking and was always comforted by her conviction that it served him right.

Now Cynthia stood between them, looking from one to the other, and Patrick was still squinting, being the noble blindman—not blind at the moment, however. Mag almost accepted the drink before she decided she mustn't be drunk or even the least bit hazy when the Marines came; she owed Percival at least that. "I'd love something," she said, "but I guess I won't, not right now."

Patrick winked at her, thinking she had refused because he couldn't drink with her. "Ah, acts of charity," he said. But it wasn't. She had rolled around in bed with him all those years and hadn't been able to help it. But that was over now. Her sons were born, grown, dying. At a certain point the father was no more important than a tomcat or papa bear, essential at the moment of conception and then of no consequence at all . . . and the mother was alone, raising them, caring about them, waiting for them to die. And afterward she would be condemned to care for a blindman who strutted around like the emperor without his clothes. She turned away from Patrick and Alfred and Cynthia, toward the stereo. She took off *Mefistofele* and found another record.

"Don't worry," she said to Alfred. "I won't play it loud."

"I think, ladies and gentlemen," he said as the music started, "that this afternoon we're in for a steady diet of Chopin polonaises."

There was sarcasm in his voice, but Mag didn't care.

10

Simon had never been so angry with his mother. Not only was she into her loud classical-music routine, not only had she reversed herself on the matter of his ear, but also she had turned his alarm clock off this morning so he hadn't gotten up to deliver the papers.

When he first woke up and came downstairs, she was already gone. "Off to work," his father said, which made no sense. His father had been blind again. "Don't worry, she'll be back soon," he'd said. In the meantime, no papers were in the driveway, nothing . . . only one *Freestate Sentinel* lying on the kitchen table.

"I think she delivered them for you," Izzy told him. "She was dressed like she had."

"She never does that by herself."

"Well, today she did."

They told him about Tim O'Neal calling home. They told him Tim didn't know whether Percival had been in the building that got blown up or not.

Right then he remembered everything he'd forgotten during the night. He started to sweat. There was nothing he could do—not even deliver his papers. A little while later his mother came home. She didn't speak to anyone, just went in the living room and turned on the stereo. He followed her in and yelled over the music: "Why didn't you wake me up?"

"I didn't sleep all night," she yelled back at him. "Gideon came."

"I mean, it's my route. How did you even know which houses to do on the other section?"

Some high-voiced opera lady was singing, louder than an actual person would sing in real life.

"I think I did all right," his mother screamed. "I was just sitting here half the night, Simon. I needed something to do."

His mother's skirt and blouse were wrinkled, not crisp like they usually were when she went to work. Her face was wrinkly, too. Another time he would have thought it was nice of her to get up for him. It wasn't as if she loved going out in the cold. But the papers were something he was supposed to be responsible for. His father had said so. It seemed like he ought to be able to do *something*.

"Well, if you're going to get up again tomorrow, don't do it without me," he said over the music.

She didn't apologize, only turned the stereo up louder. A little while later Alfred arrived and made her turn it down, but Simon had been annoyed all day. His mother should at least let him handle his own newspapers and his own ear.

"Some girl is on the phone," Darren was saying.

"Who?"

"What am I, your secretary?" Darren asked.

Simon got up and went into the phone room.

"Simon?"

It was Hope Shriber's voice—the Jesus freak. Shit. She would ask, in her low-voiced, gossipy way, "Heard anything yet?"— the way people had been asking all day yesterday and all day today. When he said no, Hope would go into her Christ Our Savior/Kingdom of Heaven spiel the way she did in social studies when they were doing Religions of the World. She'd say if Percival were dead, that meant he was with Jesus; it meant he was spending eternity in the Kingdom of Heaven—talking as if that was the best thing that could happen; you couldn't ask for anything better. He was so angry that even before Hope said another word, he had in mind to tell her Percival was nineteen years old and had plenty of time to think about eternity later, thank you very much. And that would be the end of it.

"We didn't want everybody in the class calling you separately because we thought that might be too much, so I'm calling for all of us," was all Hope said. "We just want you to know that we're thinking about you." She didn't even ask if they'd heard any news.

"Yeah, well thanks," Simon said. It was the first time he'd thought about how everyone else had been in school all day, how normally he himself would have been there, too—sitting in class and going to the cafeteria for lunch, eating school pizza and watching Pooter dance, almost falling asleep while Mrs. Bettleheim droned through seventh-period history. He felt as if he'd been away from that a lot longer than just one day.

He imagined Hope sitting by the phone in her house, with her honey-colored hair falling over the receiver, and her eye shadow and lip gloss worn off the way it always was by the end of the day. In some ways, except for her religious craziness, she wasn't so different from everybody else. It seemed to him now that he was the different one.

"What I want to do," she said, "is have a moment of silent prayer for your brother in home room. I was going to ask Mr. Forsythe today, but I wanted to ask you first. I don't want to do it if it's going to make you mad."

He should have known that was coming. He was surprised she was even asking permission. He guessed she knew how annoyed he'd be otherwise. Sometimes in class they really went at it, Simon saying, "A lot of times God just has *nothing to do with it*," and Hope's color getting so bright he thought she was actually going to sputter.

"That's just ridiculous, Simon," she'd say in a voice just on the edge of tears—the kind of voice the twins had when they got upset—and Simon would feel half bad about getting her so riled up and half good that he could get to her so easily.

But Hope wasn't sputtering today. There was a long pause on the phone. Then she said in a small, tentative voice, as if she thought maybe he'd hung up on her: "Simon?"

He didn't answer right away. He was thinking about how his father had said yesterday he was using the Angel Solution to decide about his ear. He was trying to let God bail him out; he was trying to make a deal. He wasn't doing that at all.

A thickness rose in his chest. His father had tried to make an ass out of him in front of the whole family. And his mother, too, first with his ear and then with the newspapers. What did they want from him? If he died under the anesthetic, he would be like Percival blown up: Simon Singer one minute and the next minute nothing at all. And that would be all right. But maybe it would never happen. Maybe they wouldn't let him do it. There was nothing he could do.

Then he thought: How could a moment of silent prayer hurt? How could it hurt to pray for Percival, just in case?

"I guess it would be okay," he said.

"Thanks, Simon," Hope said. "I'll call you tomorrow and let you know if Mr. Forsythe lets us do it. Or maybe I'll call him at home right now and call you back. Take care."

"Take care yourself," Simon said, and hung up.

Gideon had come downstairs. He was saying hello to everybody, but he looked awful. He kept rubbing his legs.

"What's the matter?" his father asked Gideon, squinting because his eyes had opened up not long ago and he still couldn't see very well. "You have a cramp?"

"Yeah, pins and needles, that's all. Must have slept in a weird position."

Simon had not thought Gideon would space out over Percival. They didn't even like each other that much lately. But everyone could see that he was in a bad state.

Darren came walking into the family room. "Visitors," he said to Simon. For a minute Simon was glad for an excuse to get out of there. Then he realized it was probably Hope. Of course if it was Hope, her father must have brought her—her father the Jesus Freak—and they'd want to come in and pray right now, not wait for a moment of silent prayer in class tomorrow, and that would make everything even worse.

But it was Pooter and Boozer standing at the door. They never came to his house. They couldn't drive yet, and it was too far from J Street to walk over here.

"Hey, man, how'd you get here?" Simon asked.

"Come see," Boozer said.

They all went out on the front walk. There was this '64 Chevy convertible in the driveway, one Simon knew belonged to an older guy name Marcellus, and there was Marcellus himself, sitting in the front seat.

Pooter and Boozer fidgeted around on the walk. "I bet you're really freaked out, Simon," Pooter said. It was the kind of thing Percival always used to say. Pooter got a real uncomfortable look on his face when he spoke, and it made Simon feel a little better.

"All of you can come inside," Simon said. "Marcellus, too."

"No, man," said Pooter. "You come down here and take a look at this car."

They all walked down into the driveway. Marcellus's convertible was some car. It was twenty years old and shinier than the new '84s. It was too cold to have the top down on a day like this, but they had it down anyway. Marcellus pointed out the upholstery and the rebuilt engine.

"He put fifteen coats of wax on this baby," Boozer said.

Simon admired it all. Pooter and Boozer had talked about this car a lot at school, but Simon had never thought to go see it. He remembered Percival's old car. It was just this shiny, though of course not a convertible. In summer Percival took off his shirt and washed the car in the driveway. Simon always helped. They washed it in the sun, letting the water from the hose slosh over their bare feet. Then Percival pulled it into the shade under the sugar maple where they waxed it, rubbing circles of thick paste wax onto the metal and then rubbing it off until the dark green color of the car shined through from underneath. When Percival went into the Marines, Izzy took that car down to College Park, but he was too busy with his research to wax it or even change the oil. Percival had been using a different car last year when he taught Simon how to drive.

Thinking about all that might have made Simon sad right now, but with Pooter and Boozer standing there, it didn't.

"Listen to this sound," Pooter said, turning the car radio on and letting "Beat It" boom out onto the driveway. Then Pooter must have decided it wasn't right to turn Michael Jackson up so loud under the circumstances, and he quickly turned it off.

"Don't worry about that," Simon said, thinking about his mother playing the stereo twice this volume. He turned the radio back on, lower, to show Pooter it was all right. Boozer moonwalked backward on the driveway.

"You don't see chrome like this no more," Boozer said.

"You sure don't."

"Of course, it don't get no gas mileage," Marcellus told him.

"Yeah, but who cares?"

"That's what I say, man, who cares?"

Simon could see how proud Marcellus was.

It was getting dark.

"Hey, Simon, you hang in there," Pooter said.

"I hope your brother's okay," said Boozer. He said it in a way that made Simon think he would be.

They waved when they drove off. Simon felt a lot better.

Back in the house, Cynthia said, laughing, "Percival *said* all you really cared about was being black. Until now I didn't believe it."

Simon was thinking how Pooter and Boozer would help Marcellus shine the car. He remembered helping Percival, watching the metal begin to glow.

Cynthia winked at him. He knew he must look silly, a long-haired white boy looking at a car with three short-haired blacks. But he didn't care.

Then the phone rang, and the knot came back into his throat. It was probably Hope, calling to say she'd talked to Mr. Forsythe about a moment of silent prayer. But it was only one of the neighbors, calling to find out if there was any news.

After that, every time the phone rang, Simon answered, even after he finally talked to Hope. If it was the neighbors, he gave the phone to his father. If it was a radio or TV station or a newspaper, Merle or Darren talked. As people started getting off of work, more neighbors began dropping by. Alfred became the one who answered the door. Cynthia stayed in the kitchen, accepting the food everyone brought. She offered each one coffee or tea and something to eat. Izzy and Gideon sat in the family room talking to the guests. Simon supposed Gideon stayed seated partly because he was having so much trouble moving around. But still, it was comforting knowing everyone had a particular job. Everybody, that is, but his mother. She stayed in the living room. The stereo was lower now, but she didn't turn it off. She put on record after record, craning her neck toward the speakers. Cynthia and Alfred got supper out, but his mother wouldn't come in to eat.

"Should I bring her a tray?" Cynthia asked.

"No, let her listen to her music, if that helps her," his father said.

His father was letting her get away with a lot more than he would have let Simon get away with, that was for sure. Why did she think she had a right to turn his alarm clock off and deliver his papers? Why did she get to act like a spoiled brat when no one else could? They cleared the table and washed the dishes, but his mother was still sitting there when the ten o'clock news came on.

Mag could not listen to music anymore. It wasn't doing her any good. She wandered into the family room to see the news. A woman was being interviewed—the wife of a Marine.

"We called headquarters, but they told us their lists are just tentative. They really don't know . . ." The woman's voice cracked. "We really don't even know how to feel."

Mag was annoyed by that. She herself knew exactly how to feel. Twice, Alfred had called the Marine Corps hotline to check on the tentative lists of survivors and had been given the same runaround, and she had felt helpless and furious at the same time. Then Tim O'Neal's name had appeared on the list and Percival's hadn't, and that had infuriated her, too.

"It was his life," the woman on TV said.

"His life," Mag repeated out loud.

"What?" Patrick asked.

"Nothing."

The interview was over. A tape came on, of a reporter talking to one of the officers in Beirut. Identifying the dead was "a tedious process," the officer said. "It's made even more difficult by the fact that some of the bodies were badly crushed." She saw Percival crushed, Patrick blind, Simon earless, forever and ever. "And because the personnel records were blown up," the officer was saying, "we're just now getting a handle on which men are away on leave in Egypt."

"It's possible he went to Egypt," Gideon said, with a thread of hope in his voice.

Gideon looked worse than anyone else in the room. Mag remembered all that had transpired between him and his brother. But she thought: No, let Percival not be in Egypt. Let him not be dead—God, not that—but let him not be absent. Let him be right there, at the airport in Lebanon, and let him have survived. For Percival, worse than not winning, sometimes, was not being there at all.

The night before the cross-country championship his senior year, Percival did not come home. It was not the first time. He sometimes stayed at Tim O'Neal's house, and several times he had been with his girlfriend, Jill. Girlfriends had been a by-product of the belated dark beauty Percival had finally developed, leaving him almost as handsome as Izzy without Izzy's mournfulness. Mag even drew comfort from the idea of Percival in womanly arms. It was better than being out on the streets with Tim—speeding, wrecking cars, taking drugs. Mag found Jill's belt in Percival's room and hoped the girl wasn't pregnant, but she never resented her the way she had Tim, or worried about Percival's staying away with Jill. Maybe she simply had no energy to fight about it. A difficult child could drain you; you always had to be on guard. What surprised her was his staying out that particular night. He had never stayed out all night before a race.

Percival didn't win much anymore, although he did well in comparison to everyone but Gideon. And sometimes he surprised them. Patrick said he was inconsistent because he didn't train properly, and he blamed Jill for interfering with Percival's workouts. This struck Mag as unfair because Patrick had never blamed *Tim* for interfering and because Percival had worked out irregularly for years. Even so, Percival was not doing badly. Along with his sudden belated beauty had come muscles, a man's body, surprising strength. Patrick did not discuss this, but he believed Percival had half a chance to beat Gideon in the championships. It never occurred to anyone that he would miss the meet.

Mag made pancakes that morning as she always did before a race. Gideon and the twins stuffed themselves with carbohydrates because they believed it would help them run; Simon and

Patrick ate because it was a long drive to Howard County and a long time before lunch. Everyone kept watching the door, waiting for Percival to come through it. He still hadn't arrived when the dishes were cleared, when Gideon and the twins had to leave for the bus that would take the high school team to the race.

"Where the hell is he? Call Jill's house," Gideon said.

"No," said Patrick. "He didn't forget what day it is." His voice was low and flat, detached.

"What if something happened to him?"

"Nothing happened to him. This is the same as cutting class."

For a year, ever since Gideon beat Percival at Brunswick, Patrick had been saying to Percival, "At the top levels, it's ninety-nine percent want-to." Mag believed he encouraged Percival not because he loved Gideon less, but because he had been training Percival longer. Because he had made the RipOffs for Percival so he would not spend his winters inside. Because time was running out on Percival, who would graduate in the spring, while Gideon had another year of high school.

But that day of the state championships, Patrick said, "The hell with Percival then. We can't wait for him forever."

Mag thought: We could wait. Then a calmness descended inside her. It seemed to her that, after all, Patrick had been waiting for Percival for too long. All the years of training he had devoted to him, the bits of running lore, the RipOffs—all were part of Patrick's plan to make Percival tough and strong. But Percival understood them only as a test he could never pass. And all the time, it seemed, he had been following some separate agenda which none of them understood. So on the day of that state championship, Patrick gave up on Percival, let him go. Patrick got into the car with Simon and drove to Howard County to watch his other sons.

Mag had planned to go with them. She'd planned with perfect assurance to watch either Percival or Gideon win the championship. She would watch her son pull in front of the others late in the race—Percival's dark hair or Gideon's blond curls blown back by the wind as he passed the others. She would bask in fall sunshine and watch one of her boys triumphant, golden; she would ride on that tide of joy.

Then a little nub of worry swelled inside her, larger than her anticipation of joy, and though she knew Gideon would win, she stayed behind to wait for Percival.

He came home, finally, in the middle of the afternoon. He saw their station wagon was missing from the driveway and must have assumed they had all gone to the race, even Mag. In his room, thinking he was unwatched, he emptied change and a pack of rubbers and a little plastic bag full of marijuana onto his bed.

"I think I've spent the last five years of my life," Mag said to him from the hallway, in a low voice which nevertheless made him startle and turn around, "telling you guys what I think of smoking dope."

Dark eyes are not usually cold, usually opaque, but Percival's were then. "How can you be so self-righteous about marijuana if you've never even smoked it?" he asked calmly.

"I can deduct from your behavior what it must be doing to your brain for you to miss the bus to Howard County."

"I wasn't going to win."

"You never know."

"Another area," he said, "in which you speak from wide experience."

"All right, light me up," she said.

"Huh?"

"Light me up, I said. Light me up a cigarette. A joint. Whatever you call it. If you're not going to listen to me unless I speak from experience, then far be it for me not to seek out experience. Later maybe I'll run a mile or two."

"Mother, I hate to say this, but I think you've lost it," Percival said.

"Not at all. I see that you respect only hands-on knowledge of an issue. Come on, roll one of those things. Go on."

He smiled then, at her anger, and got some white cigarette paper out of one of his drawers and began to roll a joint. "I know you won't really smoke," he said.

But she did. They sat on Percival's unmade bed, backs against the wall, looking out onto the floor—a sea of running shoes, jock straps, textbooks, a radio they called a box, the detritus of teen-aged boys—and beyond that into late-fall sunshine, a slanting, amber light. At first she felt awkward—at being in the room and not in the process of cleaning it, as much as at smoking the joint. Percival instructed her how to inhale, to hold the smoke in as long as possible—even how to pass the cigarette back and forth without dropping it on the bed. After a time she no longer felt so awkward.

He turned the box on; she knew music was supposed to sound different when you were stoned—she remembered the Beatles and the wavery sound of "Lucy in the Sky with Diamonds"— but if the station Percival played sounded different than it normally did, or more wavery, she wasn't sure, being unaccustomed to hard rock. If anything, the sound annoyed her less. "That song isn't so bad," she said.

"See? I told you."

"I'm not making a final evaluation until I'm sober again," she said.

"Oh, no. I wouldn't expect you to."

He was no longer angry with her. His real anger, she saw now, was not with her but with himself, for missing the race. But he had chosen not to go. And now no one was angry.

"Are you passing all your courses?" she asked him. "I hope so, because I know you're cutting a lot of school."

"I always pass everything," he said.

She supposed that was true. It was just that his grades were so unpredictable. Izzy had gotten As in everything, and Alfred had done almost as well, but while Percival consistently made As in math, he could easily come home with Cs and Ds in everything else. It all depended on whether or not he liked his teacher. This had been going on since middle school, and each

— 185 —

year Mag expected it to stop, believing that Percival would reach a point where he would be less affected by personality than by subject matter. But so far it hadn't happened. She was perennially disappointed—*stunned* might be a better word—when she saw his grades.

"I'm always surprised that a space cadet like you is good in math," she heard herself say. Normally they didn't talk about his airheadedness or his school work except on report-card days, but it seemed all right while they were smoking the sweet thin cigarette; it seemed as if their discussion was outside of them and couldn't do any harm.

"Einstein was considered a space cadet," Percival said.

"I'll try to keep that in mind the next time they put you in detention." The high school had a system of demerits for crimes such as being unruly in the cafeteria or cutting classes. After a certain number of demerits, a student had to spend a day in the detention hall doing homework. Percival sat there with rough boys from the slums, boys who spent their school hours practicing for lives of petty theft and stints in the county jail.

"Einstein got into college, didn't he?" Mag said. She frowned. "The teachers aren't necessarily going to be more benevolent in college. I had a few doozies in my time." The little cigarette was getting smaller as they passed it back and forth. She held it between her thumb and forefinger; her hands looked very adroit. She thought she had seen a beautiful actress holding a joint just this way in an R-rated movie.

"Maybe I won't go to college, then," Percival said in a calm voice.

"That seems logical. First you quit the running team, then you quit school. That seems very logical." She said this without anger or concern; all of it seemed rather absurd to her now—she assumed this was an effect of the marijuana—and even Percival seemed amused.

"I mean, that's the way you think, isn't it?" she went on. "You think, well, I'm not at that race today; it could have been awful but I passed it by, so now I'm out of the woods. There's this hard test coming up, but I won't take it; as long as I don't do it, I'm out of the woods. There's your mistake, Percival. You think you're out of the woods, but it's never true. Some new hard thing keeps coming up. Even disappearing into dope isn't something you can do forever. Life *is* the woods."

"That's very poetic, Mother. You're very poetic when you're stoned."

She was pleased with herself. "I am, aren't I?" Percival put out his hand and slapped hers the way he did when his friends said, "Gimme five." She didn't feel heavy and dizzy as she did when she drank liquor; she felt light, floaty, not at all bleak inside.

She began to feel hungry. "You want some chicken soup?" she said. Percival had remained picky about his food as he grew older, but he would always eat Campbell's chicken noodle soup when it was offered. He liked the appearance of the golden-yellow broth and uniform white noodles, which he believed were clean-looking. Mag's homemade chicken soup, by contrast, was sometimes polluted with gray (not pure white) bits of chicken, shards of celery and carrot, unidentifiable things.

"What I really want," Percival said, "is a banana split."

This sounded like a clever, even a wonderful, idea. Mag realized that all along she had been yearning for a banana split.

"I think we have some bananas," she said. Bananas usually lasted in the house longer than other fruits because the boys refused to take them in bag lunches to school. They looked too much like penises. But they didn't mind eating them secretly at home.

They went down to the kitchen and made banana splits. They put scoops of vanilla and chocolate ice cream on top of the bananas, then dribbled caramel and chocolate syrup on top of that. She had never before eaten such a large banana split. The ice cream tasted better than she remembered ice cream ever tasting.

"This is delicious," she kept saying. She wished she kept whipped cream and maraschino cherries in the house.

"It's always delicious when you're stoned," Percival said.

"When you're drunk," she told him, "you can't appreciate a banana split."

"Maybe we should introduce Dad to grass," Percival said, "since he can't drink."

"Oh, I don't think so."

They ate the banana splits and cleaned up the kitchen. She still felt mellow and a little floaty when the others came in and told them Gideon had won. Percival gave her such a look then: a half-amused, sad, I-told-you-so look. If you were absent from the race, there was no chance to win, and still you felt just as bad about losing. She did not know if Percival's look was of shame or resignation or acceptance. It was the only look you could give someone when a part of your life had passed and you had been absent.

Later, when she was not floaty anymore, she said to Percival, "I think marijuana's probably no worse a high than drinking alcohol, but I don't think you should use it any more than you would use alcohol—on the weekends or whatever. Not during the week. Not when you're supposed to be in school. Or racing, or whatever." She sounded stern and authoritarian, like one of his teachers.

"And, Percival—I speak from experience," she said.

He smiled a little then, the small mischievous smile she remembered from when he was a boy. She thought her lecture might have done some good. Then he said, "Pot is no longer the drug of choice, you know, Mother. People are more into coke."

Her expression dropped and Percival laughed—an open, genuine laugh. "Don't worry," he said. He patted her arm. She didn't know what to think at all.

After that he was more discreet. She checked his room occasionally for cigarette papers or packets of white powder, but she never found anything. Percival broke up with Jill and found another girl named Helen—girls came easy to him then—and sometimes cut classes to take her to his bedroom while she and Patrick were at work. His grades stayed mediocre, but he did well on the SATs and agreed for Mag's sake to apply to the community college for the following year. But the spring he was a senior, he refused to run track. He refused to go to his own graduation. Later he refused to study at the college any more than he had studied in high school. It was not that he was not capable. It was more that he was absent. Those last few years, he became an absentee in every respect. He was absent until he joined the Marines.

And she thought now: Let him not be in Egypt. Let him not be absent. Let him be present at this bombing, and survive it, and let that give him the strength to attend the other major events of his life.

The ten o'clock news was over. They would wait to hear it again at eleven. Alfred had not let Jason and Joshua fall asleep in the family room tonight; he had carried them upstairs to his old room. Everyone was quiet. Even Simon was not pacing the floor, but sitting motionless in a chair. His fingers lay still and silent. They all felt that they would hear something soon. It was a pulse, growing inside them, almost as if a bullet had been aimed at them but was coming in slow motion, letting them steel themselves before it hit.

Mag was filled with a sense of bitter irony. Percival was just coming into his own. Finally becoming a man. It seemed to her that his rebellious stage had ended when he joined the Marines, though they had not understood it. At first they had all been stunned—that Percival, who had never followed anyone's rules but his own, should sign up for *that*. But it was different than she expected. He went to boot camp at Parris Island and to infantry training at Camp Lejeune in North Carolina. He went to a school where they taught him about those armored vehicles he drove, and then he was in his unit. When he called, he sounded calm and easy inside himself. Later, home on leave, he talked about explosives and demolition and warfare as if those were games he had always wished to play. He was no longer an absentee. Having endured whatever beginning Marines go through, he looked grown up, handsome, relaxed. Even his skinhead haircut suited him. Last summer, on his last leave before going to Beirut, Percival got up early most days to run with Gideon—slow daybreak runs through rising summer light. There was a peace between the two of them, and a peace inside Percival, and Mag had thought: He will finally be able to do something with himself now. The ultimate irony.

The phone had all but stopped ringing. Its sudden jangling startled everyone. Simon leaped up. Mag stopped him by raising her hand. When she lifted the receiver, the first thing she heard was the long-distance static. It was Tim O'Neal.

"They've set up these phone lines and are bringing the units in one at a time to call home," he said. "I already called my mother, but they're letting me use it again because it's four-thirty in the morning here."

"You've heard something, then," she said.

"Not really." His voice sounded unsteady.

"What do you mean?"

"The unit I thought Percival was with . . . They came back a little while ago."

"I see."

"I mean—he wasn't with them."

"No."

Of course she had always known.

"But mainly . . . everything here's such a mess," he said. "There are a lot of guys I haven't seen." His voice was thin.

She felt perfectly hollow. It no longer mattered that Tim had alienated Percival from Gideon. All that seemed distant and petty. She was empty. Tim's death would not have made Percival's easier.

"There are a lot of line companies still out," he said. "He could still be out there."

"But you don't think so."

"I don't know." His voice cracked like the voice of a child—any troubled child, even her own. "I just don't know," he said again, and then the connection was broken.

11

Izzy was interested in the fact that his father's eyes did not seem to be affected by Tim O'Neal's call. It was very curious. This morning, he'd been convinced that stress played at least some part in his father's blind spell, after his eyes started to close while he was reading the paper. Studying the paper later, Izzy had seen how jarring the news stories were.

The death count was up to 161.

The crater left by the explosions was thirty feet deep by forty feet wide.

Gunnery Sergeant Herman Lange, one of the first to get to the site of the explosion from a nearby barracks, told reporters that bodies were lying all over. He could hear them screaming. They were saying, "Get us out. Don't leave us." The gunnery sergeant "just started digging, picking men out and taking them away on a jeep."

"It was total devastation," he reported. The area was peppered with personal items—a can of deodorant, a jack of hearts, a quarter.

Some bodies were thrown fifty yards.

That was this morning.

Later, after his father's eyes shut down, they said on television that a chaplain rescued from the rubble about noon on Sunday was the last person known to have been pulled from the explosion site alive. Rescue operations were continuing, but only dead bodies had been retrieved so far.

Hearing that, his father had taken more aspirin. Izzy assumed stress was causing at least the headaches. He remembered his own headaches when he'd killed the Biolab dogs. Then, though the situation hadn't improved, his father took a shower and came downstairs able to see again. Izzy reasoned that the shower had a powerful calming effect, which let his father overcome the psychological component of his illness.

But later he was not so sure. By midnight, more than an hour after Tim O'Neal's call, his father could not only still see, he had put the situation back in perspective for the entire family.

"Tim might be on the scene over there, but judging from what's been on television, he has even more limited view of it than we do here. You can tell from the film clips that he's right about everything being a mess. I'm sure there are more people he hasn't seen than he himself realizes, given the chaotic state over there and what he's been through. I would say, in terms of what we know and don't know, nothing's changed."

That seemed to Izzy a powerful statement for his father to be able to make, considering the circumstances. After that he was not sure, after all, that the blind spells were influenced by stress.

When the eleven o'clock news ended, his father had sent Simon to bed. Alfred and Cynthia decided to stay over, to camp out on the floor of Alfred's old bedroom, where Cynthia's boys were already asleep. Alfred went up to find blankets, but Cynthia stayed in the living room with his mother, which seemed odd, considering how his mother felt about her. Everyone else shared a final pot of tea around the kitchen table. Merle let the cat in, and his father picked it up, using it as a prop to make his final statement for the evening. "I'm turning in," he said, in such a tone that everyone else realized they were expected to do so, too.

Now it was probably only one in the morning, but Izzy felt like the night had gone on forever. He still had no idea what was wrong with his father, and he was annoyed with himself. He saw himself focusing on his father's problem like the sun focusing on paper under a magnifying glass. At any moment the heat would light the paper and he would know what to do. But nothing had happened. He could hear Gideon breathing in the other bed, and knew he was awake. Even Gideon's breathing annoyed him.

"What the hell's wrong with you?" he asked. "Here you are, this great runner, and all day you walked around like some physical-therapy patient in the process of being retrained to move your limbs. Just what we need around here, another medical case."

"What's *your* problem? One of your girlfriends dump you?"

"Don't you wish."

"Flu, asshole," Gideon said. "You think I should have made a big deal of it with everything else going on? You know how it makes all your muscles ache."

"Ache, yes. Turn you into a robot, no."

"Fuck off," Gideon said.

But Izzy didn't care. All day, Gideon had been rubbing his ankles. It had been bizarre. Everything was bizarre. Gideon rubbed his ankles, Merle rubbed his mustache, Simon rubbed his ear. Everybody was rubbing something. His father was rubbing his eyes.

Which brought him back to the fact that he still didn't know dogshit about what was causing his father's problem.

"Hey, man, I'm sorry," he said. Gideon only grunted, which

meant he was on the verge of falling asleep. Christ, he couldn't even apologize. Except for today, Gideon was never even unpleasant unless he lost a race. Then he'd sulk about it for a day or two until their father made him stop. "You spend so much time building up your power, but even then sometimes it doesn't come through," Patrick would say coldly. "If the power isn't there right at the moment you need it . . . then it isn't much good to you, is it? So what I suggest is: Stop feeling sorry for yourself and go back to work." Izzy felt like his father might be saying that not to Gideon right now, but to him, with the same stern expression in his voice.

Shit.

This morning, blind, his father had looked the way the dogs did at Biolab, watching the other dogs be killed. The way Rusty must feel, caged up and about to go back to the pound—the same helpless feeling Percival would have, if he was trapped. And there wasn't a damned thing Izzy could do about it.

He felt hot, though the room was cold. He kicked the covers off and reached over to the night table for his glasses. His father had turned the heat down when they went to bed, and still he felt like he was burning up. It wasn't normal.

For two days he'd gone around studying his father as if he were a specimen under a microscope, looking weird as hell. Nobody said anything about it because they expected him to come up with something. They'd expected it from the time he'd conned his mother into letting him keep Henry the snake. He was wizard-brain Izzy, training to be the great scientist who would make some important discovery. But now that the time had come, his mind was blank.

He was so hot, his glasses kept sliding down his nose.

Christ.

What if Jocelyn was right?

He'd end up an old man someday, still cutting up dogs—Izzy the Vivi. He'd be living with some woman twenty years younger than he was, a different woman every year, working in an animal lab, inflicting cruelty after cruelty—and in the end, when he died, maybe that was all he ever would have done.

The heat began to radiate out from his chest, into his arms and his legs. There was no pain in his chest, only heat. But maybe he was having a heart attack.

When he was at Biolab, he thought his headaches were caused by an aneurysm. He hated being neurotic. Tomorrow Gideon would limp through the house and he, Izzy, would go around clutching his chest.

No way.

If he could not help his father, at least he could take other action. He could give up his assistantship when he got back to College Park. It would be crazy to keep caging up animals just because nobody ever told him not to. If there was no point to it, it would be just as crazy as if Percival had kept running after all he did was lose.

He was sweating so much that his glasses would not stay on his nose. His nose was like a waterslide, letting them slip all the way off.

He would keep away from women, too. He was not going to be some neurotic Don Juan. That was the term his mother had used: Don Juan. He wiped the sweat from the nosepiece of his glasses, but they still wouldn't stay in place. He took them off and put them on the night table. What was wrong with him anyway, that he was wearing glasses to stare into the darkness in the middle of the night?

He pulled the sheet up over him. The heat kept building in his chest. It didn't make sense. There was no reason to be having a heart attack at the age of twenty-two.

His skin was hot to the touch. He probably had a fever. He hated being neurotic. He closed his eyes because he couldn't stand himself anymore.

He supposed what happened next was an act of self-preservation. All of a sudden, though he certainly didn't expect it, he fell sound asleep.

He didn't know what time he woke up. It was probably only a few minutes later. The heat in his chest was still very powerful, but it didn't frighten him the way it had before. Even a little bit of sleep could sometimes calm you.

An image floated into his mind. It was of everyone sitting around the table just before they'd gone up to bed. He saw Merle letting the cat in, wiggling his nose above his stupid mustache as he did it. He saw the dramatic way his father carried the cat off to bed, to indicate that everyone else should follow. He saw exactly what had actually transpired, except for one change. Now he understood what was going on with his father's eyes. He knew what was causing it, and what would happen next, when his father woke up in the morning.

His moment of certainty didn't last. His misgivings and despair returned to him in a sudden rush, and his skin felt hotter than ever. He did not want to become a dirty old man in a dirty old lab. There was no way he could be sure until morning.

He reached over to the night table for his glasses. He would not be able to sleep. If he was wrong, he would stay away from women and animals. He would not deserve them. If he was right, he would keep on with his work. The heat in his chest let up a little. In a few hours he would know. Already a coolness was seeping through his body. He was onto something. It was like a rainbow.

Mag and Cynthia were the only ones still downstairs. Mag hadn't meant to be drunk at a time when the Marines were likely to come, but after Tim O'Neal's call, that seemed foolish, the sort of gesture Percival himself would scoff at. "What difference does it make *now*, Mom?" he would ask . . . and he would raise his glass to hers, offer a toast, get roaring drunk. So when Cynthia came into the living room with glasses and a decanter of wine, Mag accepted.

She felt the liquor at once, because she had eaten almost nothing all day. For a time they just sat there, drinking and not saying much. She grew hazy. It was a relief. She was too fuzzy to think of Patrick blind, Percival crushed, anything. She studied Cynthia instead. She had never had a chance to be with her like this, without Jason or Joshua or Alfred at her side. All she saw was a pleasant-looking young woman, being polite and courteous to an older woman whose life was in the process of being shattered. She felt fairly objective. She wanted to see what it was about Cynthia that Alfred loved so much, enough to ask for Mag's house.

Cynthia smiled and poured them both another glass of wine. It was a studied gesture, more practice behind it than grace. "Here," Cynthia said. It was the first word she'd said in seven or eight minutes, and Mag wondered how they'd passed so much time together in silence. Even her grown nieces—the young women she'd felt closest to—would have felt the need to say something at a time like this.

But Cynthia was not like the nieces. She was more confident and self-assured. Mag could not imagine her as the sort of lash-batting, nail-painting teenager the nieces had been, observing with disapproving frowns while Gideon ran through the rooms dangling his underpants at the twins, who screamed, "Oh, no! It's disgusting. It's crispy. Save us!" The nieces had clutched their hands to their mouths when Percival yelled, "Tell Izzy to stop burping!" and looked down their noses as if the boys were creatures of an inferior species. Cynthia seemed too rational for that. And certainly Cynthia was nothing like the nieces now that they had grown up, languid and feminine as cats.

"I guess we're a little alike," Cynthia said suddenly, which seemed the worst kind of *non sequitor* to what Mag had been thinking. Cynthia ran a finger around the top of her wineglass. "Both of us having children so young," she said. "When you had Alfred, you were even younger than I was with Jason."

"I never wanted children," Mag said. She was going for shock value. Cynthia narrowed her eyes as if she didn't believe her. Maybe she'd gone too far. She hadn't wanted children, but she certainly wanted Percival now. "I mean I didn't want them until after they were born," she said.

"You were so young." They both studied the air. Cynthia's voice had begun to waver with alcohol. "Maybe you were even like I was," she said. "Pregnant . . . before."

Mag wasn't sure she heard that. So drunk. "Oh, no," she began to protest. But maybe Cynthia was confessing. Maybe Cynthia had been like the nieces after all: languorous, giggling, flirtatious. Maybe she had lazed around as they had, prone to paralytic bouts of doing nothing, until her reproductive system matured and she was able to remain motionless except for a sultry wiggle of the hip that brought some man along to claim her. Mag had always looked down on her nieces for their passiveness. She had never been so narrow-focused herself. It pleased her to think that Cynthia might have been like them. And that it might have gotten her pregnant.

But Cynthia certainly didn't sound passive now. "Getting pregnant was my own fault," she was saying crisply. "I never wanted Paul so much. What I really wanted was a baby." She was twisting her wineglass with an energy more like Gideon's prerace jitters than the nieces' catlike grace. Mag was annoyed.

"I think that's the wrong approach," she said. "I think you have to want the man first." This was not something she actually believed, but she wanted to disagree with whatever Cynthia said. "First you want the man and then everything else follows."

Cynthia smiled a warm, energetic smile. "This time I do want the man."

Mag's objectivity was gone now. Patrick often said, "I can't drink because it makes me sneeze, but you, my sweet lily—you can't drink because it puts you on an emotional roller coaster." Cynthia wanted *Alfred*, for Christ's sake. Bully for Cynthia. So she thrust her big bosom into his face and he was probably still smothering. Cynthia wanted the man, big deal. She also wanted Alfred to raise her kids in Mag's nice house.

"I know you're worried about Alfred taking on two children that aren't his own," Cynthia said, reading her mind. "I can understand your concern."

Mag didn't answer, only flared her nostrils a little and let the wine-breath flow out: dragon's breath. Nastiness ran in her veins along with the liquor. Alfred must have told Cynthia everything. Why should she be surprised?

Did Cynthia think Mag was some fifteen-year-old student who needed counseling?

Well, yes, I am concerned about your two little bastards, she could say. And Cynthia, however stunned, playing the psychologist, would not be able to react.

At this moment Jason and Joshua were sleeping with Alfred in his old bedroom as if they already belonged there. Was that part of the plan? But she couldn't project her anger onto the boys because all day she'd been grateful for their presence. They were the only ones who didn't seem to know what was going on and therefore acted normal. Instinctively, everyone else tried to protect them from unpleasantness, until even Simon wiped the hang-dog look from his face and Gideon, who looked more devastated than anybody, showed them how to play Atari.

It was only Cynthia she resented. Cynthia the psychologist. Cynthia the paragon parent. Cynthia the shit. This evening when Joshua grew sleepy and whined, Darren and Merle invented a game for him, covering their lips so Merle's mustache was invisible, and making him guess which twin was which. Joshua cheered up, but Jason, the older one, looked left out. Cynthia went to him at once with a storybook to read. The display of good motherhood irritated Mag no end. She herself had never been so fair. With each new baby, her affection had transferred at once from the older child to the younger one—instinct, maybe, or madness, to which Cynthia would surely be immune. Izzy had to cling to Alfred after Percival arrived, the way Gideon would later attach himself to Percival when the twins were born. But Percival had never followed the rule. He hadn't wanted mothering from older brothers, only from Mag. If he was lying dead now, just when he was coming into his own, all she would be left with were regrets. But Cynthia would never face such a thing. She was rational, even-handed, fair to her boys the way Mag *should* have been but never was. And for that, Mag hated her.

Cynthia poured more wine. The bottle was almost empty. Cynthia's gray-green eyes were alert, even after all the alcohol, certainly not languid. Wary. "I know you're concerned we won't be able to afford other children, but Alfred and I both have good chances for a promotion . . . and I'd keep the higher pay even if I took a year's maternity leave a few years down the road."

Such logic, it sounded like Alfred himself. Anyway, Mag did not believe Cynthia would want other babies. Somewhere along the way she had swallowed her languor whole, had her babies, and gone on for her master's degree. And Mag had turned down a job in Washington because a near-collision on the highway convinced her it was a sign to stay home with her sons.

She was very drunk now, a little sleepy. The wine turned on her again and she was not angry anymore. She'd been such a fool. It was only luck that Alfred hadn't been a bastard. Why should she blame Cynthia for a little bad timing? She'd been a better mother than Mag. Why should she blame Cynthia for anything?

"I made a few smart decisions," Mag said, suddenly wanting to defend herself. "At least I finished school."

Cynthia nodded but Mag could not tell if her expression was approving or only benign. She wanted to go on but could not think of a single other thing she had done intelligently. As to her grand idea of a career . . . she had jettisoned it the minute Patrick stared at her suntan, hadn't she? And jettisoned it repeatedly during those years he was coming home drunk all those times. She had always felt superior to her nieces because she believed their passivity was a condition of being female in some undesirable way that she was not. But now it seemed she was just like them. It was Cynthia who was different.

She sighed, as if she'd finally come face to face with herself. God.

She'd let her jobs come to nothing. She'd used up her energies tangling with Patrick under the covers—swearing she wouldn't but doing it anyway. She'd gotten pregnant with Simon in the moldy shower stall because the bathroom door was the only one that locked against the children. She'd sat in her living room listening to music, reading books, ignoring the boys' laundry, letting them go to school without finishing their homework, refusing to take a job in Washington. She was such an ass. Screwing Patrick, wanting to be near Patrick, having his kids. Her inactivity was not a condition of being female, but a condition of being Mag.

Even drunk, Cynthia did not look as if she would ever be so foolish. She looked like a woman who would find a birth-control method that worked, carry on with the business of being a psychologist, and never allow herself to be trapped, even by Alfred.

Good for Cynthia.

The idea wiped the alcohol right out of her.

Cynthia's eyes began to close. There was not a single line in her face. Mag felt ancient.

To come this far—to the possible death of a grown son. And to be able to change nothing.

She felt a little ill. She remembered Patrick blind this morning . . . yesterday . . . and saw him blind all the days to come— bumping against the walls, carrying the cat in his arms, pretending it was perfectly normal to walk like that, acting as if the blindness was a mere inconvenience. She saw herself pointing out that no, the fork was on the other side, dear, the shirts in the other drawer . . . forced to tend him the way she had tended children, only this time with no way out, because he would never grow up and leave her alone. If Alfred moved into her house with Cynthia, she would be banished to the Keys with a blindman forever. And Cynthia—younger, wiser—would be free.

Cynthia opened her eyes and smiled again, in a pleasant, bleary way. Even drunk, she looked so capable.

Mag's mind was working slowly because of the wine, but the idea that came to her was very clear. Cynthia and Alfred did not have to be her downfall. They could be her salvation. Even if she agreed to relinquish her house—she did not have to go to the Keys. She had always sunburned so badly, except for that one summer when she was seventeen. She could tell Patrick that. Patrick would not admit to wanting a babysitter, even in a subtle, unmentionable way. He wanted to think he could do everything—even blind—by himself. She could make an excuse. That was what Cynthia would do. She would say she couldn't bear to be twelve hundred miles away from Simon. She would like a vacation from the house—she would be gracious about Alfred's taking it—but she would not go very far from Simon. Patrick would agree to it. He would go to the Keys alone. She must not spend the rest of her days taking care of a blindman.

She was not drunk anymore. She knew exactly what she must do. She would take a little apartment near Rock Creek Park in Washington, in one of those older buildings that was not so expensive. She would spend her winter looking for a job. She had always known she could not bear to be sitting at home if something happened to one of her sons. She had waited for years to have her career, and now she must have it. There was nothing left to lose.

She had always thought freedom would feel light. She had waited for it for so long. She thought she would feel like a girl again, all her possessions in a backpack and the world opening at her feet.

She felt as if a cave had opened up inside her, and she was falling into it, like a stone.

TUESDAY

October 25, 1983

12

imon meant to get up the first time his alarm clock rang and not push the snooze button at all, but his eyes just wouldn't open. He'd slept through his paper deliveries yesterday and now he was going to do it again if he wasn't careful. He just couldn't get himself all the way up. Merle rolled over and said, "Turn the damned thing off, Simon," and later Darren grumbled, "What is this—reveille?" But Simon dozed on. Then his mother was in the room, poking at him, smelling just like Percival used to smell when he had a hangover, and he got up all at once, with a start, thinking: This is the day we're going to hear something. This is the day for sure.

"You don't have to help me," he told his mother. "You did it two days in a row." It was his paper route, not hers. He wished she'd go back to sleep. He was sick of her treating him like a baby.

"I'll help you," she said. "It's late. It's light already."

It was. Gray and cloudy. In Beirut it was after noon, the sun was shining on the rubble of the headquarters building. Simon had two clocks in his mind, one on Maryland time and the other on the time in Lebanon. "Get out of here while I put some clothes on," he said. His mother was already dressed. She went.

Downstairs, his mother didn't talk to him as they rubber-banded the papers. He figured she was too hung over. At the same time she seemed wrapped pretty tight, like an SS soldier in a Nazi movie. It wasn't like her.

They didn't talk as they drove over to Applewood Place, either. Not that he expected it. Their routine was old and es-tablished, and of course she smelled like she'd been drunk only a few hours before. But it was weird.

The day was chilly, but not cold like it would be a couple months from now. One thing he'd learned was not to concen-trate too much on the weather. He'd learned just to bundle up and gut it out, so that even if it was dark and snowing, pretty soon he would be finished. Now he was sorry he was so good at that. Even the weather didn't occupy his mind this morning. He thought about his ear, which nobody was going to let him fix because he was still under age. He thought of his father giv-ing him the Angel Solution lecture. He thought about what Hope had said last night when she finally called him back.

"It took me maybe half an hour, but finally I convinced Forsythe to let us have the moment of silence tomorrow," she told him.

"What's the big deal?"

"Well, he stalled for a long time on the phone and finally he said 'I'm afraid I can't give you permission for a moment of si-lent prayer because it's against the law to do that in a public school. But I could let you have just a *moment of silence*.' But really—if you're being silent—I mean, you can pray if you want to. Right?"

"Right," Simon said.

At the time, he'd been touched at Hope's bravery, to argue with Mr. Forsythe until he agreed to let her do something that was illegal. But now all that seemed a little silly. Last night on the news, one Marine had said that after the explosion there were so many guys trapped and calling out that it sounded like the ground was crying.

"Then you'd get there, and sometimes it was just quiet."

The cameras had gone to a shot of one of the rescue teams, carrying bags with bodies in them. He did not see how a moment of silence could change that. It would take something bigger.

He began to run, racing from house to house. He tried to get himself so out of breath that there would be only that in his mind, but as soon as he got breathless, he felt the way he had after his tonsils were out, coughing up the gook in his lungs, no more able to get enough air than Percival would be, crying out from under that rubble. He didn't throw the papers from the sidewalk, but bounded up onto the porches and dropped them at the doors. At least his customers would be happy, having their papers sitting at their feet. Across the way he could see his mother running, too, even with her hangover. He figured she was running for the same reason he was, but he was still so angry with her that it filled up his chest. It was partly her fault that there was nothing he could do for Percival. He couldn't even offer up his ear.

A guy Simon knew came out of his house and headed for the bus stop. That was how late he was with the papers. Normally he'd be on his way to school. He didn't nod to the guy; he didn't want to talk to anybody. He realized nobody else was out yet; this one kid was leaving pretty early. But he ran his papers faster, he wanted to get finished. He started to load his bag and take the footpath over to Trevor Circle. There was no bus stop on Trevor Circle and he wouldn't see anybody there. Then his mother yelled at him, "No, Simon, drive over there with me in the car. I'm almost finished here." She sounded so upset that he couldn't even go by himself. She would have a hyperspasm. He couldn't even *walk over there* by himself. He couldn't do anything. He didn't want her to freak out now, with people coming out of their houses, getting ready to go to work. So he got in the station wagon and they drove.

She parked at the bend of Trevor Circle. He would go one way and she the other. He was all loaded up, but she stood by the tailgate of the station wagon stuffing papers into her bag with no great sense of urgency. She looked like she was running out of energy.

Simon started to walk up the street. Just then the dog began barking. Honest to God, he had forgotten about Monster until that moment. Any other day he would be ready for him. He would be walking on the other side of the circle, carrying a paper in his hand like a baseball bat, just in case. But today he was thinking of so many other things.

The dog appeared from behind a bush, standing at the corner of its driveway. That was where it always hid. He had seen it next to this same bush both of the times it bit him and a couple of other times when it missed. His heart was beating fast, but the thoughts inside his head were slow and clear. There was still time to get away or to fight, either one. If he ran fast enough, he could get out of the dog's territory before it reached him. Normally it would chase him for a while and then turn back. The other choice was to get a paper out of his bag—it would only take a second—and fend it off. He was pretty good at playing bullfighter with the dog, waving the paper back and forth. Soon the dog would get frustrated and give up. The only times he'd been bitten, he'd been taken off his guard even more than he was this morning.

In the gray morning light the dog was yellow, ugly. It was baring its teeth. At the very moment it started to come at him, Simon thought: Running is too easy. Standing still is not. Staying right where he was and not fighting back would be no easier than having his ear fixed, letting them put him to sleep. It went against every instinct he had. It was something he could offer.

He made himself freeze in place. He had to grit his teeth to keep himself from moving. In the end it was no harder than playing statues had once been, locking into position, becoming cold as stone. Let the dog have at him, slash him with its teeth, make him bleed. He could not offer his ear, but he could offer that.

Mag was almost finished loading her bag with papers when Monster started to bark. She had a headache from the wine last night, and after running her papers on the last block, her temples were throbbing, making her awkward and slow. The odd sensation of complete freedom was still with her, as it had been from the moment she had sat across from Cynthia and decided what she would do. It was a cool, logical feeling. She was a stone, heavy but unfettered, falling through a dark cave. Her son was dead. Patrick would go blind. She was free.

At first, the dog's noise was simply an intrusion on her thoughts—a sharp, angry sound cutting into her headache. She was annoyed. The dog had been inside yesterday—because of her run-in with the owner on Sunday, she supposed—and she thought the exchange would keep the beast cooped up at least a couple more days.

Then it came into sight, almost beside her, barking its lungs out and running toward Simon—a dirty, yellow crazy thing.

She expected Simon to run away. Simon didn't budge. He remained perfectly still, in the strange motionless stance he had adopted several times since the bombing, with his fingers hanging limp and silent as a statue's, as if they had never been alive, never snapped. The dog almost touched her as it went by, growling and baring raw teeth at Simon's hands. Simon didn't move an inch. Mag was heavy, a rock inside, but molten. She watched Simon's stillness and felt the fury of the attacking dog. She dropped her paper bag and ran. She threw herself forward, and at the very moment the dog lunged toward Simon's hands, she tackled it.

She caught it around its hind legs. The dog didn't stop entirely, only slowed down. Simon stayed where he was, but Monster's teeth missed him. Mag hung on. The dog pulled her forward a little, then stopped and yelped. Beneath its short fur she felt hard muscles, tension, anger. Nothing moved; it seemed to be regrouping.

Then it turned swiftly and came at her face. She was holding too far back on its body to prevent it. Her face was pressed to its side just above its hindquarters. Her instinct was to let go, protect her eyes, but she held fast. She smelled dark hot dog breath and hate that had been meant for Simon. She saw its teeth. In the fraction of a second before the dog bit her, she propelled herself clumsily up and forward, pressing her belly against the dog's spine and grabbing its chest higher up. Her right arm went around its neck and her left hugged its rib cage. The dog's teeth missed her face because of the way she had moved. They caught dully at her leg, then let go.

She was straddling the dog now, her head tight against its fur, her legs sprawled out behind her. All her weight was on it, but the dog stayed on its feet. It growled, low and intense. She could feel the vibrations in her arms and chest.

Suddenly it tried to lunge forward, to rid itself of her. Its paws bit into the spongy ground while her own feet dragged free and useless. As long as it had a foothold and she did not, it was stronger than she. Its mouth was open, slavering, working to get loose. She hung on, being pulled forward; she would not have believed a dog could be so powerful. In a second it would be rid of her. She became aware of the pounding of her heart, the aching in her chest. She was about to let go when in the corner of her eye she saw Simon's legs, long sticks in gray RipOffs, and his mute, motionless fingers in exactly the same position they'd been before.

Burying her face in the dog's neck, she squeezed harder. The smell of damp fur engulfed her. It was the smell of every enemy she'd ever had—Susan Durrell with the spoon held aloft, ready to strike the toddler Percival; schoolteachers who had been unkind to him; circumstances that had left Alfred soulless and Simon earless; a terrorist bomber in Beirut. She found the ground with her knee, lifted, dug in. With all her strength she heaved herself over, onto her back. The dog's feet kicked wildly in the air. She held it to her, squeezing tighter with the arm around its chest and the hand at its throat. She still didn't have a foothold, but now the dog didn't, either. It thrashed, trying to roll her over and get its paws on the ground again. She didn't let go. Its muscles bore against her; she felt every movement of the dog's body in her own; they were one creature, blond and angry. Seconds passed. Mag's arms ached, but she held on. The kicking diminished. Simon was speaking to her. She didn't hear him clearly.

The dog made a sound—a high whining moan, terrible to hear. She squeezed harder, listening to the pitch go higher. Then the sound stopped and the kicking stopped, too. The dog was a weight against her, foul-smelling, wet. She didn't trust the silence. Finally she heard Simon.

"Mother! Listen to me!"

Her arms hurt, and her chest ached from the weight of the dog and the effort of squeezing so hard, but she held on. She lay on the ground with the dog in her arms, and above her Simon was tall, speaking to her, the sky behind him gray.

"You can let go now," he told her. Monster didn't move. Simon bent over her, his fingers moving again. He was taking the dog. "Let go now, Mother," he told her. "It's over. He's dead."

13

Patrick dreamed he was smothering. At first he dreamed he was running behind Percival when he was still in middle school, helping him train. He held a stopwatch in his hand and checked it as they passed certain points. At the end, he'd tell Percival his times. He'd say he looked strong coming out of the trees but that he needed to lean forward when he charged the hill.

It was hard to tell if Percival was listening. He was running with the long, easy stride he'd had when he was younger. It was pleasant to watch. Patrick understood that terrible things would happen as Percival got older, but in the dream it seemed possible to avoid them before they occurred. He was trying to explain this as they ran—that the future held no danger, because all the time in front of them was free.

Percival did not want to hear. He ran faster, to get away from the sound of Patrick's voice. Time passed, and Percival grew. His legs stopped looking like pipe cleaners and muscles formed in his chest. Patrick had to work hard to keep him in sight. He stopped being able to see the future in front of them, though he was running as hard as he could. Percival was getting away. Patrick was having trouble catching his breath. His head began to hurt. Still, he did not slow down. Slowing down or stopping did not seem to be options. You never stopped in a race. Percival was out of sight but Patrick kept running. His head pounded, and he was smothering as he ran.

He was still smothering as he came into consciousness—slowly, with no power to speed the process up. When he finally opened his eyes, he realized he was lying on his side, with something fuzzy against his face. The fuzzy thing was Lucifer. He reached up to swipe the cat away. Lucifer jumped down onto the floor. Patrick's head was pounding. On the night table the clock said 8:06. He never slept so late. He sat up in bed, still with that sense of everything happening in slow motion. Finally he stood, feeling for his slippers with his feet. He knew what his lethargy signified, and the odd sensation of moving as if under water, unable to function at a normal pace. He knew what the headache meant. Mag was gone, and that was just as well. He did not want her to see this. He got his feet into the slippers and went into the bathroom for his pills before he became completely blind.

His heart was as audible as a metronome. He'd thought he'd gotten hold of himself the other day, but it was no better than ever. To go blind just as you woke up gave no time to prepare. The light was almost gone now, a steady gray—and he felt suspended, caught. Trapped inside himself. His dream came back to him. Percival running. Graceful, *fast*. And the explosion. He was a little dizzy. Traveling at great speed in one of those amusement park rides that goes so fast gravity holds you against the wall, keeps you from falling just yet—aware that eventually you'll slow, and either the floor will rise or you'll tumble down.

He clutched the sink with his hand to stop the spinning sensation. Opened the medicine cabinet. A bottle against his hand. Valium? He was pretty sure it was. He squinted, but he had no vision at all, so he emptied some of the pills into his palm, feeling them—the right size, right shape. Heart drumming. Cup in hand now, spigot on. Valium, two aspirin. Down the hatch. Now think about the Keys until the mechanical calm came— think about hot sunshine, the water (ironically, when he thought of the ocean, what came to him was its turquoise blueness, the visual component), fish flapping under his touch, scales rough, cold against his hand. A deep breath. He could clean a fish by touch only. He would not need to see.

A new timbre to the headache now, reorchestrating itself toward the back of his head. What did he care about fish? A note for the logbook: Even if he could get rid of the headache, which ground away at his reason, he was not sure he could control his panic over this unbearable sense of being trapped.

He turned around, stubbed his toe on the toilet, but not hard enough to distract his attention from his head. Next would he roar and beat his chest to try to get outside of himself? There had been an amputee who'd begged in front of the movie theater where he went to Saturday matinees as a child. The man stood with his stumps on a cloth mat and held his cup up to the waist level of adults coming out of the theater, the chest level of children. Patrick had no money to give him, but in any case his pity was mingled with disgust. In such circumstances, he himself would surely have fashioned a pair of wooden legs, maybe to walk around on and certainly to raise him up to face people eye to eye, let him maintain a semblance of dignity. Why didn't the amputee do that? What was his excuse?

Heart rate still up, but he could breathe more freely; the smothering sensation was gone. Even blind, even with the headache, he was going begging. At worst, there were practical possibilities: a cane, a Seeing Eye dog, Braille, whatever would get him out of himself. Never the possibility of being trapped.

And when the Valium worked, he would analyze the events of these past three days—try to figure out why he'd been blind three days in a row—and particularly now, just after waking, after a troubled sleep.

Wary because of the stubbed toe, he nudged his shoulder against the bathroom wall and walked out, making his way across the bedroom to the doorway and into the hall. He was getting better at negotiating the stairs. He supposed it was useful to know how to traverse the house in the dark whatever happened, a good skill to have in case of a major storm or another energy crisis. He felt for the tread with his toe.

He was counting: seven steps to the landing, one step to the edge of the landing, seven more to the bottom. Someone was standing a few feet from him, at the entrance to the family room: Izzy. He didn't know how he knew someone was there, or why he knew it was Izzy.

"It's happened again, hasn't it?" Izzy said.

"Yes."

"I thought it would. It's getting worse." Izzy's pronouncements had the clarity of incisions. "Come sit down. I have a theory."

"It must be some theory, to get you out of bed before noon." Izzy hated getting up. He'd fallen off his bike because he was half-asleep the morning he'd broken his ankle delivering papers in high school. He wouldn't admit it, had insisted the bike had jumped a curb, but everyone knew the troubles he had, getting up.

Patrick hugged the wall going toward the family room. Izzy had the grace not to help him.

Someone else was there.

"Who's that?"

"It's me," Gideon said.

"What, did you go out to run?"

"No."

Of course Patrick knew Gideon hadn't been running. He could barely walk. Everyone had been careful not to mention it: Gideon, of all people, limping around because he was so upset about his brother.

A page of the paper turned. Patrick placed Gideon now—at the kitchen table, the paper spread out across it, Gideon leaning over it, reading the front page.

"What do they say?"

"They say identification of victims has been slowed because some of them, quote 'had not been wearing their combat identification tags and because records of many had been destroyed in the blast' end quote. No shit, Dick Tracy. 'What we have, in effect'—this is some Marine officer talking now—'is a couple of thousand next-of-kin who don't know whether their sons are alive or dead. Worse, it's going to be a while before some of them get any word.' Does that mean if they're all right, we should have heard by now?"

"It doesn't mean anything," Patrick said. The Valium was beginning to work. Red panic giving way to a beige calm, the headache losing its grip.

"You want to hear what Reagan says?" Gideon asked.

"I might as well."

"'The delay in notification of the families must be a cruel additional punishment for these people who wait in suspense.' I'd agree with that. Wouldn't you agree with that Dad?" Gideon sounded odd, as if his tongue were swollen.

"Maybe you better go run," Patrick said.

"Not today."

"It's the best thing you could do for yourself," Patrick said. But Gideon didn't answer, and Patrick didn't press it.

"I see no one's too fired up about my theory," Izzy said. "But you're going to hear it anyway. I think it's a combination of Lucifer and too much tea."

"What?"

"The blindness. I think it's from the cat and all that tea you've been drinking."

"Izzy, spare us," Gideon said.

Izzy ignored him. "Remember the first time it ever happened?" he asked Patrick. "We'd gone to take Lucifer to the vet, and then you drove me back to school. It was a long drive—a whole hour— and the car was full of cat hair. At my apartment we had a cup of tea and then you left."

"I'm not sure I follow you," Patrick said. He felt completely isolated inside himself. Outside, his sons were talking. Seeing gave the illusion that other people were with you, but they were not. Of course he'd always known that.

"I'm saying I think the blind spells are an allergy to cat fur and tea leaves," Izzy said.

"With all due respect, the people at Hopkins ruled out allergies a year ago."

"Allergy to one specific thing. But think about it. Number one, ever since Percival left, the cat has been sleeping with you, and it was just about that time that this thing started. Number two, ever since the explosion in Beirut, the cat has been in a panic state, practically sitting on your head all night, and the blind spells have been coming every day. Also, ever since the explosion, we've been drinking tea by the quart. Number three, every time the cat goes away, you improve a little."

"Not really."

"The first day I got here Mom threw him out and ten minutes later your eyes started to open up," Izzy said. "Yesterday the cat was around, but at first you were all right. Then you drank tea and about ten seconds after that you went blind. Later you went up and took a shower, which washed some of the dander off. After the shower you could see. Think about it."

Patrick's heart was hammering again. He was like a child, seized with wild hope. He swallowed, breathed slowly, made himself doubt.

"You're at your worst in the morning after the cat's been with you all night," Izzy said. "And what do you do first thing in the morning? You drink tea. And last night you drank tea right before bed. Then the cat slept with you and here you are."

— 217 —

A confusion gripped him. Impossible. And yet a logic of sorts, a bizarre sort of logic. He couldn't think of a clever reply.

"Some people get hayfever and other people get these weird things. How about those sneezing fits when you drink alcohol? Most people would get a stomachache or some kind of hangover. Most people don't react by sneezing."

"That doesn't explain cat fur and tea," Patrick said.

"Remember the summer I was working on that experiment with puppies? When we had to kill all those puppies with the pentobarb?"

"The summer he had a three-month migraine," Gideon said.

Patrick remembered hearing about the puppies; he didn't remember Izzy's having a three-month migraine. He supposed Izzy was sensitive enough to, getting attached to snakes and dogs the way he did. Still . . . "I don't see the connection," he said.

"We were testing them for allergic reactions. Don't you remember? They were from a strain of dogs that had food allergies—they got sick from just about everything they ate. I know I told you about it. And afterward we studied their kidneys and their adrenals. Anyway, the point is, I read seven thousand articles about allergies that summer. I probably knew more about allergies than almost anyone in the country that summer—and I'm telling you what you have sounds like an allergy to a combination of cat fur and tea."

Patrick did not let himself take it too seriously yet. He was trying to picture Izzy with a three-month headache. Back . . . when? When he was trying to patent the RipOffs, probably. He'd been so preoccupied that summer; he couldn't recall. Cat fur and tea, so simple.

"The main thing is that it takes both components to trigger the reaction," Izzy said. "There are people who get a reaction if they drink chocolate *milk*, but not if they eat plain chocolate. I mean, it can be anything, it can be totally bizarre. There was a case where a guy broke out if he was around dogs, but only if he ate tuna fish right before. He was always eating tuna fish. Or maybe you would break out only if you breathed Old Spice fumes and then went horseback riding. All kinds of weird combinations. Have you tried cutting out tea?"

"No." He had tried everything else, of course, changed his diet in ten different ways. But he had not stopped drinking tea. Stupid. His sons no longer seemed to be talking outside of him. They were right there, in the room, he could feel just how far away.

"You also have to remember that any allergy gets worse when you're under stress," Izzy said.

"It still seems a little farfetched," Patrick said. But why not? Izzy was an expert on allergies. It might be perfectly sensible. He would like it to be.

"In which case you better go shower the cat fur off before Simon gets back and uses up all the hot water," Gideon said.

"Yes, that would certainly confirm it—if a shower has the same effect it did yesterday, once we get the cat out of here," Izzy said. "Of course you have to remember there's still cat fur all over the house."

Patrick believed it then. He made himself move slowly and deliberately, but the blood came to his face, his heart beat fast, he might have been liberated. Always before he had solved his own dilemmas, had not thought anyone else could. Cat fur was so simple—and tea!—but sneezing from liquor was simple, too, and abstinence had stopped it. Maybe Izzy had broken the code this time—no telling. It would be nice to think he'd passed his good inventor's genes on to one of his sons—especially the one named after the Isaac Singer who'd invented the sewing machine. Nice not having to depend on himself entirely . . . being able to have moments of weakness, when someone else could help.

It was as if, after all, there might be some hope of getting help from outside himself. All kinds of possibilities in that. Then he thought of Percival and knew he was not liberated, still alone; Percival too. All of them. But he was leaning on Izzy.

"Don't say anything to Mom yet," he said. "It's bad enough, this waiting. Don't tell her about the cat until later."

"Oh, I wouldn't," Izzy said with a voice that had a kind of exultation under it.

"Me either," said Gideon, in a voice that didn't.

Patrick turned around and put his hands out to feel where the walls were. He knew they saw him groping against the walls, but he didn't try to joke about it; he only followed them to the stairway, found the banister, and made his way upstairs to take a shower.

Gideon watched his mother and Simon come in from the paper route, but he was so preoccupied that he didn't notice anything unusual at first. He had just figured out what his creeping numbness felt like. It was like tar sticking his muscles together and then gradually solidifying like glue. Every day the glue was getting harder, and pretty soon he wouldn't be able to move at all.

"What happened?" Izzy asked.

It was then that Gideon saw his mother's RipOffs all crusted with mud and her face smeared as if she'd been in a fistfight.

"She fell," Simon said.

"I fell," his mother echoed.

Both Simon and his mother looked grim, as if she'd fractured something.

"She tripped over that rock on the Swansons' lawn," Simon said. Gideon remembered that rock from when he had had the route. It was right in your path as you went from the Swansons' house to the house next door. He'd fallen over it a couple of times himself.

"I'm okay," his mother said. "I'm going up to take a shower."

"Dad's showering," Izzy said.

"Then I'll use the other bathroom." There was something very deliberate about his mother, very cold. She went upstairs and Simon did, too.

"I'm taking the cat to the kennel to get him out of here for a while," Izzy said when they were gone. Gideon wished someone would stay here to talk to him. He did not want the paralysis to become complete while he was alone. "You vacuum the cat fur off the furniture," Izzy said.

Gideon walked to the closet and got the vacuum cleaner out. He vacuumed the family room couch with the cannister hose. He vacuumed all the chairs and then the carpet. It took great effort. His fingers were so tired, they didn't want to stay closed around the vacuum hose. When he turned around he saw that over the noise his father had come down again. He turned the vacuum cleaner off.

"Can you see?" he asked.

"A little. I'm starting to." Sure enough, the beginnings of pupils were returning to his father's eyes.

"You ought to go outside," he said to Gideon. "Run a couple of miles. That's what you do these days, isn't it?"

His father sounded sarcastic. With Percival it was quips and jokes when it came to running, but with Gideon it was always seriousness or sarcasm or anger.

"I couldn't run today."

"Why? Because you think vacuuming is more important? Read my lips, Gideon: It isn't."

In practice, Percival used to drop behind because he didn't like to run with anybody, and his father would say cheerfully, "The only place to run by yourself, Percival, is in front of everybody," and Percival would laugh, saying, "I thought I got plenty of practice running in front when I trained with you, Dad." And his father would laugh, too. But if Gideon dropped behind, his father got irritated. "You're losing ground because you aren't striding out properly right from the beginning, Gideon. You have to stride out right from the start."

Couldn't his father see how slowly his hands moved, how his legs dragged, the right more than the left?

"Gideon, I'm serious," his father said. "Go out. Don't hang

around here, it's not good for you. It's not good for anybody, but at least you have a legitimate reason to leave for a while."

"Maybe later." He could not say he was sick, because his father would tell him that was just an excuse.

His father's face was set in angry lines. Gideon knew it was because Percival, not Gideon, was dead.

Then his father said, "You know, Percival could have trained harder once he grew, if he wanted to be any good."

"What?"

"He could have been good if he kept at it," his father continued.

His father had always thought Percival was the one who should have been good.

"The point is, he wasn't because he didn't train very hard, any more than he kept up with his schoolwork," his father said. "He was fine when it was easy, but as soon as there was trouble, he always backed off. You were never like that. I wouldn't want to see you start now."

Gideon could not move his hands.

"What I'm saying is, if he wasn't any good, it was his own fault," his father said. There was a clipped, precise tone to his voice. His pupils were half opened and half shut, not the creepy all-blue of the blind spells, but not exactly normal, either. He was watching Gideon, but he seemed to be concentrating on something else. He was doing what you had to do when someone was dying: pull your love away from them. It had nothing to do with Gideon or the way his legs dragged. His father was not seeing him at all.

"Gideon," his father said again. "Go out and run."

When he was younger, his father's anger had frightened him. It had made him obey. Now it did not frighten him, but there seemed no point in fighting back. He went out the door.

Outside the air was cool and still, the trees mostly bare, the cloud cover low, giving off an almost-Novemberish light, gray, as if the day were in mourning. Gideon felt so heavy, he didn't think he could make it around the block.

He walked at first, like an old man. Concentrating on his every step, no normal kind of walk; his body wouldn't take care of itself. He made himself think about small details so he wouldn't have to stop: right foot down, left foot down. "Break the problem into small components," his father had always said to Izzy, but he had said it about running, too. "It's impossible to think about running a whole mile, but it's easy to think of the pace you're going to run for the next two-twenty.

"Sometimes," his father had said, "you make yourself keep moving by thinking of other things."

He was not sure he could. He tried to concentrate on his brothers—Merle's mustache so scraggly and thin it was like a dandelion puff waiting to be blown away, Simon pacing around with his hands hanging at his sides, Alfred's fatherliness with Cynthia's kids. But it only made his legs feel heavier. His family was not really a unit anymore. From now on they would gather only for weddings and funerals.

Than a few little things separated out: Alfred touching Cynthia every chance he got, guiding her around the kitchen by the shoulder, by the waist. Alfred in love. The twins trying to talk to reporters, then looking to him, Gideon, for approval. After a while it was possible to think of those small things by themselves: the gestures, the jokes.

He was walking a little easier. It was as if his father's anger and his father's advice propelled him, both at the same time. In high school Patrick had joked with Percival but said sternly to Gideon, "For God's sake, you're kicking your butt every time you take a step. Propel yourself forward. Don't waste all that energy on the back-kick." And Gideon had propelled himself forward, helpless not to. Like a child.

Angry at his father now, at his father's anger—but he didn't have to think about his feet so much.

His father had said to Percival, "You've got to lift those weights if you want to develop the strength for a good kick at the end of a race." But Percival never did. He only struck his Mr. America pose. "Don't you think the biceps are getting bigger anyway? I think they are." His father laughed. "Let me put it this way, Percival. This is the first time I've ever seen a toothpick make a muscle."

Gideon lost a race and his father said, "If you don't have that upper-body strength, you can pump those legs from here to kingdom come and it still isn't going to get you in fast enough."

Jogging now . . . As if even now, his father's anger propelled him.

He had shown them both.

He'd never thought of it that way before—he'd thought somehow he couldn't help it—but there it was. His father had been angry with him, and Percival had stopped speaking to him, but he had shown them both.

It was no accident.

A memory: his father helping to coach him, senior year, so annoyed with him. "The arms, Gideon. Pump your *arms* on the final sprint, for Christ's sake." And this morning, years later, the same emotions ruling him, commanding Gideon to go out. Hating Gideon.

Or did he?

His father's absentmindedness as his pupils began to focus rang false—that preoccupied manner as he watched Gideon clutch the kitchen table and vacuum with stiff movements of his hands. His father was never absentminded.

He had known perfectly well what was wrong with Gideon's limbs.

Odd—his saying Percival could have trained harder just before he ordered Gideon outside to run. He would not be that cruel, even in anger.

And then Gideon understood. His father had made jokes with Percival because he had understood all along that he was not going to be a champion. And that Gideon was. Maybe it was not hate that made him stern but a belief that, even this morning, Gideon could run. Maybe anger was its own kind of love. Or maybe he was never going to know.

He was moving faster, though he might have had weights in his shoes. Time was doubling back on him. The twins were babies, crying in the other room. Gideon couldn't find his socks. He felt so helpless; his socks had disappeared and his mother wanted him dressed. She didn't want to help him; she was busy minding the twins. "Gideon, you're bigger than they are, you can do it yourself." But the socks were gone, and he was cold, wet, standing in an empty white light. Percival came over. They were . . . how old? Three years old and four? Three and two? Percival gave Gideon one blue sock and one white one. The light around them softened. He put them on.

A broken trophy, leaking sand.

"Talk about *tacky* . . ."

Summer now—last summer—Gideon waking early to run before work. Percival, home from the Marines, running beside him, together, friends, stride for stride in the rising light. They ran for almost six miles. A good feeling, peaceful, no envy inside of them—and a good thing, too, because maybe that was all they were ever going to have.

Tears on his face. Wet, cold beneath the October sky. His father, angry, would say, "Suck it up, buddy."

He would suck it up.

The heaviness began to lift. He watched the gray sky and the gray road, matching colors, and felt himself moving across it, fast, pulling his RipOffs open, tying them around his waist. He was running. There was light in his thoughts, and darkness. The light was hope that Percival would come home, and the darkness was a bruised place that would always be there if he didn't. The paralysis was gone.

14

Mag was showered. Dressed. Perfectly composed. In the kitchen, Alfred and Cynthia had finished the dishes. The twins had done the wash, and someone had vacuumed. The house was clean. Even Lucifer, who could be such a pest, must have been outside all day, because she hadn't seen him. Everything was in order.

Her sense of free-falling was still with her, but she felt she had it under control. It had not gone away even after she killed the dog. Ordinarily she would have expected to be punished for such an act, though her intentions were honorable. But now she felt only that it was a vicious, rotten dog and deserved to die. She had felt that way even as she lay on the ground holding it, when she knew it must be dead but could not make herself move because she was in shock.

Finally Simon took the dog from her arms and put it in the street.

"We'll leave it out there," he said. "We'll let people think somebody ran it over."

He bent to touch her arm. "Get up, Mother," he said. "It's late. People are going to be coming out of their houses. We're lucky no one's out now."

In a dull, mechanical way, she rose. They walked back to the car.

"We should go home," he told her. She realized she was sitting in the driver's seat but had not turned on the ignition.

She came back to herself a little then. "Let's not tell anybody at home about this," she said.

"They'll hear anyway."

"Yes, but not until later. Today we're sure to hear from the Marines. The dog can wait until after."

"We'll tell them you fell," Simon said.

"Yes." She could not think at all, but decisions came to Simon quite easily.

"We should go now," he said. She started the ignition. She had killed the dog for him, but he seemed quite capable of fending for himself. For a moment as they drove home she was afraid he would say he wanted to have his ear fixed, and now that he had taken control of their actions, she would not be able to refuse. But he said nothing. The matter seemed to have been deferred, not just by the situation, but also by the way—since the moment Simon told her to get up from the damp ground— he seemed to have grown and changed. He told everyone she had tripped on the Swansons' lawn, and everyone believed him, as if he were to be trusted absolutely.

After she had showered, she broached the subject of his ear, afraid not to. But Simon only said, "You know that girl, Hope Shriber? She's going to have a moment of silent prayer for Percival in school today. She said she didn't know if it would help. I mean, she was always so sure you could get what you wanted by praying, and now when it comes right down to it, she's not.

Until yesterday I was completely sure I didn't want the ear fixed. Then I was sure I did. Now I'm not sure of anything."

For Simon, that was a long speech. Mag nodded. He sounded so grown-up.

She felt as if she were falling headlong into her future. After she dressed and came downstairs again, her course of action seemed clear. When word came about Percival, Patrick would say, "We should still go to the Keys." He would say that whatever the news turned out to be. She would reply, "You go; you deserve some time to yourself. I think it's finally time for me to get that job in Washington." And he would not be able to refuse.

In the meantime, observing the proprieties was all that was left. Cynthia's boys were watching cartoons in the family room. The news updates on TV had nearly stopped. She supposed that for most people, Beirut was no longer news. Fewer neighbors were coming to the door. The only thing Mag noticed about the ones who did was whether or not they appeared to be Marines.

A young man in civilian clothes had come up the walk. When he rang the bell, Darren and Merle went together to open it. Mag could tell from the exchange that it was another reporter. A second man appeared, holding a minicam. Something about the tone of the conversation made her go closer. She noticed the twins in a detached way: two tall lank-haired men, identical down to their voices, which for the first time were suddenly deep and assured. The ridiculous mustache was gone from Merle's upper lip. A moment later the two of them were leading the reporter outside, Darren flanking him on one side and Merle on the other, escorting him down the walk toward his video-equipped van. The man with the minicam had no choice but to follow. The twins kept talking to the reporter, first one and then the other, and the reporter, baffled by their doubleness, was going where they led.

Back in the house, she heard them telling Gideon how they'd

decided that Merle should shave his mustache so they could look exactly alike again as long as the reporters were around. Gideon was laughing. He seemed all right now, better than he had since arriving. Mag forgave the twins for caring more for Gideon than for Percival. Maybe Gideon needed their devotion. She was not sure she loved any of them, was not sure in her present state that she was capable of that. But she forgave them everything.

In the living room, she put *Pictures at an Exhibition* on the stereo. She sat close to the speakers but didn't turn the volume high because she didn't want to keep Cynthia's boys from listening to their cartoons.

Cynthia came in. "I hope whatever happens," she said, "you and Patrick will still go to the Keys for the winter. Maybe if he relaxes . . . if you both relax . . ."

"I envision myself with a third-degree sunburn," Mag said. She would not speak of the impossibility of going to the Keys or anywhere with Patrick any longer; she would only prepare Cynthia for what she would say later, about giving up her house.

"I think it might be a lot for you," she said, "having the responsibility for Simon."

"It would only be for a few months. You'll come back when it gets warm—you'll want to, even if you decide to move to Florida later." Cynthia's voice was controlled, showing good breeding. At least she was well bred. "What we'll do is sublet the apartment for six months or whatever, so we can have it back at least by June. That way when I get out of school I can take the boys to the pool."

"The pool?"

"Well, yes . . . you know, the swimming pool at the apartment. It's our primary form of recreation in the summer. It also tires them out so they take good naps."

"Here they would have the yard," Mag said.

"Yes. It's a lovely yard. But I think by summer they'll be ready for the pool."

Could it be that Cynthia didn't want her house? She must be misunderstanding something. There was so much on her mind; of course there were things she was probably missing. No matter, she would be gracious for now and not dwell on it. She smiled. Kindly, she thought. It was easy to be gracious when it didn't give anything away. Cynthia smiled back and left the room. Mag could not rid herself of the all-consuming sense of falling.

Joshua came in, running from Jason. Their features were angelic . . . but their expressions! Mag knew well enough when one brother intended to kill the other.

"Okay, guys." Alfred came running in after them. He grabbed Jason by the arm. "Hey, guys, listen to me now. If you're tired of cartoons, let me tell you about this music. Do you hear this music?"

The boys nodded. The record was almost over: "The Great Gate at Kiev" was playing, the last section, her favorite.

"Well, there's a story to it. Did you know that music can have a story?"

The boys shook their heads.

"A lot of times the composer wants to tell a story just like someone who writes a book, and so he tries to make the sounds fit it. This piece describes the gate that leads into a city in Russia. I used to imagine that it took place on Easter morning, when the people were coming into the gate going to church." He went into the family room and returned with the encyclopedia, showing them a picture of the church in Red Square.

"A church like this one," he said. "When you listen to music, you can imagine anything you want, but I used to think the music sounded like springtime, and the people were coming to this church on Easter."

This struck Mag as so odd that her sensation of falling left her for a minute, suspending her in midflight. She had not thought that Alfred could imagine things like Easter. It was one thing to joke about *Mefistofele* giving him a religious education, but really his mind didn't work like that.

Joshua was beginning to fidget. He was turning the pages of the encyclopedia, looking for other pictures. "Is Easter one of the times when the world is decorated?" he asked.

"You mean the house—like at Christmas?" Alfred said.

"No, the world."

"Well, I guess the world is decorated with plants and flowers coming up." He put one hand on Joshua's head and the other on Jason's. "And with you."

The boys laughed. He winked at them. "Come on, you two roughnecks. Outside." She understood that he loved them. She did not think that was possible. But clearly he did.

Alfred followed the boys into the other room, to get their coats. Mag felt numb. To imagine Kiev at Easter, Alfred would have had to let the music move him in a way she had not thought was possible. But why not? He had always been a thoughtful child. Perhaps he had cared for it all the time and did not say. It was a mistake to judge people by their surfaces, she knew that. But Alfred's surface had always been so smooth. She saw the music having some lasting impression on him, saw him loving Cynthia's boys, loving Cynthia. It seemed extremely odd.

A memory came to her of Alfred's birth. She had been in labor a long time, and she was tired. The pains swept over her with increasing frequency and intensity, until they seemed to come one after the other, with no rest in between. She tried to do what she had read in the childbirth books, but the pain was in control of her and she could not breathe. She knew she would die. Then she thought: It is out of my hands. Immediately she felt calm. She said, "Please help me," and relinquished control. At that moment—*at that moment*—someone told her to push, and as soon as she did the pain stopped. It was replaced by an enormous, healing effort, and a few moments later Alfred slid howling into the world. Seeing the beauty of her son and feeling the sweetness of her own unencumbered body, she immediately remembered a scene from *The Potting Shed*, where the girl dreams she meets a lion. The man asks her, "Did it eat you?" And the girl says, "No, it only licked my hand." And it seemed to her that was what had happened the moment she relinquished control.

She must relinquish Alfred, she supposed. She had feared a moment when the boys would be snatched beyond her, hurt, killed, when she would not be able to call them back—but perhaps mostly they just grew up, out of control, and maybe the moment had come and gone and she had simply not known.

Even Simon—the way he had acted this morning with the dog, and now his admitting to being unsure about his ear. When he finally made up his mind, it would be a man's decision. And Izzy with his lab animals, Gideon with his maniacal running . . . Even if they ran into trouble—they were out of her control. Her freedom was not something she had wrenched from them, it was real.

But Patrick . . .

Oddly, Patrick was standing beside her. She hadn't heard him enter because of the music.

"Come into the other room, Maggie," he said. "Come help me get through the rest of this day."

It was a strange thing for him to say. He was not blind, for now, and his eyes were turquoise blue.

He sounded troubled. For three days he had not once sounded as if any of this troubled him, and now his voice was weak.

"Come here, I have something good to tell you about my eyes," he said.

"Oh, Patrick, don't. No jokes." If he joked right now, she would announce her decision to leave. She would not wait another moment.

"No jokes," he said softly. He touched her arm.

Whatever his good news was, it did not deflect his pain. She remembered then that jokes and coolness were what he always hid behind—when there were too many babies to tend, when Percival refused to run well, and now again. It was the only mask he had. And she had confused it with uncaring so she could listen to music alone. She was ashamed.

"What about your eyes?" she asked.

"Come into the family room, Mag. Turn this record off."

She knew that whatever it was about his eyes, that wasn't even the main thing. The main thing was that Percival might be dead. Their child. Their lives, braided inextricably. Even if she could have been as logical as Cynthia, nothing would be changed. Why did she think, then, that she could leave him to go blind alone in the Keys?

She was no longer falling. A sort of solidity reappeared beneath her feet—nothing absolute—and when she identified it, she saw that of course it was only sand. In the Keys, she and Patrick would walk on the beach and spend the too-hot noons in bed. After a time they would both grow bored, and he would begin to concoct sunblocks for her, even if he were blind. She would help until the house was as familiar to him as this one, and then she would find a job. There must be interesting jobs, even in Key West.

She did not think even Cynthia, with all her reserve, would escape. The web was woven of lives.

In the distance the doorbell was ringing, and also the phone. She could not see the door from here and thought at last it would be the Marines. Or perhaps not; perhaps it was Percival on the phone, calling to say he was all right. It could be either. The twins would get the door and Simon would answer the phone. It was the way they did things, and it was out of her control.

In that last second, she envisioned Percival whole, rescuing other men from beneath the rubble. Saw him in action—he had always been graceful and light. Saw him performing the sort of act that would fill him, calm him, perhaps for years. Or if not . . . Patrick tightened his hand on her arm, and she leaned into him. Alfred was calling them from the other room.

"Someone wants to talk to you," he said. Mag could not tell if he meant the person at the door or the person on the phone. Neither Mag nor Patrick moved.

"Hurry up, this is long distance!" Simon was yelling. Mag lifted the needle from the record. "Hurry!" he yelled. They began to run, she and Patrick, toward the phone room. His hand was still on her arm. In the distance they could hear Simon saying, "We knew you'd be all right, man, we knew you were too ugly to die." He spoke in a clear, light voice that was not even his imitation of a black man's voice. And they could hear, very clearly in the distance, the sound of him snapping his fingers as he spoke.